SKIN AND BONES

THE EVER CHACE CHRONICLES, BOOK ONE

SUSAN HARRIS

SKIN & BONES

ISBN: 978-1-63422-185-6
Cover Design by: Marya Heiman
Typography by: Courtney Knight
Editing by: Cynthia Shepp

Everything that I am,
And everything that I aspire to be,
I owe to my parents.
This one's for you guys.

PROLOGUE

THE DAY WAS JUST ANOTHER ORDINARY DAY, DULL AND overcast, the grey clouds threatening to unleash a torrent of rain down amongst those who meandered about. In the heart of winter, the night drew in quickly as evening approached.

A rumble of thunder grabbed his attention as he studied his next victim while she rounded the corner. Vibrant and full of life, the young girl was on the cusp of her maturity, reaching the tender age when all creatures came into their powers. He licked his lips in anticipation as he scented the ambrosia in the air. After weeks of preparation and patience, it was finally time for action.

His ruby-haired girl hugged her companion, a human girl, and bade her farewell. Straightening up in the seat, he slowly guided his run-of-the-mill car into the terrace. He knew his Carly's routine, he knew it by heart, and he had everything planned down to the last second. He was nothing if not meticulous, and it had never steered him wrong before.

Adrenaline pumped in his veins at the thought of feasting on unbridled power as the curly-haired teen bent over to stick her laces back into her shoes. Teenagers these days were willing to put their safety at risk by wearing unlaced sneakers. Her stalker slowed his car to a stop. His mouth watered as rain began to dance on his windshield. He would enjoy this, he always did, and as time went by, he realized he craved it more and more.

As Carly straightened up and, almost on instinct, cast her gaze in his direction, he smiled, drinking in her frightened, green eyes and opening the car door...

Chapter One

Derek Doyle slid under the police tape, his heavy footsteps crunching over the gravel as he made his way down to the crime scene a short distance from the Garda station where he worked. He held back the growl that clawed at his throat. The smell of blood and urine disturbed his already-heightened senses, and he clenched his fists as the lingering scent of fear threatened to unleash his temper. Going all wolf in front of a dozen or more cops with silver rounds in their guns might not be such a good idea, but Derek wanted nothing more than to catch the crazy monster who had slaughtered an innocent. The idea of making the perp scream like he had his victims was running rampant in his mind.

Traffic had halted on the bridge above him as crowds gathered to catch a glimpse of what had happened. Derek cracked the bones in his neck as he nodded a greeting to some of the uniforms, who, in turn, eyeballed him. The world might have come to terms with the fact that werewolves, witches, and all the in-betweens existed a few years back, but there would always be bigots, especially on the force.

Ignoring the officers, he let his nose guide him. His eyes soon focused on the teenager's body. She lay half in, half out of the little stream of water, her vibrant hair tangled with blood as her green eyes stared blankly up at him. The growl he had been holding back bubbled to the surface. His chest vibrated with the sound. The few men and women who were not in his special task force took a step away, none of them eager to be near an angry werewolf. Not that he really blamed them. As old as he was, Derek had a handle on his inner beast, but a human would never be a match for a pissed-off werewolf.

He held his hand up in apology. They relaxed, the tension evaporating slightly from their scent. Derek slipped down the short embankment, digging his heels into the muddy ground. The medical examiner for all things paranormal—a young witch who had a knack for seeing inside a victim's body and assessing the damage—was examining the girl. She looked up as he stepped up next to her.

"Poor dear, whoever did this wanted her terrified, Derek. It leaks from her... just like the others."

Derek put a hand on her shoulder. "We'll get him, Anna. I swear it; I will get justice for all of them."

Anna brushed a tear from her eye with her arm and nodded. This was the third body in three months, and they were no closer to finding a suspect. From the trauma, it was obvious a supe was responsible, but why attack human teenagers? Most of those in the supernatural community wanted to live in harmony with the humans and would not do anything to jeopardize that, especially considering a few years back, when their existence had become known and the world leaders had wanted to round them up and tag them like animals so they could keep tabs on them. Well, that was until one of the most powerful men in the world had turned out to be one of his kind.

Derek squeezed Anna's shoulder before he dragged his gaze from the slain girl and headed over to join his partner. Tall and thin, with black hair pulled back into a ponytail, Richard 'Ricky' Moore looked like he was a member of a Goth rock band rather than one of the finest cops and supes he had the pleasure to work with. He and Ricky had been teamed together and had quickly become friends. The other members of the Paranormal Investigations Team, or P.I.T. as Ricky liked to call it, were like Derek's family. He would die for any of the men and women on his team.

"Yo, D, we really need to nail this monster."

"Preaching to the converted, Ricky. What have we got?"

Ricky narrowed his eyes as he spoke. "Young female, age approximately fifteen years old. Been out here maybe four to five hours—tops. Rainfall overnight washed away most of the evidence, so not even your keen smell can pick up on much. Unsub must have dumped her during the shift change. Same dumpsite as the other two victims. All three drained of blood with bone marrow extracted."

Ricky stopped as another snarl rumbled from Derek. This unsub was sick and twisted.

"D, I have more bad news. There was a girl took about a mile from her house in Waterford. He dumped her schoolbag with her, and this time, we got an ID. Girl's name is Carly Saunders."

Derek raised an eyebrow. "As in Graham Saunders, head of the Munster banshees?"

"One and the same. Anna needs to do more tests, but it looks like the girl hadn't evolved into her powers yet. She wants to go over the tests again to see if the other two vics come from supernatural families, ones who may still be in the closet."

Derek nodded. "It's possible. The perp has never taken a victim from Cork, but he has dumped them here. We have to assume this is his comfort zone. It helps. Let's just hope it helps enough to track this sicko down."

A beep interrupted them. Derek pulled his phone from his jean pocket and read the text before looking back at Ricky. "Sarge wants us back at the station for a briefing. Anna's going to be taking Carly back to the morgue now anyway... Come on—the uniforms can keep watch."

Without another word, Derek turned and headed up the embankment. Flashes of light blurred his vision as the social media nation on the bridge above him took snaps of the grisly murder to upload to the web. He shook his head in disgust. Making his way up the grassy hill, he soon stood on the concrete bridge amongst the vultures.

The reporters spotted him. Their voices melded into one entity as they screamed at him and asked him for comments or information. Not even bothering to say *no comment*, Derek crossed the road and jogged around the corner to the Garda station.

The brazenness of the killer bugged him. He dumped the bodies five minutes away from the police station as if to taunt them. Things had been much simpler in his day. When he had been human, the bad guys were the bad guys and the good guys were the good guys. Nobody had had a clue that werewolves and vampires existed. After a childhood where it seemed possible that he was more likely to end up on the opposite side of the law, he had joined the army at eighteen. Being in the army had straightened him out. When he was just twenty-four, he was recruited to a special operations team. He had gone on many covert missions, but one night in Cambodia had changed his life forever.

After he was made lycan, he had been forced to serve under a brutal alpha who demanded he keep the fact he was alive a secret. So Derek told no one. He'd made no contact with his family, not because Neville had ordered him to do so, but simply because Derek hated what he had become—a monster who reveled in blood and death. He had fought through the ranks until Neville became afraid of him and set him free.

He'd wandered for a bit, unsure if he would be welcomed home, but when Derek had shown up at the barracks back in Ireland, the men who had once known him were stunned that he had not aged a day in ten years.

After intense questioning and debriefing, and after telling his commander the truth about what had happened to him, they honourably discharged him due to PTSD. It was something they did not put in his medical records, however, which allowed Derek to apply to the guards. This worked out for him for a couple of years until questions about his youthful looks threatened to unleash his secret, and he was forced out. At that point, the world had found out about his kind and wanted to hunt them down. It wasn't until Sarge had phoned and offered him a job on the new task force that he'd felt like he had a purpose again.

Living until you were almost a hundred while looking twenty-seven would do that to you.

Derek shook off the demons of his past as he walked through the gates of the station and bounded up the steps with a gasping Ricky hot on his heels. Silently, they shuffled down the hallway before coming to their operations room. Derek pushed the door open with a loud creak, and Ricky slipped in under his arm, flopped down at his desk, and propped his muddy boots up on his desk.

"Sarge will have your guts for brekkie, bro."

"Pffft. D, you worry too much."

"And being your partner has aged me like ten years."

Ricky grinned up at him. "D, you're older than most of us combined and look younger than all of us. Stop flaunting your youthful grace at us, pretty boy, and sit your fine ass down."

Derek smirked despite the horror that still lingered in his mind and eased himself into his own chair. Checking his email, he frowned as he spotted another 'invitation' from the Munster pack to come speak with them. Derek had been a lone wolf for half a century, keeping himself free of pack politics as much as possible, but the latest alpha seemed overly keen to have him join the pack. Derek deleted the email as the door flew open. In filed the rest of the team with Sarge hot on their heels.

The rectangular room had one solitary window, and because everyone had a desk, the tiny space often became cramped. There was a series of whiteboards on the wall behind each desk, with the main suspect board freestanding in the center of the room. It didn't leave a lot of elbowroom.

Sarge must have called them all in because even members of the night shift had braved the sunlight for this. Donnie and Caitlyn, the resident vampires, wore dark sunglasses and heavy clothing to hide their skin from the sun. Hollywood directors had gotten some of the truth right—vampires had fangs, had an aversion to sunlight, and needed to drink blood—but they tended to exaggerate a little. While his friends preferred to be one with the night, the sun did not reduce them to ashes on the wind. It did burn their skin so they looked like victims of a terrible fire, but kill them... it did not. However, a stake to the heart would do the job nicely.

Donnie was built like a rugby player, all broad shoulders and thick thighs. He had played professionally for Ireland until one night of celebration had ended with him getting stabbed and turned by Caitlyn. They were loyal as hell to each other and the team, but as far as Derek knew, the two weren't romantically involved. Caitlyn held all the grace of a movie star from the fifties—à la Dita Von Teese. Even now, in ripped, faded blue jeans and an olive-coloured, hooded sweatshirt, the female oozed sex appeal. Black curls framed her face, and eyes of slate grey were behind those sunglasses.

The vampires perched on the edge of Ricky's desk, Caitlyn pushing his muddy boots off the desk with a *tsk*. Ricky muttered something in Latin under his breath, and his boots instantly cleaned themselves. The warlock grinned and set his now-clean boots on the table again. Derek grinned as he waited for Sarge to speak.

Melanie quietly slipped into the room and sat down in front of her computer. Unlike the rest of the team, Melanie was human. She was gifted with computer skills. The youngest member of the team at twenty-two, the girl had been recruited to join just about every task force in Ireland and more. But she had settled on their little operation. Derek had never asked why, and Melanie had never offered an explanation, but he thought she was brave. She was a tiny wisp of a thing with Christina Hendricks' red locks and big-rimmed glasses that took away from the subtle beauty behind them, and she had the courage to join a team full of supes.

Just as Sarge cleared his throat, the forever-late Fionn burst through the door. Derek wrinkled his nose as the smell of cat stabbed the air. The ginger-haired cat flushed the same colour as his hair. "Sorry, Sarge."

Their boss just snorted as Fionn padded to his own desk and tucked his legs under himself as he sat, resting his chin in the palm of his hand. When the unit had first started out, they'd had almost a ten-member team from various backgrounds, but some had died in the line of duty and some in conflicts from their own species. Now there were three shifters, a warlock, two vamps, and a computer geek, giving the team seven unless Anna was included as a team member, which rounded them to eight.

Sarge cleared his throat again and the room hushed, the bear discernible in that authoritative voice of his as he said, "Three vics in, and we're still no closer to getting a hit on the unsub. Mr. Saunders has already barged in here, demanding we pull our heads out of our..." Sarge paused, glancing at Melanie before continuing. "Anna is running tests on the previous two victims to see if there are any traces of supernatural in their DNA. Ricky, I want you and Fionn to drive to Clare and ask the family of the first victim what they are, face to face."

Ricky made to protest, but Derek caught his eye and

shook his head. Fionn and Ricky did not get along, and it was quite possible the two would kill each other before they reached the victim's house. Donnie and Caitlyn smirked.

Sarge stared at the vampires. "I need you two to stay here until dark and help Melanie try to see a connection between the victims. We know they all come from different counties, different sections of society, but there has to be something that links them all together. I've got people from all over breathing down my neck about our lack of progress, so we need to find this SOB now."

Fionn hissed but got up and headed for the door. Ignoring Ricky, he let the door slam behind him, and Ricky groaned.

"C'mon, Sarge, you know the cat hates me... let one of the vampires go instead."

Sarge stared him down, and Ricky lowered his gaze. "Maybe if you hadn't broken his sister's heart, he might like you more. You have a job to do, so do it—that's an order."

Derek stood and clasped his friend on the back. "If you told Fionn the truth, he might feel more receptive."

Ricky shook his head, keeping his secrets to himself before turning and storming out as well.

Derek spied Melanie watching as Ricky left, and the young girl blushed when she noticed she'd been caught. Poor girl would get her heart broken if she ever became the subject of attention from his friend. Derek loved him, but Ricky had more demons than he did, and that was saying something.

As the vampires began rearranging the suspect board and putting up a school picture of Carly Saunders, Sarge beckoned Derek forward. He followed Sarge's lead, sitting when the bear sat, folding his arms across his chest.

"Ricky and Fionn don't work well together."

"Ricky will have to get used to working with a new partner in the near future. I'm easing him into it." Sarge sighed. The bear was younger than Derek by almost twenty years, but something about the aging process with bears meant his lifespan was shorter. Sarge, whose real name was Tom Delaney, had been threatening to retire for years and wanted Derek to take over; Derek was happy being a cop and did not want to be a leader.

"We'll see. What do you need me to do?"

"I need you to go speak with a consultant. She teaches various subjects over at the College of Paranormal Studies and is expecting a rep from the team to escort her here after her twelve o' clock lecture."

Derek groaned as his wolf growled inside him. "I'm not a babysitter, Sarge... let me work the case."

"Derek, it is four days from the full moon, and according to reports, you have been a little on edge this week. All I need you to do is bring the woman here so I can babysit her. Maybe you will change your mind after meeting her."

Snorting, Derek asked, "Why this lecturer? What is so special about this woman?"

Sarge stretched his arms over his head. "Girl is all kinds of smart and has an eidetic memory. She holds degrees in criminology, psychology, paranormal anthropology, and paranormal species. Our unsub leaves no trace of himself and drains the vics of blood and marrow. A fresh pair of eyes may help."

Derek wanted to catch this monster as bad as Sarge did. He let out a defeated breath and said, "Tell me the details."

Chapter Two

Derek cursed a blue streak and tightened his grip on the steering wheel as he drove. Perhaps Sarge had been right, that his control was stretched to the limits at this moment. His wolf clawed at the edge of his mind, and he eased off the steering wheel as he heard it crack under the pressure. Blowing out a breath, he counted to ten to try to calm himself. However, being this close to the full moon hammered at his self-control.

If he were being honest with himself, Derek hated what he had become. Sometimes, when he thought hard about it, he considered the reason why he had joined his team was because he believed himself to be as much of a monster as those he chased down. He had explained this to Ricky one time, but his friend had shot him down. Ricky told him he could never be a monster like the ones they hunted down... that he would never let him be.

As the College of Paranormal Studies came into view, Derek turned on his right indicator and pulled into the first parking space he saw. The building loomed in his vision as he rolled up the window and popped his sunglasses on. It was a rare sunny day in Ireland, but Derek was worried that his wolf would come to the forefront and show in his eyes. All he needed was for some poor student to piss themselves at the sight of him all wolfed out.

His wolf snorted at the thought, liking the fact that they had power over mere mortals. Derek shook his head, opening the car door. His skin ached, so he stretched out his muscles. Despite the fact that he could channel his wolf at any time and change whenever he wished, for the most part, he tried to suppress that part of himself. This made the days leading up to the full moon more painful and the change excruciating on the night of, but he needed it to remind him that he was still human... to some extent, anyway.

He shut the car door and rolled up the sleeves of his shirt. Behind the shade of his sunglasses, he could still see the admiring glances from the students bustling around campus. They smiled and batted their eyelashes at him, but he swiftly walked past them. Derek knew he was considered good-looking, handsome even, but he knew the wolf genes made him appealing to others. It made him more attractive with pheromones or something like that.

Striding forward, Derek made his way across the campus to find out where he could find his consultant. Sarge had barely given him any details at all except that the woman's name was Ever Chace and she had helped him out a few times with different cases. If Sarge said she was the right person for the job, then Derek was inclined to believe it. Sarge had earned that from him—

from all the team.

Derek paused for a moment to take in his surroundings. The college was a newly built facility, barely a decade old. When the supes had been revealed to the world way back in the 90s, Cork City center had gone through a metamorphosis. Originally, the college had been a small building with just three floors, and a vast array of businesses on the outskirts of the city centre. When the government had passed a motion to create a new college where humans and supes alike could study whatever they wished in paranormal studies, a lot of the businesses were bought out. A vibrant, state-of-the-art facility that was four stories high and spanned about four blocks stood in their place.

Both humans and supes studied there, and they even had night classes for the nocturnal creatures. Derek had been pleasantly surprised that the world had accepted them as openly as they had. Of course, there were those who'd said they were abominations, creatures spawned from the devil himself and set forth upon the earth. The largest group was called Humans Matter, and they staged protests and rallies all the time trying to sway people to their cause of banning supes out of Ireland altogether.

His wolf bared his teeth, snarling at the humans' way of thinking. Derek sighed and shook his head as if he could somehow shake the wolf from his brain. As he moved forward, his heavy boots crunched on the asphalt. He had never been inside the college before. Glancing around for a sign that would lead him to a reception area, all he saw were building names. The Dracul Building made him smirk, while Wolfsbane House made him itch.

Derek was so busy trying to figure out where he

was going that he walked smack into something... and the most amazing thing happened. His wolf instantly stilled—calmed and laid down in his mind's eye. For a moment, he didn't know what to do. He blinked away the confusion and stood there like an idiot for a few heartbeats.

His mind was clear, and he could think. Derek's thoughts were just his thoughts; he wasn't competing for headspace with his wolf. For the first time in a long time, he was just Derek. He felt human.

Then he heard a groan and shook the shock away as he gazed down at what he had collided with—or actually, *whom*.

Papers had scattered all over the ground, and a woman in her mid-twenties tried to scoop them up before they blew away. Derek knelt down and gathered up some before handing them to her. She cursed in German under her breath, and Derek's lip curled up. He rose when she did and was about to apologize when the woman spoke.

"You'd think, being a wolf, you'd be a little more observant."

"And if you're smart enough to be attending college, then you should be smart enough to watch where you're going." The words left his mouth before he had the chance to think. He was about to apologize again when the girl burst out laughing.

It was then Derek had the chance to take her in—this girl who had calmed his wolf. She stood around 5'6" with silky smooth, golden-blonde hair that shimmered in the sun and blue-grey eyes that sparkled as she laughed. Her outfit made her look older than he imagined she was, but the faint hint of sneakers underneath faded denim jeans intrigued him. A black blazer over a loose, sky-blue blouse accentuated her eyes. With pale skin that matched her hair, she was classically beautiful, and Derek was captivated by her. She smelled of sunshine and sand; he could almost taste it on his tongue.

He was struck by a primal urge to taste her, to press his lips to hers and see if she tasted as good as she smelled. Although calmed, his wolf whimpered in agreement, and Derek had to take a step back to prevent him from acting untoward.

"I'm sorry for being so rude," he began, but she waved him off.

"That's okay. I probably shouldn't be rushing around. Lost track of time... Are you lost?"

Derek bobbed his head. "I'm looking for the reception area."

She came to stand beside him and pointed straight ahead. "If you cross the quad and go into the main building, it's just inside the door. You can't miss it. Look for a heavyset woman who looks like she could eat you alive. That's Norma."

His grin widened. "Should I be scared?"

She smiled back. "Nope, I don't think wolf is her idea of a good meal. You should be safe."

She swept her hair off her face, and Derek wanted to run his fingers through it to see if it felt as soft as it looked. What the hell was wrong with him?

Before he had time to articulate another word, the woman looked at her watch. "Shit! Sorry, I'm late for class! Nice running into you."

And with that, she was gone, the scent of her lingering as his wolf whimpered.

He watched until her golden hair disappeared from

sight, and that was when the wolf-rage punched back inside his head. Derek stumbled with the brunt force of it, grinding his teeth and clenching his fists to his sides. People around him gave him a wide berth, moving farther away as he tried to calm himself so he wouldn't change.

When he had reined in his wolf, Derek wondered just who the hell that woman had been and how he was going to track her down to see her again. His phone beeped, dragging him from his thoughts. Pulling it from his pocket, Derek slid down his shades and squinted to read a text from Ricky. After claiming he had not killed the cat yet, Ricky told him they should make it to the first victim's house by one.

Glancing at his own watch, he saw it was twenty past noon. Thrusting thoughts of the mysterious woman to the back of his mind, Derek focused on the job at hand. He followed her directions after crossing the quad, pushed open the heavy oak doors, and stepped inside. The corridor was dark, so he removed his shades and crooked them in the V-neck of his shirt.

He almost smiled as he laid eyes on who could only be Norma, glaring at him from behind a high desk. It was evident straightaway that Norma was a witch; he could scent the sage that clung to her clothing. She was indeed a heavyset woman whose shoulders gave Donnie a run for his money. A crooked nose and beady eyes watched him from behind thick glasses as he walked forward and leaned an elbow on the edge of the desk.

"Can I help you?" she croaked.

"Yes, I believe so. My name is Derek Doyle. I'm with the Paranormal Investigations Team." He flashed his badge, and Norma's frown deepened. "I'm looking for a

Ms. Ever Chace. Her presence has been requested by my captain to help with a case."

Norma cleared her throat. "You just missed Ms. Chace." As she started tapping away on her keyboard, she left him waiting for a few moments before she responded again. "Ah, yes. Ms. Chace is in the middle of a paranormal offenders lecture over in Dracul Hall. You'll find her there."

He flashed his most charming smile, but it seemed to have no effect on her. "Thank you so much, Norma. You have been a great help."

The quad was now quiet, with just a few stragglers rushing to get to class. Not bothering to shield his eyes, he made the short trek across the quad in only a few minutes. He held open the door for a young student, who blushed profusely as she thanked him before she melted into the darkness of the hallways.

Derek checked the board and spied the name and room number he was looking for. Taking the steps two at a time, he bounded up the stairs and strolled down the hall as the time on his watch indicated he was far too early to collect Ms. Chace. Derek came to a stop at the open door of the lecture theatre, and his wolf silenced once more. He couldn't stop himself from going in, as if a siren song were calling him and his actions were not his own.

The lecture theatre was massive and packed with about two hundred students. The stage loomed below him, and his eyes wandered down until they landed on his mystery woman. He swallowed hard and leaned against the doorframe. His wolf curled up inside him, content to listen to her voice as she spoke.

"There are many misconceptions that can happen

when it comes to paranormal profiling. Not all vampire killers drain their victims of blood. Not all shifter deaths are a result of dominance fights or loss of control of their animal. Like humans, serial killers and murders exist in the supernatural community as well. Sometimes, a human will even use a typical method of killing used by a supe to divert suspicion away from them."

Derek inclined his head and listened intently as she continued to speak.

"For example, take the case of Philip K. Bourke, who raped and murdered seventeen men in the UK. Philip managed to use a nail to hammer two identical puncture wounds into the neck of his victims to give the impression a vampire had committed the murders. He even figured out how to drain some blood from the victims, but after good police work and investigation, it was soon discovered that the murderer had been human all along."

Derek remembered the case. In the end, it had been Bourke's cocky ego, thinking he could not get caught, that had done him in. He'd created a blog and posted detailed stories on how the murders had gone down, information only the murderer could have known. Bourke was now doing life in prison in the UK.

"When it comes to profiling a person of paranormal descent," she continued as she walked from one side of the stage to the other, "we must leave our prejudice and beliefs to one side as we would if the offender were human. Some of the supernatural communities are as human as you and I. They have the same rights to a fair trial and to be innocent until proven guilty."

There was a pause and a nod before a new voice piped in. "But isn't there an increasing chance in the days leading up to the full moon that violence amongst the werewolves is increased, and thus can only indicate most murders that happen around the full moon are indeed done by wolves?"

Derek snickered; he couldn't help it. Eyes turned in his direction, and her eyes danced mischievously as the woman on stage peered up at him.

"Brendan, we have a unique opportunity to have a wolf with us so close to the full moon. Now, I know we usually ask Declan about wolfie matters, but he is too young to be around us this close to the full moon. Would *you* mind?" she coyly asked Derek, but her facial expression betrayed her as she grinned.

Derek straightened and smiled back at her. "Not at all. Brendan, is it?" he asked, flashing his teeth at the poor boy. "Any occurrence of violence would have happened way back before the supernatural community came out to humans. When wolves are forced to conceal a vital part of themselves, reduce shifting to when necessary, and basically never fully accept their other halves, that, of course, could lead to violent outbursts and losing control of their wolves. But, having alphas and being part of a pack strengthens the human half and lessens the spate of murders that could occur if a wolf is not properly disciplined. Any person, wolf or human, can succumb to rages if they bottle up their emotions. Wolves just tend to use claws when they lash out."

"Thank you, sir."

Derek nodded, barely taking his eyes off the blonde.

A bell chimed, signaling the end of class, and the students clambered free of their desks and hustled up the steps. He waited until the room was almost empty before he descended. His mystery girl stood talking to a grey-haired woman, who he assumed was Ms. Chace. The woman was small with a kind face. She smelled human, and Derek wondered how she had ended up being a paranormal studies professor.

He came to a halt as both women glanced in his direction. Remembering his manners, Derek held out his hand and addressed the grey-haired woman. "Agent Derek Doyle of the Paranormal Investigations Team. Tom Delaney sent me to escort you to the station. He speaks very highly of you, Ms. Chace. It's a pleasure to meet you."

The woman clasped a hand over her mouth and giggled. He raised an eyebrow as she doubled over laughing. The golden-haired girl next to him just shrugged and smiled. His wolf inclined his head, intrigued. When the woman had finally regained her composure, she waved a hand, and Derek wondered if Sarge knew his consultant was crazy.

"Dear, I'm afraid you have the wrong person. I'm not Ms. Chace."

Derek wondered if he had read the board wrong and frowned. "Oh, I'm sorry. Can you tell me where I could find Ms. Chase, please?"

"I'm right here."

Derek turned and looked into cobalt eyes. This time, she extended her delicate hand and said, "Ever Chace. Nice to see you again, Agent Derek Doyle."

Derek took her outstretched hand, and his wolf wagged his tail at the simplest touch of skin. He pulled back, raising his eyebrow again. "You're Ever Chace—*Doctor* Ever Chace?"

"Guilty. Now, shall we go? I don't wish to keep Tom waiting."

His wolf bristled at the casual way she spoke of Sarge, purely jealous of the familiarity and evident fondness in her voice. He backed away, the confusion of being in such close proximity with Ever beginning to unease him.

Ever said her goodbyes to the other woman and gathered her bag before following after Derek. They walked in silence until they were out in the fresh air again. Even though his wolf watched Ever with an intensity that shocked him to his core, Derek wondered how she could calm his wolf so much as to turn him into nothing more than a puppy dog.

"So... are you going to speak to me again or not?" Ever smirked as she caught up with him despite his long strides.

"Depends on if you knew who I was when you ran into me."

She snorted. "You were the one who ran into me, Mr. Agent. Besides, other than knowing you were a cop, how was I to know you were the one Tom had sent to bring me to the station?"

He blew out a breath and stomped out to the car park. Derek had no clue why he was so pissed off, but he knew he needed to get Ever to Sarge and leave before his wolf decided he didn't like being docile anymore. He could feel the rage build up inside him, and he longed to punch something. It was not a good feeling for a wolf on the cusp of a full moon.

Derek went to the passenger side of his car and opened the door for Ever. Looking surprised, she gave him a genuine smile and slipped into the seat of his BMW. As he closed the door, he gave himself a minute before getting into the driver's side. After putting the keys in the ignition, Derek started the car and reversed out. It was a little after one and the lunch traffic was beginning to build up.

"If you're going to be all silent and broody, Mr. Agent, can I at least turn on the radio?"

Derek grunted a *yes* as he maneuvered his way through the traffic, groaning as Ever turned on the radio and an overly poppy track vibrated out of the speakers. She tapped her fingers on the window and hummed along to the song. Both man and wolf were utterly captivated by her.

This was going to be a long day.

Chapter Three

"How well do you know Sarge?"

The question seemed to startle Ever after the long, uncomfortable silence. Derek had barely opened his mouth as they'd trudged their way through traffic. She stole a peek at him, and he felt her curiosity heightened as she ran her haunting blue eyes over him. The possibility of being so close to a wolf would be too much of a draw for a scholar like Ever. She surveyed him now like he imagined she would a textbook—hungry, fascinated, and eager to devour all she could.

Ever swept her hair off her shoulder and smiled as she spoke. "I've known Tom since forever. Tom asked my parents if they wanted to adopt me when I was abandoned as an infant. Because of him, I grew up in a loving home with parents who adored me. He's my godfather in every aspect... like my uncle."

The tension that had caused Derek's knuckles to whiten as he drove seemed alleviated somewhat by her words, and Ever relaxed into the luxury of his car. Comforting black leather that shouldn't have been as soft as it was allowed her to snuggle into the seat, and when she sighed, his wolf echoed her sigh, delighting in bringing her pleasure.

"Someone abandoned you at birth?" Derek asked, a slight edge in his voice.

Ever shrugged her shoulders. "It's something I came to terms with a long time ago. My parents were open and honest about how I came into their lives, and I've only ever felt grateful to whoever it was who felt they could not keep me. I had a wonderful childhood and an amazing life. What do I have to complain about?"

As the car came to a halt in the midst of the jam-packed traffic, Derek opened the window and exhaled. He looked over at her then, and he felt the slight amber slip into his eyes that betrayed him as a deadly predator.

"I'm surprised, Ms. Chace, that you have such a positive outlook on your past. I feel slightly envious."

"Ever," she said.

"I'm sorry?"

Her lips tugged up into a smile. When she smiled, her whole face lit up in a radiant, otherworldly beauty that caused Derek's heart to skip a beat. He wasn't sure what the hell was going on, but every minute he was near Ever Chace, he liked her more and more.

"Call me Ever," she replied, warmth in her voice. "If my students get away with calling me Ever, then there's no need for the Ms. Chace bit from you—makes me feel old!"

Derek chuckled for the briefest of seconds before he caught himself, and Ever watched as something flashed over his features before disappearing. He saw her struggle not to giggle as his jaw ticked, and he didn't blame her. As Ricky often put it, Derek liked to pretend he was closed off and abrupt, laughing very little and smiling even less. But somehow, this siren had pulled from him a laugh that was usually reserved for his friends and family.

"If I'm to call you Ever, then I insist you call me Derek. Seems only fair." His own words shocked him, the slightly teasing tone shocking him even more.

Derek edged the car forward at a break in traffic. His wolf stretched out in his mind, at ease with whatever it was that made Ever have this effect on him. He could hear the rapid beat of her pulse as she studied him, his wolf preening at her inspection. *Down boy. Keep your head in the game.*

His wolf snorted at him and shook out its fur. Derek felt eager to know all about the girl—no, the *woman.* The little smidge of information she'd shared was not enough for the man.

"What made you want to specialize in paranormal studies, especially in paranormal offenders?"

Ever leaned forward in her seat and rested her chin in her hands. "My parents are supernatural, and I grew up in that world. It was hard for me when all my friends were of that world and I felt like an outsider. But, with my mind retaining information like I do, I watched my friends and my parents' friends and became fascinated to learn anything I could."

She broke off for a minute, her nose crinkling. "It was my own insecurity at first, but when the world found out that the things that go bump in the night were real, I thought it would be easier for a human to explain things to others. I couldn't be biased against the monsters if I'd grown up with them."

Derek bristled at the slight irritation in her voice. Someone had hurt her in the past because of who she was or who her parents were, and damned if the wolf in him didn't want to sink his teeth into some flesh and tear that idiot limb from limb.

"Anyway, I was one of the first students in the College of Paranormal Studies. When I graduated a few years later, the dean asked me to teach while I studied. And now, here I am, working as a consult for P.I.T."

A car honked from behind, and Derek bared his teeth in the mirror as he inched forward, so caught up in Ever he hadn't realized the lights had changed colour. In the last half hour since they had emerged from the college, the car had barely moved as the steady flow of cars tried to maneuver the busy city streets. At this rate, Ricky would be back from Clare and they would be still stuck in this abyss.

Derek steered the car into the correct lane as they came to another frustrating halt outside City Hall. He thrummed his fingers on the dashboard with impatience.

"Why do you bother driving if you get this annoyed over a little traffic?" she teased at his obvious discomfort.

"Driving, I love. Being stuck in traffic, unable to move, frustrates my wolf and me. This close to the full moon, we're always at loggerheads for control."

Her cobalt eyes sparkled with interest. "Most werewolves, bitten or changed, talk of their wolves as an extension of themselves, while you speak as if your wolf is separate from you."

It was Derek's turn to shrug. "I dunno. I think I've always referred to my wolf as just that—my wolf. When we are in human form, I'm the one who is most in control. When he's in control, then I allow him the freedom to be a wolf without the leash of my conscience. There are things the wolf likes to do that at times disgust me, while he is vocal about things I do that piss him off. I keep thinking one day I'll accept what I am and learn to be one with my wolf. And I have absolutely no idea why I just told you that." His jaw ticked again.

Ever bit her lip. "Were you changed by force?" she inquired, her curiosity shining on her face.

Derek's grip on the wheel tightened as the car lurched forward and made good progress before the lights changed. "Yeah, it's not a choice I would have made. I guess I carried a latent form of the gene. When a werewolf tore out my throat while on a mission, it triggered the change, and here I am."

"From your words, I take it you wish you had never survived the bite. Why do you talk like being a werewolf is a curse?" Ever asked, still looking curious.

The lights changed and Derek accelerated, the traffic now beginning to die down as their car reached the outskirts of the suburbs. Even though there were still more vehicles than usual on the road, the journey to the station would only take about twenty minutes at most. Glancing at the clock on the dash, he blinked when he saw that it neared two o'clock in the afternoon. Time had flown in the cramped confines of his car, too quickly for his liking. He still hadn't answered Ever's question.

Derek leaned his head to the right. "Isn't it?"

She gave a little shake of her head. "Some consider it a blessing. To stay young, to remain strong for hundreds of years. To watch history unfold before your eyes and see all the wonders that the world has for you to experience. I think it would be a privilege."

He looked at her then—really looked at her—and held her gaze. "And then there are those who, after centuries on this wretched earth, claim that this is punishment for our past sins. That staying young and strong while we watch those we love wither and die around us is a fate worse than death itself."

His statement, though brief, held an abundance of emotion, of loss and sorrow entwined with secrets that Ever was eager to discover. "Do you really believe that? Do you honestly think being a werewolf is your penance? And if it's a curse for past sins, then can you not look at it as some sort of redemption? A way to balance the scales?"

Derek remained silent for the moment; the only sounds were their breathing, the hum of the car's engine, and the world that continued around them. He had never looked at it that way, but he couldn't agree with her positive outlook on being a wolf. Ever was too young, too optimistic, to see the darkness that blackened the world. He hoped she stayed that way—hopeful, eager, looking at the good rather than the bad—but he didn't have it in him. The darkness had latched on years ago, drenched itself in blood, and taken host in his soul. It had become a part of him that he couldn't escape, no matter how much good he did.

"I don't believe in redemption, Ever," he sighed, sad but resolved, "but I was made lycan, and I've learned to live with that much like you learned to be the woman you are today. If I can use my abilities as a wolf to do some good and catch bad guys—the monsters humans are afraid to hunt—then I can be content with that, with my life."

Ever opened her mouth to speak, when a sharp buzz stopped her. Derek pressed the answer button on his phone, not needing to put it to his ear to hear the caller. "Doyle."

"D! I swear on all that I hold dear in this world that I'm going to shave the cat bald and use him as a rug in front of my fireplace!"

Derek grinned, and Ever looked at him, unable to hear the words his friend spoke.

"Fionn could claw your eyes out in a second, my friend. Then how would you be able to spot a beautiful woman coming your way?"

Ricky cursed and Derek laughed, his wolf liking the way Ever smiled to herself when he did. His wolf licked at its paws, as if he were making himself more presentable for their travel companion.

"So we spoke to the first vic's parents, and it looks like we finally got a break. Sandy Goldsmith was, in fact, a supe who had yet to come into her powers. Her parents were merpeople, and Sandy was coming up on the age of maturity, to develop her sea legs. D, she was their only kid. It takes mermaids centuries to have one kid."

"It's safe to assume that the boy was supernatural also. At least we've an MO now, Ricky. We're gonna get this bastard," Derek said, a growl rumbling deep in his chest.

"Chalk it down, my furry friend. So, you get with the consultant yet? How's she looking?"

Derek's growl found its way up his throat so it echoed throughout the car, much to his friend's amusement. Ricky had enough women running around after him, Ever would not be one of them.

"Easy, D. No need to scare the pretty little teacher

with your scary-ass wolf routine. Down, boy."

Derek ground his teeth together. "If the cat doesn't kill you, Ricky, I may just have to do it myself."

But Ricky just laughed harder. "Love you, too, D. Right, the cat is back now. We should be back in under an hour. We're halfway there already."

Hanging up with a grunt, he stole a quick look at Ever. Her golden-blonde hair seemed to lighten her face and make her eyes a dazzling shade of blue, like the purest of water that allowed you to see the bottom of the ocean. He struggled to restrain his wolf as the beast in his head demanded he claim her as his so that no one would dare touch her without losing an appendage. He wanted to yank off her seat belt, pull her into his lap, and kiss her until they were both drunk with passion. He had never felt this possessive, this hungry for someone before.

"Tell me more about your parents." Derek genuinely wanted to know more about Ever, and his wolf seemed to behave when she spoke. He kept his eyes forward as he steered the car around the city suburbs mere minutes from the station.

"My mother is a high Wiccan priestess and my father a highly respected Druid. They met one winter solstice as teenagers. My father says when he first laid eyes on the gorgeous, raven-haired beauty that was my mother, as she danced amongst the others in her coven, that no other girl would suffice."

She smiled at the memory with a look many women got when they spoke of marriage and love. He hadn't understood the reaction before... until right now.

"He courted her for many months until she gave in and went out on a date with him. They were inseparable after that, married a few months later, and decided to travel the world. They had wanted to share their love of each other by having a family, but we both know witches and warlocks cannot have kids with one another."

Her voice wavered, sorrow flooding her words as she continued. "When Mom sat me down and told the story of how I had come into their lives, I cried at the sadness in her voice when she spoke of the children she could never have. But Mom brushed away my tears and simply said, *"Mo chailín leanbh*—my baby girl—*just because I did not give birth to you, that does not make you any less mine or your father's. We are blessed that someone else brought you into the world for us. Our grá—our love—for you is not diminished because I did not carry you."*

Derek signaled and veered the car around the roundabout, trying to avoid the disgust in his stomach at the media vultures who circled around the murderer's dumpsite. They were waiting, watching, for a chance to catch something—anything—they could publish. After he made it through and edged the car into the station, he pulled into his parking space and brought the car to a halt.

Killing the engine, he pulled the keys free and went to open the door. Ever went to do the same, but Derek's voice stopped her.

"I think your mother is a wise woman, Ever. From the way you speak of her and the words she told you, she is your mother in every way except blood. And believe me, sharing blood with someone doesn't necessarily make you closer. The family we choose as our own matters far more than the family that is forced upon us."

He was out of the car before she could answer him.

Ever quickly followed suit, grabbing the bag that she had stashed under the seat when she had gotten in. She closed the car door behind her as Derek waited for her to emerge. As she flashed a smile, he started to smile back when the main door to the station opened and out strode his boss.

"Uncle Tom!" she squealed and ran into the arms of the aging bear. A chortle escaped him, a familiar sound. She hugged him fiercely, and Derek understood why. This was the man who had ensured Ever hadn't been lost to the system, one of those kids who went into foster care and never emerged. He'd forged a life for Ever that she may have never had if he hadn't been the one who had found her on those church steps.

"How's my favorite niece today?"

"Here to help as much as I can."

Her words seemed to sober him and he stepped from her embrace, his eyes darting to Derek.

"And has Agent Doyle behaved himself?" Sarge teased his second-in-command, basking in delight as Derek growled.

Ever laughed, sweeping her hair back off her face as the wind began to gust. "Derek has been nothing but a perfect gentleman, haven't you, Derek?"

Derek muttered under his breath and stormed off ahead of them. Both Ever and Sarge laughed as they followed him up the steps to the station. Derek waited for them to join him, his temper fraying a tad. The muscle in his jaw ticked, and Sarge watched him brace a hand against the wall.

Derek moved to open a door for Ever, and she slipped inside under his watchful gaze. He ran his eyes over her curves and cursed when Sarge punched him lightly on the shoulder, a grin on his face.

Derek felt his wolf stir and snarl, snapping at the inside of his mind as Ever moved farther away from him down the corridor. She linked her arm with Sarge, and the pair chatted away as Derek stalked after them. In a few days, he would be off the case for forty-eight hours while he lost control to his wolf. He needed to get his head in the game and focus on finding that monster before another child was taken far too early.

Gritting his teeth, he mentally slapped his wolf on the nose as he growled and followed the pair in front of him, his eyes firmly watching only one person—and it certainly wasn't Sarge.

HE WATCHED THE DAMN WOLF PULL INTO THE POLICE station and felt the urge to dissect the beast who had made it his mission to capture him. This creature and his team wanted to stop his fun and games and take his prizes away from him.

He wouldn't allow it.

His shoulder bumped against the journalists who swarmed around him with no idea that the man they sought was right in front of them. He could kill them all, bathe in all their bloody glory, but he had other things to do. He had a plan, and he had to stick to it. Timing was everything.

Grudgingly, he left the crowd and made his way to his own vehicle. He spied the cop speaking to a stunningly beautiful woman before the bear came to meet them. It intrigued him to see the look on the hard-nosed cop's face. Maybe he would have to spend some more time watching him and his new golden-haired girl.

However, now was not the time. Tearing his gaze from them, he slid into his car, his body shaking in anticipation. He hadn't had enough time with his Carly; she had faded too quickly. She wasn't as strong as he would have liked. His body trembled in pleasure as he remembered how she had tasted... and how she had screamed and begged for her life.

But it was over too soon. The next one would last longer; he would make sure of it. His hunger was growing, and his need was insatiable. He didn't have time to waste. He wanted to feel the taste of young, tart blood on his tongue once more.

He needed to live. His lust for blood only elevated the need for survival. He hadn't expected to enjoy it so much, hadn't meant to fall so far that even if he managed to stay alive, he would be a slave to the bloodlust. But he didn't care.

Regaining his composure, he drove the car into the steady stream of traffic, blood on his mind and another victim in his sights.

CHAPTER FOUR

DEREK SIPPED HIS LUKEWARM COFFEE AS HE KEPT AN eye on Ever. She was hunched over the case files, scouring for information. After a brief introduction to the rest of the team, she had gotten sucked into things right off the bat and hadn't looked up even when Melanie set a cup of something warm down on her desk.

He tore his gaze away from her and went back to concentrating on his own work. His lust to spill the killer's blood sharpened when he looked at the crime scene photos of Carly Saunders. Matted hair, her dirtied and bruised body, and those cold, dead eyes staring back at him. Derek's fist clenched and he fought the urge not to slam it down on the desk. Turning over the photo, he read through the findings of the scene in frustration. The murderer had left no trace of himself. No fingerprints, no hair, nothing.

The room suddenly went silent, and he raised his head from his report. The entire station was watching him intently, Melanie with a tinge of fear laced in her scent.

Caitlyn waved off the others and came to stand by the edge of Derek's desk, resting her hip on the edge. She let her lips tug up on the edges before saying, "*Mon ami*, my friend, this moon cycle has you on the very edge. If you need to sit this one out, we can handle this."

Derek reached out and patted her arm. "I'm fine, Cait. The wolf is just a little tetchy right now. I can't let this one go; I have to see it through."

As she twirled a decadent black curl between her fingers, the vampire let her eyes wander and seemed pleased that everyone had gone back to work. "Then I'd suggest a break. Growling your frustrations in our workplace doesn't do much for staff morale."

"I was growling?"

"Like an angry wolf."

Derek smacked a hand to his forehead. In his time on this earth, he had never felt so on edge with his wolf. Sure, he could satisfy it by changing before the full moon, but this close and this angry could lead to the wolf taking over for the next four days. He couldn't chance it.

"Thanks, Cait. I'll try to rein him in."

The vampire nodded and rose, moving with the grace of a predator until she stood next to the male who rarely left her side. Donnie shot him a glance, and they locked eyes. If anyone knew how hard it was to rein in the monster behind the mask, it was Donnie. But that wasn't Derek's story to tell.

The phone on his desk rang, and Derek answered on the third ring. "Doyle."

"Derek, its Anna." The medical examiner's voice was

grim.

"What you got for me, sweetheart?"

Derek listened as Anna explained that after vigorous testing, she could only conclude all three victims were of supernatural descent but had not come into their powers yet. Marrow had been taken from their bones, as well as patches of skin. Enough blood had been drained from each body that the victim would have lost consciousness shortly after. Anna didn't have to say it, but he knew the teens had suffered.

"Was there any indication of...?" his voice trailed off because he really couldn't say the words. The teens had been murdered in a horrific manner, knowing that they had been violated as well would be too much.

"No. The animal at least left them that bit of innocence. Derek, there was something I noticed on the last body. There is bruising on her arms that could provide fingerprints or tell us what kind of monster we are looking for. I sent my findings to the lab."

"You're a star, Anna. Let me know if you find anything else."

"Will do. Greg Saunders has rung a number of times asking when his daughter's body can be released. I told him to contact P.I.T., as it's an open investigation. I suspect you or Tom will receive a call from him soon."

"Appreciate the heads-up. Talk to you soon."

The M.E. hung up without another word, and he rested the receiver in its cradle. Sarge motioned him over, and Derek stretched out his tense muscles when he stood. Ever and Melanie were deep in conversation. As he scratched the stubble on his chin and made to give Sarge the information he'd received, the door crashed open to reveal a red-faced Ricky storming in.

Oh, the warlock was angry. So angry that the pulse of his magic swept around the room and lashed against Derek's skin. He saw a flash of red in Donnie's eyes before Caitlyn laid a hand on his elbow. Derek's own wolf snarled at the power play and wanted to show his friend who was boss. The only person who seemed unaffected was Ever, who calmly got up from her chair and walked right up to Ricky.

"Hi, I'm Ever. Nice to meet you."

Ricky stared at her, blinked, and all at once, the power he was lashing out rescinded and the charming Casanova was back.

"Ricky Moore, darling. Ever—such a beautiful name for a beautiful woman." He took her hand, but instead of shaking it, Ricky turned it over and pressed his lips to her skin.

Ever laughed, a sound so pure and joyful that it made Derek's chest ache.

"Well, you certainly are a charmer. Let me guess—Mr. Broody over there is your partner? Nice yin-and-yang thing you have going on there, Tom."

"I try." A gruff response from the bear.

Ricky glanced over at Derek. Something in Derek's expression must have made him release Ever's hand, but the smug grin on his face refused to budge. Derek became even more intrigued by Ever. Not only could the girl quieten the wolf in him, but she had also somehow tamed the storm that brewed inside Ricky. Derek would ask him about it later, but he suspected Fionn hadn't kept his mouth shut and had laced into Ricky for mistreating his sister. And of course, Ricky kept the real story quiet.

"So, sweet Ever, have you gotten caught up on the case? Because I can stay late and run through things with you if you need me."

Ever smiled. "Nah, I'm good. Besides, I don't think your charms will work on me, Ricky."

"You wound me. My charms work on everyone."

"My mother would disagree."

Ricky blinked in surprise. "Your mother?"

"Perhaps you've heard of her. Samhain Chace?"

Ricky backpedaled and shook his head. "Damn girl, you know how to burst a man's bubble. No way am I going to upset Samhain's baby girl. I like my balls where they are!"

Derek had heard the name Samhain Chace before. She was the overall leader of all the covens in Ireland and one of the most powerful witches of her time. It was hard to believe that the golden-haired beauty was the child of two of the most influential supes in the world. Samhain gave off an aura of power and confidence when she entered a room. Was it any wonder that her daughter did the same?

Ever simply waved him off. "It'll be our little secret." She strode back over to Sarge's desk and sat back down, waiting for Derek to speak. Derek moved forward, elbowing his buddy hard in the ribs as he did. As he came to stand at the front of the room, everyone fell silent, all waiting for his report.

"Anna rang through to say she can confirm that all three victims were indeed supernatural. Bone marrow and skin samples were taken from the victims, and a large portion of blood was drained from them throughout their torture. Ricky and Fionn were able to confirm that Sandy Goldsmith was a mermaid who had not come into her powers, and we know the perp messed up by killing the daughter of a high-profile banshee. I would say it is safe to assume that Philip McRae was also a supe."

"What does he get from kidnapping and torturing young, not yet matured, supes?" Donnie asked.

"Life."

They all looked in Ever's direction. "He gets to take their life from them. These children are on the cusp of adulthood. He takes away their chance at a full life. Takes away what they've waited their whole lives for. The chance to finally be a supernatural creature."

Derek considered Ever's words. He couldn't understand the anticipation of finally being who you were meant to be, but he appreciated that these teens had spent their entire lives knowing what they could become and now never would. The perp was literally stealing their life from them. But why?

"So it's safe to assume the children in the supernatural community are in trouble. Do we have anything else that could narrow down the search?" Derek queried, needing to get a head start on this so his team could work while he was out of commission.

Ricky came to stand by the evidence board. "Sandy Goldsmith's father wasn't supernatural. He was human, and..." He broke off, leafing through some papers before he seemed to find what he was looking for. "Gotcha! And guess what? Maria Saunders was latent. Her banshee powers never manifested. Greg Saunders may lead the banshees, but he doesn't have the ability to sense death—that's the female's job."

"Neither the Goldsmiths nor the Saunders had typical supernatural parentage. How does that help us find the killer?" Sarge asked.

A sense of foreboding cascaded down on the team. It seemed no matter how many steps they took forward, they tended to take a hundred back. Derek strode over to the window and peered out toward the bridge. The gaggle of reporters still hung around waiting for scraps. Not even the darkening sky could lure them away from their pursuit of the ultimate story. He closed his eyes, breathed in, and then exhaled. Letting his thoughts fade away, he just was. He had learned meditation many years ago as a young wolf, and if he'd ever needed a clear head, this was the time.

"If one of Philip McRae's parents turns out to be human, then it's safe to say that the killer is after half-breeds or latents," Derek mumbled.

"That's it!" Ever exclaimed and went to the board. She positioned the victims' pictures on the board and grabbed a dry-erase pen. "The first victim—Sandy Goldsmith. How old was she?"

"Fifteen," Derek replied, the details imprinted on his brain.

Ever wrote the age on the board before turning back to him. "Philip McRae?"

"Fifteen also."

"And how old was Carly Saunders?"

"Seventeen."

That bugged Derek about the MO. Most killers stuck to a certain victim type, but this killer crossed both gender and age brackets. The only thing that seemed to be consistent now was the fact that he took supernatural teens who had yet to mature.

"How close to their next birthdays did they die?"

Caitlyn reached out and grabbed a folder from the desk. Scanning her eyes over the pages, she looked up. "The first victim died two months before her sixteenth birthday. The second was two weeks from turning sixteen, and the most recent was a month away from turning eighteen."

"Latent or half-breed supernatural beings mature or come into their powers at different rates. Unless they are born full-fledged supernatural—or, if you like, purebred— they come into their powers at different times. Banshees tend to hear the first call of death on their eighteenth birthday. I read somewhere that a halfling mermaid grows her first fins on her sixteenth birthday. Could this be how he's choosing his prey?"

"Damn it, Ever... you could be right. It's the closest we have come to finding a pattern," Sarge barked.

"I can only predict that he has selected his next victim already. The time frame between kills has shortened each time. Can we see if we can narrow down how he chooses his targets? Can we try to find a link between all three kids to see if there are any people who overlap with all three victims?" Derek rubbed his temples, suddenly tired.

"I set up an algorithm that will alert me to any similarities in their Internet activity and social media. It may take a little bit of time for something to ping, but I've created an app on my phone that connects me to my work PC. I can call one of you when it does," Melanie piped up in her quiet manner.

"Good work, Lanie," Ricky said in praise, causing the tech's cheeks to blaze a vibrant red.

Sarge checked his watch and cleared his throat. "Okay, folks. It's a little after five. Let's call it a day for now. We can meet again at 0700 and focus on trying to narrow down a suspect pool. Go get some food and rest. None of us can work on fresh air and little else."

The vamps were the first out the door. They didn't

need sleep, but they did need to feed, so Derek assumed they would be hitting up one of the vamp bars in town for nourishment.

Melanie gathered up her laptop and bag. With a quick goodbye to Ever and Sarge, she made to leave unnoticed. Ricky held out a hand and offered to drive her home. Even though they were friends, Derek shot him a look that clearly stated his opinion. Ricky rolled his eyes, took Melanie's bag, looped it over his head, and held out an arm. Melanie bravely linked her arm through his, and they strode out.

Sarge embraced Ever, and she pressed a kiss to his cheek. He stayed back as they chatted for a few minutes and made promises of a catch-up soon with their respective families. Ever gathered up her own stuff and looked up to see Derek watching her.

"Can I drop you home on my way, Ever?" Sarge asked, his gaze wandering between Derek and Ever.

"I can do it," Derek said before Ever could answer.

"You sure?"

"Of course, Sarge. I'll make sure she's home safe."

Ever's phone rang, and she spoke calmly into it. Derek tried not to listen in, but it was hard not to. He heard her ask whoever was on the other end to sub in for her classes for the rest of the week, as she would be continuing to consult with P.I.T. His wolf approved of the fact she was seeing this through to the end, as did the man.

"Take care of her, Derek. She's family."

Sarge stared him in the eye, and Derek knew he was getting the protective, hurt-her-and-I'll-kill-you look. He nodded and replied, "I'll protect her with my life, Sarge."

"Good. I would hate to have to train another replacement before I retire. Took me long enough to train you."

The bear clasped Derek on the shoulder and waved his goodbye to Ever, who was still on the phone. Derek leaned on his desk and waited for her to finish up her call. He watched her with the ferocity only a wolf could. The curves of her body fit snugly into the clothing she wore. She wasn't small, but with his height, she would fit comfortably against his chest. Derek moved his gaze to her face. Those cobalt eyes of hers were the first thing that pierced him when he looked at her.

Her heart-shaped face was framed by her golden-blonde hair to perfection. There was a slight kink to the sides where she had tucked her hair behind her ears. She seemed almost faeish in appearance, but he could scent no hint of fae from her—only a cocktail of summer and sun. She shivered then and turned in his direction, as if she sensed him watching.

Derek was used to being alone and had spent most of his adult-wolf life by himself. And while he had dated a few times, he had never felt this pull, this yank, toward a woman. Never had he had such a primal need to strip a woman naked and claim her for himself.

The woman in question finished her call and advanced to meet him. "Sorry about that," she said, a yawn halting her. "I had to get someone to cover my classes for the next few days so I could concentrate on this. I want to help as much as I can."

"Believe me, you've helped more than you know."

She grinned at him. "Shall we go?"

He nodded and held the door open for her. She walked past him into the corridor, where they fell into a comfortable silence. Derek wasn't one for small talk, and he waited for Ever to make the first step. The gorgeous professor stifled another yawn, and her eyes looked heavy with tiredness.

"I don't know whether I'm tired, hungry, frustrated, or all of the above."

"I'd go for all of the above," he said, a lazy smile playing on his lips.

"Should we get some food on the way back to my place? If I weren't so tired, I'd offer to cook. I make a mean steak."

"Sure; sounds like a plan."

His wolf yipped in agreement, but Derek wasn't sure if it was because it was getting fed or spending more time in Ever's company. They left the station and made the short journey to his car. Again, he opened the door for her, and she slid in with an easy smile. He rounded the car and slipped into the driver's side. Derek started the engine and reversed, edging the car out of the parking spot before he snuck a peek at Ever.

Her eyes were closed, and the faint sound of her breathing was all he heard as Ever fell asleep beside him. He had no idea where she lived, and he was loathe to wake her.

Home, take home, the wolf spoke to him, projecting his thoughts into Derek's human mind.

With little option left, he drove the car to his house close to the airport and parked. Getting out of the car, he went around, opened the passenger door, and very carefully hoisted Ever up into his arms. She wrapped her arms around his neck and rested her head on his shoulder. His wolf howled its approval as the soft heat of her breath danced on his neck.

He shuddered under the intense feeling of pleasure that rippled through him, instantly feeling guilty because of the horrors the poor teens had been subjected to. But as Ever's breathing deepened and dusk began to settle on the city, Derek strode into his house, startled by a stunning realization. This woman in his arms called to him on a most primal level and captivated both man and wolf.

Goddamn it—he wanted to keep her.

CHAPTER FIVE

THE FORCE OF HER HAIR WHIPPING AGAINST HER FAIR skin was sharp enough to draw blood, but she felt no pain. Sand swirled in the desert, and the dense heat was enough to draw a small bead of sweat from her forehead, but neither bothered her; she was no mere mortal. She wiped the blood from her sword onto the body of the slain at her feet and continued. This one had not been worthy.

Eyes blazing a radiant shimmer of cobalt, she paced down the sand dune, avoiding the multiple bodies that had been laid to waste. The ones who were still alive watched her with awe and admiration, as if she were a goddess. Perhaps she was, but right now was not the time to consider her divinity. Dressed in the finest of clothing from her tough, bear-hide skirt to the cropped bra top she wore underneath the hard, impenetrable breastplate woven from the toughest metals from her land, she tended to wish that those beneath her would consider her one of the fiercest of warriors of all time—so much more than a mere goddess.

Brushing the cutting strands from her face, the warrior paused as she surveyed the landscape before her. Her fellow sisters fought battles of their own, each warrior so gloriously beautiful in their dance of death that she paused for a moment to admire them. The wind gathered around her, sand entwining with it in little bursts before settling on the barren wasteland once more. She nodded her approval as her sisters chose the victors, those worthy and battle ready. War was coming and good soldiers were needed in order to level the playing field.

Halting her observation, she moved forward, the harsh glare of the too-bright sun and the grit of sand slipping in between her sandals causing a mild yet noticeable irritation. Blood soaked the sand, a reminder of all those who had been slain here this eve.

Reaching the end of the dune, she made her way over to one of the other warriors who had come halfway to meet her.

"Have we reached our quota on this cull, Systir?"

"We are but a few soldiers short. Mayhap our sisters will have more luck in the ocean lands," her sister replied.

She let a dangerous smile curl up her lips. "We have little time before he attempts to storm our home. We will have enough strength to defeat him, I am sure of it, but we must not get complacent. Take the worthy home and begin their training."

"Do you not fear that they will be too tired from the trials to commence such a rigorous training regime?" There was concern in her sister's voice—not for the warriors, she guessed, but for the loss of soldiers should they not survive the training.

"In battle, there is no rest. We fight until our enemy is defeated, or we bleed our last drop of blood. Our enemy will crush us if we do not have the stamina to last a day of fighting. Then it will be the blood of our kin that will be spilled onto the sands of time, and we shall perish, mere mentions in a history book."

"Understood." The warrior pulled out a curved horn and blew sharply into it. The shrill sound made her fellow sisters' ears twitch as they stood, gathered the worthy, and with a fist over their chests, faced her. She bowed her head, mimicked their actions, and then they were gone; the only evidence they had been there were bloodstained footprints in the sand.

The hairs on the back of her head stood to attention, and she spun round, her sword in hand. Metal clashed against metal as her attacker snickered at her. The startling white of her attacker's hair shone in the unforgiving sun as he thrust his weapon forward, the warrior able to dodge with seconds to spare.

"I would have thought you more careful, daughter mine."

"And I would have thought you had more sense than to take on a warrior of my caliber, Father. Mother has trained me well in the art of spilling blood."

The white-haired man chuckled. "It is nice to see you inherited your mother's cockiness and self-importance, daughter. I shall enjoy bleeding it out of you as I once bled it from her."

Fury became lightning in her veins as she charged him, her body and sword hungry for blood. They danced the dance of warriors, each taking tentative strikes to find a weak spot in their opponent. But they were both seasoned warriors—weakness was not in their vocabulary.

She pivoted to the right, hoping to sneak her blade in through his ribs, but he spotted her advance, familiar with her movements. Knowing that immature reactions would only lead to her own bloodshed, she cursed to herself and focused her energies on defeating the man who threatened to take away all that her mother had built—her legacy. That was something she could never allow to happen.

With poise, speed, and precision, she struck out with her sword and caught her foe on the upper arm as he tried to avoid the strike. The smell of copper hit her nostrils, and she bit back a smile at her little victory.

But her father was not happy. In fact, he began to tremble with rage that his own daughter had been able to draw blood from his flesh. Arrogant as he indeed was, her father did not believe he could be thwarted in his goals. As they stared at each other, the intensity of her own blue eyes was mirrored in the pale blue of his own. They held each other's gaze, neither willing to yield to the other. She felt the call of her sisters reaching out, beckoning her home.

"Shall we end this now, Father? Do you yield and live to fight another day, or would you like to know what it's like to feel the blade of a warrior slice through bone?"

Her father ran his fingers through his chest-length beard. "We shall call it a draw this eve, daughter mine. Next time, by the Gods of Old, I will grieve your passing as you finally lay dead at my feet."

She sheathed her sword at her waist and dismissed him with the flick of her hand. "The Gods of Old hold no sway over me. Your power will not be enough to defeat my mother's army. I look forward to ending your rein for the good of all of our people. Until the next battle, Father."

She gave him her back and realized far too late that she had made a stupid mistake, one she would have punished her subordinates for. Her father was behind her in an instant, using his sheer power to punch through her back and wrap his hands around her heart. The pain made her cry out, a weakness her body would not allow her to clamp down.

"As I said, daughter, you hold your mother's arrogance within you. You will not die from this wound; that would be cheating, and I would never allow that. But I will rip your heart from your chest, dear daughter, and if you should die then, I will see you in the next life."

He pressed his lips to the top of her head before he squeezed her heart. She allowed her eyes to close and sent a silent prayer to her sisters. As they burst onto the sand once more, they roared at the sight of her father and charged. A battle cry sounded, so fierce that it wrung tears from her eyes.

Suddenly, there was nothing but searing pain as her father ripped her heart from her chest, and then, oddly, there was no more pain, no torment inside her. The storm of emotions she carried inside was gone, and the peace of death seeped into her very being. The edges of her world darkened as she lost control of her limbs, and she crumbled to the ground at the feet of her father as he had always wished.

Ever lurched to awareness as she sat up to the sound of screams. Her eyes darted around as she tried to locate the source. When the screaming continued, she realized she was the one who was screaming. Ever took in the strange surroundings with no clue as to where she was.

Anxiety rushed through her as she clutched her chest, the pain from her dream slowly easing now that she was awake.

Heavy footsteps thundered down the hall, and Ever searched for a way out of the unfamiliar place. How had she gotten here? Where *was* here?

The door was flung open. Light flooded the room as Ever blinked away the sudden brightness and laid eyes on the man who stood in front of her. Dressed in only drawstring pant bottoms, Derek Doyle was a vision of pure masculine force. His hair was tousled, and he watched her with hazel eyes tired from sleep.

"Hey, you okay?" he asked, concern littering his voice.

Ever rubbed the back of her neck. Was she okay? The dream had felt so real, the pain of dying even more so. Maybe talking to Derek about her parents today had dragged up insecurities of where she had come from. Ever had never had such vivid dreams before. It almost felt like a memory.

"Yeah, I think so... bad dream."

Derek snorted. "With all that's going on with the murders, I'm sure a lot of people are having nightmares. Can I get you anything?"

She hugged her knees to her chest and pulled the warm, orange blanket up to her chin. It was soft to the touch and comforting, though she still had no idea how she had ended up on a couch, covered in a soft blanket with an almost naked Derek Doyle. Ever glanced up at him again, running her eyes over his frame. He had defined muscles that she guessed he'd had before he became a werewolf and a broad chest that looked perfect for snuggling. Ever blushed at the thoughts in her mind and shook her head.

Derek padded out of the door, and Ever watched him go, surprised at the tattoo covering his entire back. She wanted a better look, but he came back into the room with a glass of water and set it down on the table next to her.

"How'd I get here?"

Derek sat down on the coffee table in front of her, resting his chin in his hands as he replied. "You fell asleep before we left the station. I had no clue where you lived, so I brought you here."

"God, I'm so embarrassed! First, I fall asleep, and then I wake you with my over-active imagination. I'm so sorry, Derek."

He grinned, and her heart did a little summersault. "I wasn't really sleeping if I'm being honest. I was going through some case files when I heard you scream. Must have been some dream considering you are as white as a ghost. Wanna tell me 'bout it?"

She returned his smile, surprised at how easy it was to be in his company. It was hard to believe that they had known each other less than twenty-four hours. "It was strange, like something out of a fantasy novel. I was a fierce warrior with sisters, though I don't think they were blood. We were holding trials of some sort. When they were over, I stayed behind while the others left with our soldiers. Then my father arrived, and we fought until he ripped my heart from my chest. I think I kind of died."

Derek whistled. "Damn, that was some dream... no wonder you woke up like you did."

"Yeah, I don't think I'm gonna sleep anymore tonight after that." She sighed. "But you go and get some rest."

He cracked the muscles in his neck. "Nah, with the full moon so close, my wolf is restless. He simply wants to become, so sleep won't come easy. I'd probably get a few hours and wake up grumpier than usual."

Ever laughed. "Not a good idea, it seems."

"Not really. I'm already an ass... no sleep will make me so much worse."

Amusement lit up his voice, and Ever guessed this was a side to Derek that very few people saw. She reached out, giving his knee a squeeze in silent thanks, and heat lit up his eyes with amber. He shook his head and the amber resided, leaving just the deep brown of his eyes.

"You want something other than water? I think I've got coffee somewhere."

"Sure. Then maybe you can tell me about that impressive tattoo on your back."

He made no reply, simply strode out the door he came in, leaving Ever alone and giving her the opportunity to take in her surroundings. The couch she rested on sat in the center of the small, square room, adjacent to a huge, open fireplace. Cream-painted walls that might have appeared dull and boring at first were decorated with a vast array of pictures and paintings that gave the room a homey, warm feel. A wide patio door to her right looked out over the city, the darkness from outside sparkling with the firefly of lights that beckoned her back to the city she dearly loved.

Getting up, Ever walked around the room, taking everything in. She studied the pictures and paintings. There were pictures of Derek as he was now with a variety of different people, including children, taken over the years. On the far wall, she spotted a picture of a young girl perched on his shoulders. Both Derek and the girl were laughing, clearly having fun. Beside it, a similar picture captured Derek again with a young woman perched on his shoulders. She was startled when she realized that the young girl and the young woman were one and the same, the birthmark on the side of her face evident in both pictures.

"That's my niece, Chloe."

His voice sounded behind her, and she jumped. He came to stand beside her, handing the hot cup of coffee sideways. Ever tried to ignore the shot of electricity that sparked when he brushed his fingers over hers.

"Do you still see her?"

Derek grinned, his eyes on his niece. "Like I'd have any say in the matter. Chloe got her mother's stubborn nature as well as her looks. When Sylvia passed, she made Chloe promise to keep in contact and make sure her kids knew me. That way, Sylvia could ensure I was never alone."

Ever nudged him with her elbow. "She sounds like a wise woman."

"Oh, she was. She and Mark, my brother, were the ones who defended me so publicly when I came back changed. I was convinced they would shun me because of the evil inside me. But Sylvia introduced me to her new baby girl, told her I was her Uncle Derek, and that I was strong, fierce, and would protect her even after her mom was dust on the wind." His voice cracked, and he cleared his throat while Ever took a timid sip of her coffee.

"She handed me that little girl, and I sat there for hours, just holding her, grateful that my family had not cast me aside. I had stayed away for so long after I was changed that I feared I'd left things too late. Now, if I'm out of contact for too long, I receive numerous phone calls threatening bodily harm if I don't turn up to a family event."

Ever sighed at his thinking that he was evil, but she decided not to press him. "How long were you gone?"

"Ten years."

"That's a long time to be away from home."

"I had to serve my alpha until I was strong enough to control myself. When I could maintain control of my wolf, I came back. I just feel lucky that it wasn't too late to say goodbye to my mother. My dad died about five years after I went missing in action."

Setting her coffee down on the arm of the couch, she leaned against it, facing him. "Derek, I'm so sorry."

He reached out and tucked a strand of blonde hair behind her ear. "Nothing to be sorry for, Ever. It is what it is. I'll continue to watch over my family for as long as there is breath in my body. Or Sylvia will come back and haunt my ass."

His eyes held hers, and suddenly she felt the urge to kiss him, to press her lips against his and taste him. She sensed the lust roll through him and chewed on her bottom lip as he froze.

"Damn it, Ever. Don't look at me like that."

She swallowed hard before she answered him. "Like what?"

"Like you wanna take a bite outta me."

Ever closed her eyes, and an image popped into her head. *She was astride Derek's lap, gloriously naked, her head thrown back as he thrust into her, the strength of his hands on her back the only thing that held her in place as they rode each other into nirvana.*

She flushed, clearing her throat and shrugging, but

her heart pounded in her chest as she slowly reopened her eyes. He shifted away from her and walked around to stand at the opposite end of the room. She was amused by his coyness and intrigued more by the wolf who tried to be hard on the outside, but was sensitive and loving on the inside.

"I got the tattoo long before I got home. I wanted to do something to remember my brothers who died when I was changed." He slowly turned to reveal the impressive artwork on his back. From the curve at the bottom of his back to the strong outline of his shoulder blades, the tattoo was a piece of art carved into skin. "The dragon is a symbol of strength and protection, while the samurai is representative of all the warriors who died that night. If you look real close, you can see the outline of their names engraved on the sword."

Ever proceeded to walk over to him and place her fingertips on his back to trace the outline of his spine. She ignored the shudder that ran through him at her touch. The skin was smooth where the tattoo sat. She traced the sword with the names of Derek's fellow soldiers. Then she began to follow the curve of the dragon as it surrounded the samurai and roared a silent scream of aggression.

"It must've hurt getting all this beautiful line work done. How did you manage to get it to stay on your skin? Most tattoos on shifters fade away due to your healing abilities."

He stepped away from her touch and faced her. "If you get it done before that full power sets in, it will work. I found an artist who dealt with supernatural beings before, and while it was twice as painful, it was worth it."

Ever began to say something, but the sound of

Derek's phone broke the spell of the moment.

"Yeah," he barked into his phone.

Ever listened as he spoke, watching as his eyes opened wide in surprise.

"When did this happen?" A pause before he answered. "Okay, we're on our way. Be there in twenty."

He hung up, and Ever could feel the nervous energy flowing from him.

"What's happened?" she asked.

"The kidnapper struck again. And close to home this time. He tried to take a young pup from her home in Middleton."

"Tried?"

A feral grin spread over his face, making him look ever so wolfish. "He picked on the wrong pup. She fought back... and escaped. She's in the hospital now."

Grabbing her bag, Ever headed for the door. "Let's go."

Chapter Six

As soon as the car screeched to a halt, Derek was out and stalking through the hospital doors. Ever scrambled out of the car and followed him. As she watched the rigid line of his spine, the hunched tension of his broad shoulders, and the pulse of the vein in his neck, she found herself blushing.

For a single moment back there, Ever had thought Derek was about to kiss her, and she had craved it, as if the alpha wolf were a magnet pulling her toward him. Growing up, her parents had warned her off dating supernaturals because she was so normal, and that had stuck with her—Ever, the normal in a world of magic. But as much as she had craved Derek's touch in that moment, Ever had only wished for one thing in her whole life—to fit in with the people she had grown up with.

So, she had shied away from dating supes. The two boyfriends she'd had were extremely normal... and boring. Ever felt as if she was going to break all the rules with Derek Doyle, and nothing with this wolf would ever be boring.

Quickening her pace, she weaved in between the bodies that stepped out of Derek's way. If Ever could feel the anger radiate from him, no doubt everyone else could, too. As Derek, in all his rush and rage, barreled through the emergency room to where the young werepup was recovering, he bumped into an orderly, causing him to drop all his charts on the floor. Derek kept going, single-minded in his actions, but Ever paused, crouched down, and helped the man collect his charts.

"I'm so sorry about my friend. He left his manners at home in his kennel," Ever said, beaming at him.

The orderly narrowed his gaze, nodded, and took the charts from Ever, rushing off into a hospital room.

Ever took in a breath and went in search of her angry wolf... *Wait, her wolf?*

Shaking that ludicrous thought from her head, Ever shoved open the door Derek went through last and skidded to a halt as she almost ran face-first into the hard muscle of his back. A low growl rumbled from inside him. For some reason, Ever knew his wolf was fighting for control.

Ever cautiously maneuvered around Derek's big body and assessed the scene. Standing with Tom and the rest of Derek's team was a man Ever knew only from his many press conferences and public appearances. Arthur de Valera stood with arms folded across his chest, his stance rigid, acting as if he were not the least bit intimidated by the raging wolf who snarled next to her. The alpha of the Munster wolves gave off the impression that he was harmless, reinforced by boyish good looks and charm. He was surfer-pretty—green eyes and blond, shaggy hair with a smile that dazzled cameras. He was the poster boy for good werewolves, but Ever knew Arthur had gotten where he was by bathing in blood and death. It was the alpha way.

Tom whispered in Arthur's ear, but the alpha shook his head. "The pup needs to know he cannot stay a lone wolf in my county any longer. He has shirked his responsibilities for too long and needs to learn his place."

Ricky shook his head. With a gentle tug on Melanie's arm, he slowly moved her from the path of destruction that would no doubt litter the halls of the hospital if these two alphas went at it. Death would be assured for one of them.

As Derek held Arthur's gaze, Ever could almost feel the wolf snapping at Derek, looking to break free and sink its teeth into flesh and blood. She tasted copper on her tongue as if she could sense what the wolf wanted.

Calmly, Ever stood in front of Derek and put the palm of her hand on the side of his face. Derek shuddered, and the weight of the eyes watching them almost burned a hole in her back. The hair on the back of her neck stood to attention as Derek snarled, the sharp canines of his wolf teeth beginning to show. If she didn't get him to calm down, they would never find out what the girl knew about her kidnapper.

"Hey, Mr. Wolf."

A growl rumbled in his chest, and Ever gripped tighter onto his cheek.

"Don't you growl at me; I'm only trying to help. Ignore the posturing from over there and remember that you came here to catch a killer. Hasn't that poor girl been through enough? If you go in there all snarly and wolfie, you'll scare her. Derek, please... we need to find out what she knows before he takes another child. If you let the wolf take over, you'll be no good to us. Or to his victims."

Wolf eyes blinked, crushing gold until brown ones returned. Although the anger still radiated inside him, Derek looked calmer than he had a few minutes ago, and Ever could deal with that. He cupped her hand in his, still on his cheek, and reluctantly drew his eyes from the other wolf to look at her.

Ever smiled at him as he released her hand and moved forward. Arthur reached out as if to thank her, and Ever shirked out of his reach. She didn't even wait for a snarl from Derek before she chastised the alpha wolf.

"Shame on you, Arthur, that you'd provoke the situation to get one-up on Derek. Any person knows not to attempt to touch a person who a wolf considers under their protection. Would you be so petty as to challenge him when lives are at stake? I thought you a better man."

With a flip of her hair, Ever went inside the hospital room, holding the door open for Derek. He glanced at her as he passed, a questioning expression marring his handsome face. Ever heard Tom whistle low then speak to the team. "I've never seen anything like that before in my life. She calmed the wolf."

"Seems like D is quite taken with your goddaughter, Tom."

"Her father's going to kill me."

Ever grinned as she let the door swing shut and walked over to where Derek waited for her. The hospital had given the girl a room to herself; her parents and a doctor were the only other people permitted to stay in the room. The teen wolf cuddled into the curve of her mother's body, the daughter the image of her mother, with an intense shade of auburn hair and olive eyes. Her father stood with his back to them, but from the trembling of his body, the wolf himself was straining for control. Her father wanted blood for what had happened to his daughter, and Ever totally understood his need for vengeance.

The doctor came forward and held out a hand to Derek, but he was too caught up in his own thoughts to notice.

Ever grasped the woman's hand and said. "Hi, I'm Ever, and I'm consulting with P.I.T. for this investigation. This is Agent Doyle, and he left his manners at home today."

The doctor laughed. "I'm Dr. Val. It's so nice to meet you, Ever. It's okay; I work with surgeons every day who seem to have left their etiquette at the door of medical school."

Derek brushed passed them, and Ever sighed. He pulled a chair to the side of the hospital bed and spoke. "My name is Derek, and I'm working very hard to catch the man who tried to take you. Do you mind if I sit?"

The teenager bowed her head. Derek sat down slowly as he placed his palms on his jeans and leaned back in the chair. Ever stayed where she was, standing next to Dr. Val. The young girl watched him with wide eyes, shaking as her mother gently ran her fingers through her hair.

"You've no need to fear me, little pup. I'm just a little cranky because of the moon's call, and I'm not acting like myself." He spoke honestly to the girl, surprising Ever that he would admit to his lack of control. He seemed like a man who was known for being strong and in control.

"S'okay... sometimes, my brothers get cranky like that, too. I'm used to it."

"You're a brave young woman, Miss. First, let me know what I should call you. I don't want to have to call you pup all day." He let the left side of his mouth curve up into a friendly smile.

The girl let out a sigh and rubbed the tiredness from her eyes. "My name is Christine, but I prefer Chrissy."

"Then Chrissy it is. Now, Chrissy, can you tell me what happened? Anything you can remember is fantastic."

Chrissy swallowed hard. "It's a little hazy. After I shifted, my wolf took over, and I wasn't me for a while. I know Papa said the wolf must never take control, but I was so scared, and she knew what to do." The girl hiccupped back a sob.

Her father turned round, wetness blanketing his eyes. "You had no choice, Chrissy. You did what you needed to do to survive. I'd never chastise you for that."

Derek reached out and took hold of Chrissy's hand. "Sometimes, we need the wolf to protect us when we are too afraid ourselves. Let me tell you a little secret about me. I was a bitten wolf, not born like you. When I was first changed, I knew nothing of the world like it is now. I didn't deal very well with what I'd become, and I let the wolf take charge more times than I can remember. He kept me alive when the man didn't want to live. So, our wolf sometimes has to do things our person wouldn't. Even your dad would agree with me."

The girl wiped away a stray tear. "Okay, I'm okay."

Derek kept hold of her hand and ran his thumb

along the inside of her palm, hoping to keep her calm. Every second, Ever was becoming even more enamored with this wolf. As if sensing her thoughts, he stole a peek in her direction before turning his attention back to Chrissy.

"I knew the change was coming for a couple of days, but I didn't tell anyone," she began. "I wanted to prove I could do it myself like my brothers do, out in the woods under the cover of the moon. I snuck out of bed and went outside through the back. The woods are at the back of our house, so I knew if I got into trouble, someone would hear me howl and come get me." Chrissy paused, taking a break before she continued with the dark and horrid story.

It suddenly hit Ever that if the girl hadn't changed, they would be looking at her body now on the cold, unforgiving table in the morgue. There would be no fight in her eyes, no spark, and no life. And that thought punched a hole in Ever's chest.

"I stopped by my favorite climbing tree, where Papa built me a tree house, and rested against the branches. My muscles burned, and the wolf was ready. But then he dropped down from the tree house and grabbed me. I screamed, and he put his hand over my mouth. I... I... wet myself, and then the wolf—she started to tell me to bite down hard on his hand, so I did. Once I tasted his blood in my mouth, my wolf took over. We changed, and she bit his leg when he let me go.

"The wolf wanted more blood, but he kicked out and hit me in the ribs before punching me in my face. He kept screaming that I was ruined, spoiled, and that someone else would die in my place. Then he was gone, as fast as a wolf could run, and I howled as loud as I could for help."

The poor girl burst into tears, and her mother hugged her close. Derek waited until the girl was composed again before he spoke. “You did so well, Chrissy. You fought back, and now he will bear your marks on his skin. You left us with clues to follow. Is there anything else he said or did that stood out as odd to you?”

The girl shook her head, but then froze. “The wolf put pictures in my head, and I remembered that when I bit his hand, he tasted wrong—like I’d eaten something bad. The wolf found it hard to believe he was human because his blood tasted of magic. But not his given magic.”

Derek stood and brushed a loose curl of hair from Chrissy’s face. “You did brilliant Chrissy, thank you. If you ever want to become a cop, come see me in a few years. You’d make an excellent addition to my team.”

The girl beamed, and her father snorted. “All she has ever wanted to be is a policewoman. You’ll see her for certain in a couple of years.”

Derek nodded and replied, “Good, and I meant every word. I’ll see you soon, Chrissy. Ma’am.”

He smiled at the two girls curled on the bed and went to speak to her father. Derek could have lowered his voice, but he seemed to want all in the room to hear. “Your daughter is strong and has the makings of a future alpha. She will survive this. And I promise you, sir, that if I can, I will rip out the bastard’s throat with my teeth and see that he gets the violent and painful death he deserves. You have my word.”

The men shook hands, and Derek headed for the door. Ever smiled at the doctor as they all headed out. Peering back, Ever saw that Chrissy’s eyes had drifted shut, but she doubted the girl would sleep peacefully.

The nightmares would haunt her for a while.

Derek held the door open for her and Dr. Val as the rest of the team waited patiently. Ricky and Melanie were further away from the rest of the team. When Melanie made to go over to the others, Ricky said something to her. She scowled and shook her head. Ricky threw his arms up in the air as the tech ignored him and came to stand beside Caitlyn. Arthur hung around on the fringes, only a rumble from Tom kept him away from Derek, for now.

"Well? Was the girl able to help?" Tom asked, running his knuckles over the stubble on his chin.

"That girl is gonna make an awesome cop one day. She bit him on the palm and the leg. He'll be hurting for a while, so we might get the jump on him. When she changed, he shouted at her that she was ruined, spoilt... something you would say about meat. Her wolf claims the blood she swallowed tasted bad—like magic, but not his magic."

"What the hell does that mean?" Ricky's eyebrows almost met as his gaze narrowed.

"I think I know why he takes the marrow and blood," Donnie said, his voice sounding like it was being raked over cut glass. The vampire seemed like the type who rarely spoke but when he did, people listened. "He is consuming their power through their marrow. I'll bet he is human but carries the sense—the ability to sense when a supernatural being is maturing. That is how he hunts them. He wants to be supernatural, yet he enjoys the torture and terror he inflicts before he kills."

"Damn, man. I think that's the most I've ever heard you speak."

The vampire swatted at Ricky, but the warlock just

grinned at him. Derek slapped him at the back of his head, and Ricky groaned.

"Where's Fionn?" Derek asked, suddenly noticing the shifter was missing.

"Fionn had to take care of some pride business. We should have a new replacement in a few days," Tom answered.

Derek nodded, not bothering to delve deeper into Tom's statement. "So, best we can do is head back to the station and work on our new leads." Glancing at his watch, he said to Ever, "Want me to drop you home so you can get a few hours' sleep?"

Ever dismissed his comment with the wave of her hand. "I couldn't sleep now even if I tried. Let's just head back so we can catch this monster while he's injured."

"I'll take you home, Lanie," Ricky said to Melanie, whose expression darkened at his words.

"I am quite capable of seeing myself home, *Richard,* if I intended to go home. I can help out more if I'm working with the team. And don't try that macho B.S. with me; it won't work."

"Come on, babe. You're not like us; you can't function without some rest."

As soon as the words slipped from Ricky's lips, the warlock knew he had royally messed up. Melanie's shoulders tensed, and despite the anger in her cheeks, her eyes glistened, obviously hurt by Ricky's words.

"Fine. I'll take my perfectly normal human ass home by myself and try and remember my place." Her voice wavered as she gathered her belongings.

"Shit, Lanie, I didn't mean it like that."

"I understand what you meant by it, Ricky, and that's the problem. I can never compete with the likes of you,

Derek, or even Ever—who is super smart and human, but Derek still had the sense to ask her what she wanted to do. I told you before, macho crap doesn't wash with me." She stormed toward the exit, turning only to hiss at the object of her anger. "And don't you dare follow me, or I will kick you so hard you'll never have kids."

Ricky stood, mouth hanging open, as Ever smiled inwardly at the girl's courage to stand up for herself. She assumed that she and Melanie felt the same way, wishing they were both as powerful as the beings they surrounded themselves with. Nobody spoke for a heartbeat, and then Ricky was gone out the door, calling over his shoulder that he would see them at the station.

With all the action, Ever had totally forgotten that the Munster alpha was still there. Power suffocated the air, and Derek took a step forward. The vampires watched and waited to back up their friend as Tom settled back against the wall. Ever raised an eyebrow. He shrugged.

Standing between the two wolves, panic began to fill Ever. The stark reality that Melanie had laid out—that Ever was perfectly human and would be ripped apart if there were a fight—was sinking in. Her gaze darted from one wolf to the other. "Derek..." she began.

"Have no fear, Ever. I would not degrade myself by having an unsanctioned dominance fight here, especially when there are cameras." He looked over her head to speak to Derek. "You have to choose, Derek—become a member of the pack or move on. Cork is pack territory, and not even your job can save you from pack laws. I'm sure if you want to stay a lone wolf that they'd welcome you up north."

"I've no desire to be alpha of a pack, Arthur, and we

both know who the strongest wolf is. Why would you want to bring that on yourself?"

The other wolf grinned. "Maybe I'm tired of being alpha, Derek. Maybe I just want to settle down and have pups with a mate. What do you say, Ever? Fancy being an alpha's mate?" He reached out and brushed his fingertips across the bare skin of her arm.

That did it. The wolf roared from deep inside Derek's being, and Ever heard the snap of bone and the tearing of flesh as the man began to become wolf. Fascinated by the change, Ever couldn't help but watch, having never witnessed a change before. It was quick—Derek's clothing ripping, fur sprouting from his skin as his bones gave way, crunching and snapping into place, until a very large, golden-brown wolf stood panting on shaky legs.

Amber eyes blazed as it snapped its teeth, and Arthur stepped back. The wolf padded forward a step and bared its teeth. Ever's heart pounded in her chest, but she knew the wolf would not hurt her; she felt it right down to her core.

"I've never seen a change that fast," Arthur said.

The wolf crouched down and readied itself to attack, and Ever did the only thing she could think of. She had get Derek to calm down. Tom went to grab her and move her out of the way, but Ever held up her hand.

She crouched down so that her eyes met the wolf's. "He's not going to hurt me, are you, Derek?"

The wolf snorted in response, as if it were a stupid question.

"See? Now that we know the only person he wants a chunk out of is Arthur, I think you should leave with the good doctor and get as far away from us as possible."

Ignoring the two as they left, Ever slowly held out the palm of her hand. The wolf sniffed her hand and then ran its tongue along it. Ever chuckled and brought her hand up to scratch behind the wolf's ear. The animal leaned into her caress and sighed contentedly.

Picking up the discarded contents of Derek's pockets, she held up his car keys. "Looks like I'm driving us back to the station." Ever rose, and the wolf instantly clung to her side. She danced her fingers over his fur, so soft and smooth, as they walked out of the hospital, the heat of the beautiful animal fascinating her on so many levels.

RAGE BREWED INSIDE HIM AS THE DAMN WOLF BRUSHED him aside as if he were nothing. He didn't even stop for a moment to look at him. Would he have known the wolf if he had just taken the time to pause and scent? What did someone like him smell like to supernatural creatures?

The woman helped to pick up the stolen charts. He had hoped to slip inside and kill the young girl, smother her, but there were too many creatures around. Soon, he would be like them—powerful and strong, no longer weak and forgettable.

He stumbled away from the woman and slipped into a hospital room to spy on them. He was used to waiting, watching—it was all part of the pleasure. The anticipation made the kill so much sweeter on his lips.

So, he waited while the little bitch that had bitten him spilled to that damn wolf. The wolf wanted to spoil his fun, end his game... and he was not ready for it to end so soon.

Doyle stepped outside, and he decided he needed something to distract the wolf from coming after him. And then, the perfect opportunity fell into his lap. She was not his type—far too human for him—but he would enjoy playing with her for a while.

He waited until the red-haired girl stormed from the room, tears in her eyes. Then he stalked her, following her out the door as she made her way across the car park and fumbled for her car keys. The girl dropped them and swore, bending down to retrieve them as he came up behind her.

She sensed the danger a mere second before he grabbed her, covering her mouth with his hand. She struggled, but he enjoyed that even more so. The girl whimpered as she tried to free herself, and he could feel the wetness of her tears on his hand.

Rubbing up against her, he whispered into her ear, "I'm going to enjoy playing with you. I've never had a human before." Then he punched her in the face, and she slumped in his arms.

He grinned as he shoved Melanie's body into her own car, leaving her bag behind, the only breadcrumb to her disappearance.

Come get me, wolf!

Chapter Seven

This had to be the most surreal moment in her life. Having reassured Tom that she was all right travelling with wolf-Derek, Ever drove with a wolf that would not take his eyes off her. Not that Ever could stop herself from glancing at Derek every now and then. She hadn't taken much notice of him after the change; there had just been too much happening to appreciate the beautiful creature.

Golden brown fur covered most parts of his body, with a faint stripe of darker brown—almost hazelnut—streaking down his muzzle. Intense amber eyes watched her with the same intensity that shone from human-Derek's eyes. He was also bigger than your average sized wolf. The top of his head came just under the top of her hips, and my God, those teeth! Ever didn't doubt that wolf-Derek would be able to rip her throat out in a single moment if he so wished. She was glad he seemed so taken with her.

Not just the wolf...

Ever flushed as the tiny voice rattled about in her head. She brushed it off, trying to concentrate on the matter at hand—catching a killer and returning balance to her world. Then she could deal with the insane chemistry and connection she felt for this complicated wolf.

Another voice interrupted her train of thought, and she blinked at the unfamiliar whisper, like a wind grazing against bare skin, as the thought repeated itself in her mind.

He is your champion; he will protect you when you need him.

Maybe she was going mad. Perhaps studying creatures that she would never be while wishing for more had suddenly pushed her over the edge, like the killer. Was it possible the thoughts of never being more than just a human had become too much for her?

Derek whined beside her, followed by a sharp bark, and Ever concentrated on the road again, slamming on the brakes as a light ahead of her turned red.

She peered sheepishly at Derek. "Sorry. I was just thinking too hard."

The wolf blinked at her, then rested his muzzle on her thigh. The wild heat of him almost burned her through her jeans, but she focused on the road and eventually drove Derek's car to the station and parked.

Ever switched off the engine and paused, unsure of what to do next. A lot of cops still had issues with supes working in positions of power. Since marriage equality for all was now legal, the bigots needed a new outlet for their anger, and the supernatural community bore the brunt of it.

"So, what do I do now, Mr. Wolf? Do we just stroll into the station as you are and risk you getting shot? I'm not really certain if you're as invincible as the Hulk, you know?"

The wolf raised his head and snorted. He inclined his head and pawed at the door. Ever sighed and slid out the driver's side. When she opened the passenger door, Derek hopped down onto the ground and waited. Heart beginning to race, Ever closed the door and moved forward.

Derek padded alongside her, his big body pressing up against her side. Opening the door to the station, Ever, after a hesitant breath, went inside. The place went from bustling hub to den of silence in an instant. Ever gulped as a couple of officers' hands went instinctively for their guns. Derek snarled, baring his teeth as the tension amped up several volumes.

"Do you really think you growling at them will help your case, Derek?"

"That's Derek Doyle?" one of the officers asked.

"Yes, the wolf is Derek Doyle, and if one of you so much as twitches a finger, not only will you have to deal with a pissed-off wolf, but you'll have to go through me as well."

The baritone of Tom Delaney's voice rebounded off the walls, echoing in probably every person's ears. It wasn't a threat per se, more like a definite warning as to where Tom's loyalties lay.

Ever strode over to Tom, and Derek trotted after her, his eyes darting from cop to cop as he moved. Tom held open the door of the P.I.T. room and ushered them in. With one final glare, the officers went back to work and Ever grinned at her godfather.

He smiled back at her. "Nice to see an old man still holds some authority with the little whelps."

Ever dismissed his comment with a wave of her hand. "Pfft... Tom, you could be one-hundred-and-fifty years old, all grey haired and frail, and one look would make these 'little whelps' want a cuddle from their mammies."

The bear chuckled. "It's so good to have you around, Ever, despite the circumstances."

There was a little huff followed by a growl, and Ever turned her attention back to Derek. He would be no good to them if he remained in his wolf form, and she knew that once the moon hit full in twenty-four hours, Derek would be lost for a good portion of the night before they could resume the search for the monster.

As the vampires slipped into the room, Ever crouched down and came nose to muzzle with the wolf. The wolf sniffed, stilling when she began to speak.

"Hey wolf, any chance we can get Derek back just for a little while? We could really use his help with all this."

The wolf tilted its head and nudged his nose with hers before turning away and padding over to the door. The wolf looked back at Tom, who simply nodded and said, "I'll make sure she's safe until you come back. Donnie, can you help Derek get to the locker room?"

The quiet vampire bowed his head, opening the door for Derek. He waited a moment, and then Derek followed Donnie, the door closing behind them. Tom's phone rang, and that left Ever alone with the hauntingly beautiful Caitlyn.

"I've known Derek a very long time and never seen a reaction like that," the vampire mused as she brushed a raven-coloured curl from her face.

"It's just the wolf in him trying to protect someone that is more fragile than him. It's purely platonic." Ever wasn't entirely sure whether she was trying to convince herself or Caitlyn.

"Men don't look at a woman the way Derek looks at you if it's only platonic. He may be as tough as nails, our Derek, but he has the biggest heart of anyone I've ever known. He'd be your champion, if only you would let him."

He is your champion; he will protect you when you need him.

The voice sounded in her head again, and Caitlyn's words were eerily similar. She chose not to say any more about it, hoping that Caitlyn would change the subject. This connection, after such a short time of knowing the man, scared her, but it was the most right she had felt in her entire life. Being near man and wolf seemed to fill the gaping hole that had grown every day since she'd found out she was adopted.

Ever, flustered that she couldn't seem to stop thinking about things that were insignificant—especially when there was a killer loose in the city—tried to focus on the details they had learned from Chrissy. The brave girl had said that the killer had tasted wrong, of magic but not his own. It was a strange way to describe it, but something clicked into place.

Donnie returned, perching himself on the edge of Ricky's desk. Ever looked up to see Caitlyn watching her with an intrigued expression on her face.

"What ran through your mind, Ever? Your scent changed."

Finding it slightly disturbing that the vampires could scent 'changes' in her moods, Ever ran over her thoughts again before replying. "I think he might be ingesting the marrow and blood. I mean, I know we said that he was trying to steal their life force, but maybe he thinks by eating their marrow and drinking their blood he'll gain some of their power. Could he be trying to turn himself magical by doing this?"

Donnie answered, his voice reserved and level. "There are many out there who wish to know the intricate ways in which one might be changed into one such as us. But we are a secretive bunch, and the... shall we say, requirements... for being made vampire or wolf, are extensive. Many other species can only be born, not made."

Ever shook her head. "So why does he think he can be 'made' by killing and ingesting body parts?"

"Perhaps he has been repeatedly denied the change, or something triggered him to need it sooner than later—like terminal cancer or a brain tumor. Nothing says desperation like death creeping outside your front door."

A look passed over the vampire's face before vanishing so fast that Ever wasn't even sure she'd seen it. Caitlyn bristled at his words, leaving Ever wishing she knew their story. Tom finished up his call and came back over to them.

"Ever had an interesting thought, Sarge," Caitlyn said. "She believes that maybe the perp is eating the marrow and blood in an effort to be made. Donnie also thinks he may have been refused the change, and that spurred the killings."

The bear let a growl rumble in his chest, and his eyes flashed a brilliant shade of green before returning to normal. Feeling angry herself, Ever could understand his anger, but now was not the time to let emotions cloud their actions. Another life could be at stake.

"Donnie also thinks he might be ill," she began, "like he got a terminal diagnosis and is clutching at his once chance to stay alive. Plus, he may have petitioned either the wolves or the vampires to become one of them and been refused."

Tom nodded. "A guy like that wouldn't have taken a rejection like that well. He might've caused a scene, been noticed." He scrubbed his chin. "Caitlyn, take Donnie and go see Chester. Ask if he was ever petitioned by someone who fits our description."

Caitlyn hissed out a breath, swearing in French. "Could we not send Ricky to deal with Chester? I've managed to elude him for decades, and now I must go to him and beg?"

"You're going in your capacity as an Agent of P.I.T., nothing else. Chester might want you to join his kiss, but we both know why he wants you, Caitlyn, and it's not because of your particular talents."

They both looked at Donnie, and the poor vampire looked totally flustered. "I don't like being used as man candy for Chester, but I want to catch this beast more than I care about being uncomfortable. It's okay, we'll go."

He swept from the room with an incline of his head to Ever, and the clickety-clack of Caitlyn's heeled boots followed him out. The door closed with a bang behind them, and Ever raised an eyebrow at Tom.

"Do I want to know what that's about?"

"Let's just say Chester isn't the easiest vampire to deal with, but he has the most information."

"Okay, so what can I do?"

Tom pulled a card from the pocket of his shirt. “Can you call Dr. Val and see if someone matches the profile of our killer? I think he’d have taken the news of his illness extremely well and stayed away from doctor’s appointments because he really believed he had the cure all along. I’m going to phone Arthur and ask him the same about someone looking to be changed. Use Derek’s phone; I’m sure he’ll be back in soon.”

Tom turned from Ever and went to sit at his desk to make his call. Ever sank down into Derek’s chair. Resting her chin in the palm of her hand, Ever yawned and picked up the receiver. Inputting the direct line on the card, Ever waited as the phone rang, twice, three times, then four. Contemplating hanging up, she had just eased the phone from her ear when she heard a voice.

“Dr. Val Frey.”

“Hi, Dr. Val, this is Ever Chace. We met at the hospital this evening.” Silence greeted her on the line. “Dr. Val? Are you there?”

A voice cleared on the line. “Of course, Ever. I apologize. It’s been a rather long night.”

Ever blew out a breath. “That’s an understatement. I was wondering if it would be okay to ask you a few questions. We may have come up with a few theories that can help us narrow down the suspect pool.”

“That’s perfectly alright. Anything I can do to help.”

“Thank you,” Ever replied. “So, we think that the killer might have been refused petitions to be made vampire or were, and that a possibly terminal diagnosis might have pushed him over the edge.”

The doctor tsked down the phone. “I work in emergency medicine, but I can speak to the radiology head of department and see if we can possibly find someone who fits that description."

Ever remembered what Tom had said. "Oh, and Tom thinks that when he or she got the news, that they took it well—too well, in fact. We think he believed he had the cure in his mind already and wasn't afraid of the news."

"That might help us narrow it down. I'm afraid we still have high numbers of terminally ill people, despite the advances in medicine. I'll do my very best to aid you in whatever way I can."

Ever sighed. "Thank you. We appreciate anything that you can give us."

"I'll prioritize that and get back to you once I get some information. Where can I contact you?"

Ever rattled off her mobile number and told the doctor that she could call anytime. They exchanged a few polite words, and as Ever went to hang up, she heard the doctor call her name.

"Yes?" she asked.

"If you need to talk... about anything... you can call me. I think we could be good friends."

The line disconnected, leaving Ever listening to the bleep, bleep, bleep. Strange as that was, it seemed the last few days had amped up the strangeness factor. Beginning to get lost in her own head again, she jumped when the door pushed open and Derek stepped inside.

The look on his face could only be described as sheepish and embarrassed. He glanced at the ground before looking directly at Ever. Her pulse quickened, urging her to go to him, the magnetic pull that stretched out between them stronger than it had been before he had changed. Now, the connection that tethered them together was pulled so tight it was close to snapping.

"Hey," she said, her voice croaking.

"Hey yourself," he replied with a coy smile.

Ever returned his smile. "Nice to see you on two legs again."

Derek snorted a laugh, very like his wolf half. "Yeah, um..." he began, rubbing the back of his neck, "I'm sorry for losing control of myself back at the hospital. Shouldn't have happened."

She shrugged. "It's the full moon. Totally acceptable."

"Yeah, I'm not sure it was just the full moon, but thanks for that."

A quick change of subject. "We may have established some links as to who the killer might be, or at least his profile. We think he's terminally ill, and his petition to change was denied. We also believe he may be eating the body parts he took from his victims in order to try and use their magic to become supernatural."

"I can't wait to rip out his throat with my teeth," Derek growled.

"Caitlyn and Donnie have gone to see if Chester knows of anyone who might've taken the refusal of a petition badly. Tom is talking to Arthur to find out the same."

Derek whistled. "I bet Caitlyn wasn't happy with having to see Chester."

"No, but Donnie said he was fine. What's their story, anyway?"

"Sorry," he shook his head. "That's not my story to tell. Ask Cait over a bottle of really expensive French wine, and you'll get that story out of her."

Ever laughed as Tom finished up his call. Derek went to his boss, and they exchanged a few words before coming back over to where Ever sat at Derek's desk. She reported in, telling them that Dr. Val was going to look into it and get back as soon as she could. Tom said that Arthur hadn't had a petition for a change in a while and would contact the alphas from other counties and be in touch.

Derek muttered something, and Tom chuckled. Shaking her head in dismay, she yawned. The men took notice and tried to convince her to go home and get some rest, which she politely declined. Ever rested her head on the desk for just a moment, letting her lids flutter closed.

The scent of wildflowers immediately assaulted her nose as she brushed a giant leaf out of her way. The sand tickled her toes as she walked around her home, the sun beating down on her, making her golden tan seem to shimmer. She could hear the sound of the waves crashing against the beach and longed for the chance to cool her body in the bliss of the salt water.

But today, she had warriors to assess, and with the war looming, now was not the time to indulge in petty forms of pleasure. As she turned through the ferns, strong arms encircled her from behind. Rather than kick out in attack, she almost melted under his touch.

"You should not be here. If mother catches us, there will be hell to pay."

"I do not fear your mother. What I fear is going another day without your touch, without the taste of you on my lips."He pressed his lips against the nape of her neck with the barest hint of teeth, sending a delicious wave of heat throughout her body. But this man needed only to look at her with those deep brown eyes, and the fearsome warrior slipped away, leaving only a woman

who craved the touch of the man.

"You cannot say such things to me. My life is not my own, and despite how much I may like you, I was made to rule. As a ruler, I must be strong; I must not let myself be given over in temptation."

Strong hands traced over the bare skin of her stomach, and she shivered. She could not resist him, this man who made her whimper with one touch. She shirked free of his grasp and turned to face him, the handsome lines of his face making her heart go aflutter.

He backed her against a nearby tree, their presence shaded by the luscious green of the trees that surrounded them. The man who demanded she make him her champion pressed his body to hers, rotating his hips so that she knew how much he hungered for her as well.

Bracing her hands on his bare chest, she made to shove him away. Any one of her sisters could stride past and spy them. But he did not seem to care. His lips traced her jaw, sending her heart hammering against her chest, and then he continued down her nape. When his lips grazed the top of her breast, she could no longer withhold the moan that escaped her lips.

The smug bastard slipped his fingers into her hair and dragged her gaze to his. Molten heat shone from his eyes, and she knew then that she was in trouble.

"Destiny has many different faces, my forever," he whispered in a low and husky voice that almost made her lose control. "And our destinies are entwined. Do not resist me, Ever. Ever..."

"Ever?"

Ever jerked up, blinking the sleep from her eyes. "God, I'm sorry. I must've fallen asleep." Memories of her dream cascaded over her, and she blushed, the feeling of Derek against her body lingering well after the dream. She so needed to get her mind out of the gutter.

Derek opened his mouth to answer as Ever tried to dampen the heat that flushed her cheeks. The phone on his desk shrilled, and he pressed the speakerphone button.

"Derek! Please tell me you're back on two feet. Melanie's gone!"

Ricky's frantic voice brought all three of them to attention. Derek was the first to react.

"What do you mean Melanie's gone?"

"I *mean,* I tried to follow her back to her place to apologize for being an ass, and she wasn't there. I scryed for her but got nothing, so I went back to the hospital. Her car was gone, but her bag was left in the middle of the car park. There was a note on the bag. He got her, D..."

"What are you saying, Ricky?"

"That bastard we're hunting has taken my Lanie."

Chapter Eight

North Main Street was heaving, the who's who of supernatural creatures and wannabes emerging on the city's supernatural quarter. Long before the world was made aware that creatures from their nightmares roamed the streets, Cork City's North Main Street catered to those in the know and those who wished to hide what they were from the humans around them.

Of course, when the supes came out of the closet, the owners of the businesses around North Main Street capitalized on the sudden influx of new customers and amped up the cheese factor. There were vampire-themed bars, where your favorite movie vampire look-alikes served vampire-themed cocktails. There was a banshee karaoke bar right next to a ghoul restaurant. And then there were the places that sometimes humans went into but never came out. But those places were mere whispers on the wind, and like the bogeyman in the shadows, places like Chester's and the things that went on inside them were myths used to scare the humans away.

On this Friday, the night sky was clear with only the tiniest scent of rain in the air. Crowds thronged the cobbled streets, searching for some mediocre thrill, either to release them from their mundane lives or to dull the ache that came with an almost eternal life. Although most humans craved the chance to live forever, the creatures who bore the curse of eternity would have given it up in a heartbeat... well, if they'd had one, that is.

Caitlyn slowed her pace as she reached the outskirts of Supernatural Central, as it was affectionately called. Moments later, Donnie halted next to her, his aura so finely in tune with her own that she could sense his presence from miles away. Reborn barely twenty years ago, Donnie had been the only vampire Caitlyn had made. She had a desire not to inflict the Hunger on another, meaning she had lived a very lonely life. But, as she glanced sideways at the companion who had failed to leave her side since he'd been reborn as a vampire, the night Donnie had been made flashed through her mind—as it did regularly—as if it had only been yesterday.

Torrents of rain fell, soaking the streets of Dublin. The throbbing sound of music itched on her sensitive hearing; the crooning of an Irish ballad filled the air as she passed a public house. Thunder rumbled above, and Caitlyn quickened her pace, the Hunger a driving force in her actions. She had left it far too late to feed, the need growing and growing until she could no longer stand the burn that forced her out on this blustery night.

Dublin's Temple Bar was suffocated with people. It

had always been a beacon for tourists, making it the best place to find a quick bite. A person straying away from their group was an easy target for a hungry vampire.

Caitlyn let her ankle-length duster fall open to reveal the leather pants and top she wore. Yes, she knew it was vampire cliché, but for speed and comfort, she needed the flexibility of it. Her thick-heeled boots, custom made with hidden blades in the soles, clattered along the busy street as she weaved in between the people with the grace of a dancer and the stealth of a prowling panther.

Leaning against a damp wall, Caitlyn's gaze wandered over the crowds that had gathered in the crossroads where pubs and fast-food patrons merged. Nobody seemed to mind the rain, the alcohol that flooded their bloodstream making them careless, clumsy even. Caitlyn clenched her nails into the palm of her hand, drawing blood as another wave of Hunger almost brought her to her knees.

Many saw being made vampire as a blessing, a reward, but Caitlyn thought otherwise. Made almost two hundred years ago in France, Caitlyn had despised what she had become from the moment she had opened her eyes as a newly born vampire. The Hunger took away all the good things about being a vampire—the speed, the beauty, the strength, and the immortality. The curse of the Hunger, and the inevitable lives lost because of it, weighed heavily on her heart, even if it no longer fluttered in her chest.

Caitlyn's attention was yanked from her thoughts as her eyes latched onto a young man being cast out of a public house by two bouncers. He landed on the ground in a drunken heap as people simply walked around him. She didn't even take in his appearance; the Hunger didn't care whose blood she drank, as long as she drank. The Hunger roared in her ears, and she eased off the wall, slowly making her way to the drunken man.

Bending down, she let her fingers dance on his shoulder. He turned and looked up into her eyes. Smiling at the lust in his eyes, she helped him to stand, leaning in to whisper false promises of a night of passion-fuelled fun. He followed her, and Caitlyn could feel the weight of his gaze as she sashayed down an alleyway. As soon as he was within distance, she yanked him into a doorway. He pressed his eager body up against hers, and she almost shuddered in disgust. Tilting his head slightly to the left, she ignored his groan as he slipped his hands inside her jacket to clasp a hand over her breast.

Quick as a striking snake, Caitlyn let her fangs extend, sinking them into the man's exposed throat. The man made to jerk away, but she held on to him by the belt of his jeans and drank. As soon as the whisky-laced blood hit the back of her throat, Caitlyn groaned her satisfaction. The monster inside her urged her to take more, to drink her fill and take his life, but after a couple of pulls, she retracted her fangs, licking over the wound to stop the bleeding. The man wavered on his feet as she placed a hand on either side of his face. The unsteady man stared into her eyes, and she commanded him to forget all about her, advising him to make his way back to his friends.

She watched the man stagger away, heading back the way they had come, and she carefully wiped the blood from her lips with her thumb. Straightening her clothing, Caitlyn went to step out of the cover of the doorway when she heard a scuffle.

Her eyes darted to a group of men who were gathered

around a body, kicking the living hell out of it. The poor man had no chance of survival, the abuse his body took a stark reminder of the night she had been made vampire herself. You could barely see the outline of the man's face through the blood pouring from numerous cuts and lacerations. Three against one was unfair, and Caitlyn itched to snuff out the lives of those who were in the process of playing God.

Two of the men had backed off; the last man lifted his leg and stomped down hard on the bloodied man's face. The beaten man stilled, but Caitlyn could still hear the faint murmur of a heartbeat. The men snickered, spitting on their victim before leaving him to face death in the alleyway. A lump formed in her throat, but she knew the man had no other chance to survive.

Caitlyn rushed over to the man and finally got a chance to see him up close. Despite broad, muscular shoulders and a thick neck, the man looked so fragile in his dying state. Full lips graced a handsome face, but his blue eyes were glazed over, his breathing shallow and wheezy.

His eyes locked onto hers. Caitlyn's breath caught for a moment. Those eyes looked at her as if she were a savior. She almost stopped what she was doing, or what she was about to do, hating the sense that this man saw her as something other than what she was.

He tried to speak, but blood gurgled in his throat as he coughed, splattering blood on the sleeves of her coat. He reached out a wobbly hand, and she grasped hold of it.

"Please do not speak. I will ask you a question, and if you say yes then you and I will be forever tied together. Blink once for yes and twice for no. Do you understand me?"

A blink.

"I can save your life, but it will not be the life that you imagined you would live. Would you be willing to live another life for the chance to see another sunset?"

The silence was deafening as she waited for an answer, and the rain began to pour down hard on them before the man finally blinked his eyes once.

Caitlyn gave him a small, sad smile and said, "I do hope you can forgive me once you are reborn. And that you do not resent me for this."

Confusion pierced his eyes as she raised her wrist to her lips, released her fangs, and scored her flesh. Blood welled on her skin, and she held her wrist to the man's lips. He struggled at first, but then the blood worked down his throat. She waited until she knew he had enough in his system before pulling her wrist away from his lips.

His eyes rolled back, his body convulsing. Placing her hands around his neck, she said a silent prayer in her mother tongue before twisting and snapping the man's neck. He stilled, dead for certain now, but in three days' time, he would rise again and she would be saddled with a baby vampire for many years. She scooped her arms under his body, lifting him with ease. Crouching low, she jumped up to the rooftops and disappeared into the dead of night.

"You must stop letting the past haunt you, Cait."

Donnie's voice slammed her back into the present, and Caitlyn fluttered her lashes on her cheeks before she looked him. "When you have lived as long as I have, then the past will haunt you as well. Shall we go?"

Without waiting for a reply, Caitlyn sauntered past the long line, coming to a halt at a red door by the side of Chester's main entrance. Sensing the ever-present Donnie behind her, she danced her knuckles on the door three times. The door creaked open, and a meaty bouncer ran his gaze over her, then Donnie.

"Agent Hardi and Agent O'Carroll to see Chester."

Holding the door open for them, the bouncer nodded.

Caitlyn continued up the stairs, normally hating having someone at her back, but with Donnie she felt safe, protected. At the top of the stairs, she veered to the left, moving forward until she came to a door that was slightly ajar. Tension tightening her muscles, Caitlyn rolled back her shoulders and cracked her neck.

A warm hand grasped her shoulder. Caitlyn peered back at Donnie. He gave her shoulder a comforting squeeze, a tiny ghost of a smile tweaking his lips, before he returned to the strong, silent guise that he had down to a fine art.

Caitlyn pushed the door fully open, her feet vibrating under the pulse of music that drummed below them. Biting back the bitter taste in her mouth as she laid eyes on Chester, Caitlyn took in the vampire's appearance. Thin and tall, he had decades on Caitlyn. He was wearing the same smug expression he always wore, like the cat about to eat the mouse after having spent hours toying with it. His long nose seemed so out of place on his pale face, and his dark brown hair slicked back to curve around his nape. Chester sat grinning at her, tapping his fingers against each other, very *à la* your typical movie villain.

"Caitlyn, always a pleasure. And Donald, have you given any thought to joining my kiss? I must be wearing you down by now."

Her partner shook his head. "As I've told you many times, Chester, I join your kiss the day Caitlyn joins. Not before."

Chester narrowed his eyes, his bleached eyebrows almost meeting. Then he shook Donnie's reply off with the wave of a hand. Leaning back in his chair, he set his feet on top of the desk. His dress shoes were so shiny Caitlyn could almost see her reflection in them.

"I really do wish you would stop following Caitlyn around like her personal guard dog, Donald. You'd have so much more power if you joined my kiss. Oh, you could still work for P.I.T.—I'd permit that—but obviously, you'd have to put my needs first and what's best for the kiss. I'm sure we could work something out."

Donnie simply shrugged his shoulders, glancing at Caitlyn with an obvious affection that made her uncomfortable. She was certain it was all for Chester's benefit, but something clenched inside her when Donnie looked at her like that.

"How about some refreshments? I have some nice beauties that taste exquisite—lovely, like a fine wine. Or would you prefer some virgin skin—never been bitten? To be the first to pierce flesh... it is the most delicious taste in the world. But, you would know all about that, would you not, Caitlyn... considering who made you?"

Donnie stepped forward, his fists clenched, but he paused when Caitlyn grabbed hold of his elbow.

It's okay. He's baiting me—looking for a response from us. He feeds off my discomfort. I'm fine.

I'd love to make him bleed for the way he speaks to you.

And I would love to see that. One day, I will see that.

Donnie relaxed his stance and stepped back in line

with Caitlyn. Chester chuckled, cracking his knuckles.

"Interesting. So, you two can chat telepathically?" When neither vampire spoke, Chester continued. "Fine, keep your secrets. But it just makes me want you in my kiss even more.

"Never mind. I have an eternity to convince you." He winked, Caitlyn cringing inwardly on Donnie's behalf. "So, what brings two of P.I.T.'s best and brightest to my humble door?"

Caitlyn folded her arms across her chest as Chester continued to rake his eyes over Donnie. "We're following a possible lead on the person who is responsible for the deaths of three children and the attempted kidnapping of another."

"Ah, yes... terrible business. Almost makes me happy that vampires cannot have young. It is a blessing, is it not Caitlyn? That we do not have to suffer as humans do and mourn the loss of a child?"

Caitlyn tried to mask her expression, the past creeping up on her again as a knife twisted deep in her gut. The smug grin on Chester's face acknowledged that she hadn't hidden her reaction at all.

Donnie spoke to Chester, dragging the old vampire's attention from Caitlyn to him.

"We believe he is murdering these kids because his request to be made was denied. Multiple times."

"We've had many multiple requests to be reborn. Can you be more specific?" Chester drawled, his eyes raking over Donnie's muscular frame.

Donnie cleared his throat. "This man would've stood out as being overly upset at being rejected until the very last time. Then, he would've been too calm—utterly accepting of your refusal. You would've remembered him."

Chester kept his smug expression, but something ran through his mind, his eyes darkening. "Timothy! Timothy!"

The meaty bouncer who had escorted them in strode in, almost taking up the entire space of the doorway.

"Timothy, remember that strange fellow who came in looking to be made? He wrecked the place one week, and a couple of weeks later tried again but left without so much as begging a word."

Nodding, Timothy replied in a soft tone, unexpected from such a stern-looking man. "Yes, he came back all apologies and asked one last time would you make him. He politely thanked you for your time and left. I remember because he gave that god-awful name, and we laughed about it for days."

Caitlyn's phone rang, and she walked outside Chester's office to answer it, brushing by Timothy.

"Derek, we might have a lead here. Chester knows something."

"Listen, Caitlyn. Melanie's missing, and Ricky is certain the man we're looking for took her. We're on the way back to the hospital to see if I can pick up a scent. I need you and Donnie there. Ricky said there was some blood."

"We'll meet you there. Derek, we know what he does to the kids..." Her voice trailed off as if she didn't want to finish what she'd begun to say; sometimes words had great power. "Ricky won't be rational in this."

"None of us will be rational on this, Caitlyn. He came after one of us. I want his blood."

"You'll have to go through me first." Slamming the phone shut with a growl, she went back inside to pull

Donnie from Chester's clutches.

As they hurried down the stairs, Chester called after them. "Think about my offer, Donald. Caitlyn will tire of you eventually. Once she does, you will crawl for me, Donald. I'll enjoy watching you crawl."

Ignoring Chester, she slipped her hand into Donnie's so her protégé wouldn't storm up those stairs and detach Chester's head from his shoulders.

"Not now. We have bigger things to worry about."

The serious tone in her voice made Donnie jerk to attention. Once they were outside, Donnie slid his hand from hers and stormed his way through the crowds that still lingered outside Chester's in the hopes of getting inside. Caitlyn had to straighten one or more drunken girls who Donnie brushed past in his rage. He disappeared round the corner, and Caitlyn had to hustle to catch up with him.

When she rounded the corner, he was leaning against the wall, his head resting on the brick, his palms above his head. His breathing was rapid, and Caitlyn could almost sense the fury that leaked from him.

"Why do you let him talk to you like that?" he barked.

"Chester and I go way back. He dislikes me for a number of reasons. One day, we'll have it out and only one of us will walk away, but now we have bigger things to worry about."

Donnie spun round, taking her face in his hands. "I would rip him limb from limb if you asked me to. You know that, right?"

She stayed in his grasp for a moment, basking in his touch, letting her emotions spill for a brief moment, and then she reluctantly eased away from him. She would never tie herself to another, never let what remained of her heart be shattered by another—even one for whom she cared.

"That was Derek. Melanie's missing, and Ricky thinks the suspect has her."

Donnie lashed out, his fist connecting with concrete as he punched a nearby wall. He bared his fangs and snarled. "Not for long... Timothy remembered who he was. We've got a name."

CHAPTER NINE

FOR THE SECOND TIME THAT NIGHT, DEREK SCREECHED to a halt just outside the hospital emergency room. The car park was packed with squad cars as well as uniformed police officers. His boots were on solid ground even as he yanked the keys out of the ignition. Sarge's car pulled in behind him, but loathe as he was to leave Ever, Ricky and Melanie had to be his main priority. He had no idea why he had reacted so intensely to Arthur's proximity to Ever, the wolf riding him like never before to protect what was his. That was it; she felt like she was his—his to protect, his to care for. And while Ever's presence calmed his wolf, it also made him more on edge when others were around.

But that was something he would deal with once Melanie was back with them. Hearing the raised voice of his partner as Ricky barked orders, Derek knew the uniforms would be doing their best to help him, but this was a supernatural issue and needed a supernatural to fix it.

The uniforms stepped aside as he came near. Whether it was in fear after seeing him as a wolf or because they knew he was the only one who could calm down the worried and angry warlock, Derek didn't know. He quickened his pace as he saw Ricky grab a uniform by the scruff of the neck and lift the poor rookie up so that his toes scraped the asphalt.

When Derek placed a reassuring hand on his partner's shoulder, Ricky's head darted round to look at him. Worry illuminated the warlock's eyes; they flashed a translucent lime-green before he recognized Derek and set the rookie back on his feet.

"He took her, D. That monster has her, and it's all my fault." His voice cracked as he spoke, full of loss and grief.

Derek gave his shoulder a squeeze. "Don't. We will find her. We'll get her back, I promise you with every fiber of my being. Never leave a man behind."

"Never leave a man behind."

Sensing the now-familiar presence of Ever, Derek released Ricky as the warlock shook himself, gathering his composure. Ever came to stand beside him but didn't speak. With a quick glance at her, Derek could see the firm line of her mouth, her eyes determined, and her posture tense.

Sarge assessed the scene. "Tell me what you know."

Ricky cleared his throat. "'Bout three-thirty this morning, Melanie left the hospital. I followed her about ten minutes later, and her car wasn't in the car park. So, I went to her place and waited, but she never showed. I assumed she was really pissed at me. I came back here to... I dunno... something told me to come back here.

Something felt off."

Swallowing hard, he paused before continuing. "I went back to where her car shoulda been, and that's when I saw it—her backpack. Lanie would never leave her laptop behind, not by choice. It was dark, so it was hard to see. I ain't got no wolf eyes or vampy scent, but when I pressed my fingers to the ground, there was blood. Is it her blood?"

He looked up at Derek, but while Derek could scent the blood, he couldn't tell whose it was. Maybe Cait or Donnie could. Turning, he focused on the two vampires who appeared silently beside them. The look on both their faces told Derek their visit to Chester's had been just as much hell as he thought it would be.

"The blood carries her scent. It's faint, but it's there. Also, Ricky, there's not enough blood on the ground to have caused death."

Caitlyn's words registered in Ricky's mind as his shoulders sagged and his chest heaved with relief. Then, as if remembering what the monster had done to the children, his body trembled, a blue streak of profanity leaving his lips—low enough for the supes to hear but not the humans.

Anger and helplessness filled the silence as they contemplated what to do next. They all wanted blood, even more than before. This monster had come into their house and taken a member of their family. As agents of P.I.T., they had some leeway to go outside the scope of the law as many supernatural creatures fell outside the parameters of normal law. The monster would not live to hurt anyone else. They all knew it. They all had to have it.

"It's personal," Ever said quietly. "Now that he has

taken Melanie, he knows it will be personal for us all. Ricky especially. He wants us distracted so he can go after another of his victims. He doesn't want Melanie—she's not his victim type. He'll strike again once he figures we're preoccupied."

"Ever's right," Derek replied, running his palm over his face. Damn, he was tired, and the nearing moon was a plague on him. He had twenty-four hours before he would be no good to them for twelve hours. "He never meant to take Melanie. It was a spur of the moment decision, a mistake, but we need to figure out why her and not one of us? He wants power, and we have it."

Donnie tapped a foot against the ground. "Chester gave us a name, but it's an alias. Like some vampires, our perp sought to become a vampire to start a whole new life, name included. Chester's muscle, Timothy, says the guy referred to himself as Stefan Darke. They looked into him when he petitioned to be made but could find no evidence of him. It's not much, but it's a start."

"Did this Timothy manage to get a description?" Sarge asked.

Donnie shook his head. "He said the name and his actions stood out, but as for appearance, everything about him seemed normal—an average Joe, apparently. Nothing distinctive. I'm sorry it's not more."

Ricky shuffled his feet. "So, what do we do now? We can't follow the blood trail; it's gone because he drove away. We have no fucking leads apart from a stupid-ass name for someone who has vampire envy. Son-of-a-*bitch*!" The last word came out in a strangled scream, and he swung out with his hand, lightning sparking, crumbling a nearby wall.

"Feel better?" Derek asked.

"No... helpless. I feel helpless."

"Join the club, buddy."

Caitlyn cleared her throat, bringing them out of their self-pity. "If we can find out who is behind Stefan Darke, then we can find Melanie. I'm not well versed in criminal psychology, so correct me if I am wrong, Ever; but if he already had a persona for his new life, isn't it possible he will have purchased items in his new name? Credit card, housing... he may even have changed his name by deed poll."

With a slight incline of her head, Ever acknowledged Caitlyn. "Caitlyn is right. He's fully confident that this would solve his problem, that he would have eternal life soon. He would've prepared for it. The person who committed the murders is who he really is. Stefan Darke is who he wants to be, who he needs to be to disassociate himself from the crimes he commits."

"I think we're ready to give the profile."

Sarge whistled, and the uniforms gathered round, a sea of navy hell-bent on reclaiming one of their own and willing to listen to anyone who could aid them—regardless if they were bigoted or not. A strike against one of them was a strike against all.

"Listen up! We have some information in relation to the child murders and the disappearance of Melanie Newton. Derek?"

Derek nodded and addressed the crowd. "Melanie Newton went missing this morning between three-thirty and three-forty. We believe the man responsible for the murders of three teens and attempted kidnapping of a fourth is the culprit."

A hushed whisper rippled through the uniforms, and Sarge raised a hand to hush them.

Loudly, Derek continued, unwilling to waste any time. "We believe the man is terminally ill and had petitioned to be made vampire a number of times before resorting to murder. He may be known in the supernatural forums or grey areas as Stefan Darke. Shake your C.I.'s for info and see if there have been any rumors circling. He is meticulous in his planning, and his preparation is down to a fine art. But, he made a mistake taking Melanie. If you find out any information about him, then contact any member of P.I.T. directly. We're in charge of this investigation, so run everything by us. Any questions?"

Silence greeted him, so he dismissed them with a nod. Ricky had gone to stand by the crumbling wall of his own doing. Derek's wolf was edgy, restless. He slid past Ever, his arm brushing hers as he passed, calming his wolf slightly. Nearing his partner, he leaned back against the wall and waited for Ricky to speak.

"I messed up, D. More than I ever did before. I made Lanie think she was less important because she was human. What if I don't get the chance to prove that I didn't mean it like it sounded?"

"You will, Ricky. Melanie's going to come home, and she will need you to be strong for her. But don't muck around. If you wanna be with her, be with her. Life is too short for all this crap."

Ricky glanced sideways at him. "Shouldn't you be taking your own advice, mate? You look at Ever like you'd conquer the world in a wave of blood and death for her. What's going on?"

With no other way to explain it, he simply told Ricky the truth. "That's something I need to figure out later, once we get your girl back. I've never felt such an intense pull before."

They remained in silence for a few moments after that. The sky was beginning to lighten, the first hint of morning breaking through the clouds. The sun wouldn't harm the vampires, but it would make them uncomfortable.

Caitlyn spoke into her cell phone and closed it. "I just spoke to a contact of mine who says no one has come in to change their name legally. He said he'd look into deeds; see if any new properties have been registered under the name Stefan Darke."

Derek smiled. "Cheers, Caitlyn. You and Donnie head back to the station and work from there. Sleep there if you must. With me out of action tonight, I need you and Donnie on point."

Caitlyn returned his smile with a hint of fang. She patted Ricky on the back and made to walk away when Derek called her name.

"How did it go at Chester's?"

The stunning vampire turned monstrous in a single heartbeat. "One day, I will rip out his throat and gorge on his blood. Parasite."

Derek heard Donnie chuckle as Caitlyn rounded him up, and the two vampires headed back to the station. Sarge also indicated he was heading out, so Derek nudged Ricky, and they walked over to where Ever waited for them. Ricky spoke to one of the C.S.I.'s before returning with Melanie's backpack. He looked at Ever, sadness in his eyes.

"She'd kill me if I left her stuff here with the humanoid cops. I'll keep it safe for her until she's back to claim it."

"I'm sure she'll appreciate it, Ricky."

The uniforms started to disperse, and the three of them quickly followed suit with Ricky clinging to Melanie's backpack. Once in the car, they rode in silence. Ever studied him out of the corner of her eye as greyish clouds darkened the sky and rain began to drizzle down.

"Are you feeling okay?" she asked Derek as he impatiently drummed his fingers on the steering wheel as he drove.

"If anything, I'm embarrassed."

"Why embarrassed?"

Derek shrugged. "I behaved like a jealous pup when Arthur got next to you. I had no right to behave like that. God, I'm over a hundred years old and have control over my wolf... except when I'm near you. Are you sure you're not supernatural? Because I've no other way to explain it."

Ever gave a small laugh, low and quiet, being sensitive to the turmoil Ricky must be going through. "Nope, I am one hundred percent human as far as I know. I feel it, too, you know. Whatever this is... we'll figure it out."

They shared a smile, and Ever leaned back into her seat and gazed out the window, watching the houses blur by. Her bones ached, and she desperately wanted to soak in a warm bath and sleep. Something gnawed at her senses, and she knew if she slept then she would dream. Confusion over Derek and everything with the case stopped her from thinking on her dreams. They had felt so real, as if she were remembering a forgotten memory.

Shaking the icy sensation that flooded her veins, Ever turned her attention back to Derek. Watching him from the corner of her eye, she drank in the sinfully good-looking profile of him. His hair seemed longer now, curling up behind his ear. Perhaps because of the change? If the change could heal wounds, then why not grow hair? The sharp edge of his jaw was kissed by the start of a beard, halfway between stubble and full-on scruff. His lips were pursed, and a muscle ticked in his cheek.

"Why are you looking at me like that?"

His words startled her. "Like what?"

"Like a science experiment that you want to crack."

"I'm not."

"You are." He growled, but it was a soft sound with no malice in it.

"Sorry. I'm just fascinated by you... I mean, your control. I've never been around a were this close to the moon. I'm sorry if I made you uncomfortable."

"It's alright. Did I frighten you when I was a wolf?" he asked, a little hesitant with his words.

She shook her head. "Not at all. For some reason, I knew you would never hurt me. I knew that your wolf would never cause me harm. Don't ask me how I did, but yeah, I knew I was safe."

"That's good. I'd never hurt you. I'd rather tear my own arm off."

Silence filled the space again, and Ever pulled her eyes from Derek and looked back out the window. As they neared the station, the car was halted by a backlog of traffic. Ricky had remained silent for the whole journey, and Ever hoped that no matter what the outcome, he could come back from the dark hole he was embedding himself in.

"Have you ever wanted to find your biological parents?" Derek asked.

"Is it strange to say not really?" Ever sighed. "I was

left on the church steps for a reason, but I ended up having an amazing childhood. I laughed, I cried, I loved, and I believe things would have been different if I hadn't been abandoned. I'm grateful to be loved by my parents. Some kids don't have my luck."

It was something that struck Ever as strange for the longest of times, that she felt no urge to find the person who had given her up—not because it would hurt her mom or dad, but there was no deep-seated need to belong. Apart from the longing not to be so normal, Ever felt nothing for the mother who had given birth to her or the father who had donated his seed.

A soft snore sounded from the backseat, and Ever turned round to see Ricky in a fitful sleep, cuddling Melanie's backpack. He seemed young that way, and vulnerable, and Ever guessed that the hard-man routine he put on for everyone else was just that, a routine. They seemed so different, Ricky and Derek. Derek was the former military man, the strong and silent type, whereas Ricky was the charmer, hiding who he was behind jokes and sarcasm.

"How long have you and Ricky worked together?" Ever asked.

"Forever." Derek chuckled with obvious affection in his voice. "Well, that's what it feels like. I joined up when Sarge came and told me the powers-that-be were gonna be revealing themselves to the world. He said he was heading a task force to deal with supernatural offenders. Be the poster boys and girls for policing the creatures. That was about ten years ago."

He smiled, as if the memories were fond, before continuing. "Ricky joined up two years after me, and for some reason, we clicked. I was beginning to feel more like myself, doing something useful, something I was good at, but I was very much a lone wolf. Ricky helped me be more social. Actually, he helped Caitlyn and Donnie assimilate into our little family."

Derek rubbed a hand down his thigh, and Ever found herself reaching out and resting her hand over his. "He seems like a good man. Despite what I said before, my mother speaks highly of him. He helped when a local witch went missing, helped track her down. Did you work that case?"

With a gentle shake of his head, he replied, "No, I was away with family that weekend, but Ricky told me all about it. It was him and one of our old team members, Conrad, who tracked her down and made sure she was safe."

"Has Conrad moved on? Where does he work now? You only have a few members now."

Cracking his neck, Derek shifted uncomfortably. "Conrad died. He was killed by a rogue shifter. We've lost a few good men and women in my tenure in P.I.T."

"I'm sorry." She gave his hand a squeeze. "I'm beginning to understand why you feel being a werewolf is a curse. So much death, so much loss."

"You get used to it."

"You shouldn't have to."

Derek sighed. "Over time, in this job, you get accustomed to death—loss, not so much. No matter how many years I'm on this earth, loss still surprises me. But we have to feel pain in order to know that we can feel anything else. When you stop hurting, when loss doesn't affect you, then you might as well be one of the monsters we hunt."

"That's a very profound way of looking at it."

"I'm not just all good looks and wolf, you know."

Ever laughed as a voice grumbled behind them.

"Can you go back to talking about how awesome I am? Like, for real, D; you should be romancing the girl, not being all morbid and shit."

Derek reached back, pretending to slap him, but Ricky simply laughed. Watching him in the mirror, Derek saw Ricky's face crumble as he remembered what they were doing.

He cast his gaze out the window. "We at the station yet?"

Chapter Ten

The three of them trudged into the station. The mood of the entire station was somber with everyone scrambling around, making calls and trying their damnedest to get a lead in Melanie's disappearance. Ever considered that this travesty could lead to something else, a harmony between the human police and the supernatural members of P.I.T. Tensions might be high, but the human police knew that Derek and the team considered Melanie one of their own, whether she was a lowly human or not.

There were no vindictive stares or bigoted glares; cops were simply being cops with an urge to find one of their own who had been taken on their watch. Derek led the way, a protective hand on the small of Ever's back, and she fought back a shiver at his touch. Even as insignificant as it was, it heated the blood in her veins. It felt oddly familiar, and Ever could not shake the feeling that she was missing something important.

"Destiny has many different faces, my forever. And our destinies are entwined. Do not resist me, Ever."

"Ever?"

Ever peered over her shoulder and realized that she had suddenly stopped in the middle of the squad room. People were looking at her, and heat bloomed in her cheeks. She took in a breath and continued moving forward.

"You okay?" Derek asked, his breath warm against her ear.

Ever felt her heart pound in her chest so hard it actually hurt. When she failed to answer him, Derek steered her to the side, letting Ricky go by and head into P.I.T.'s room. When the door closed behind him, Derek put a tentative thumb and finger on her chin and brought her head up, their eyes clashing as Ever trembled.

"If this is too much for you, then you can tap out. No one would think any less of you if you did. What we do, what we have to see; it can't be unseen. For some reason, I feel that the horror we might be faced with might be too much for you. Is this something you can't come back from? If we find Melanie and she's not alive, can you let it go?"

"I think I'm losing my mind. The dreams are following me into my waking hours, and it's as if I'm remembering things buried deep inside my mind. But they can't be memories. Maybe my biological mother was bipolar and I've inherited it. Derek, my mind is the only thing that has made me unique. If I lose that, then I lose who I am."

Derek traced the outline of her bottom lip as a tear trickled down her face. "You're not ill, Ever. If you were, I'd smell it. And your mind is not the only thing that makes you unique. I've been drawn to you from the very first moment I laid eyes on you, and that was before I knew you had such a brilliant mind. We can figure all this out together. I promise that I won't let you lose yourself."

"Thank you."

Derek leaned in, and Ever held her breath as he pressed his lips to her forehead. Taking her hand, he gently tugged her after him, and they went inside. Eyes turned in their direction as they walked in. Ever blushed when Derek directed her to his desk, sat her down, and then, before releasing her hand, brought it to his lips. Her skin tingled, and she shook her head. She knew he was letting them all know that he considered her his. And she liked it.

Tom gave Ever a brief smile before glaring at Derek. Derek kept his cool. After a few moments, he inclined his head as silent words were spoken. Ever turned her attention to Ricky, who seemed lost in thought over at his own desk. His lips moved, and Ever could feel the slight stirrings of magic—a familiar sense that she had grown up with. His eyes were shut, but she could see them moving behind his lids.

"Goddammit!" he exclaimed suddenly and shoved a stack of files off his desk. Caitlyn came over to him and picked up the mess on the floor. Ricky put his head in his hands and scrubbed hard. "I've tried locater spells, tracing, summoning, and nothing's working! Why can't I find her?"

"Perhaps, my friend, she is not conscious. It takes a great deal of power to find someone who is unconscious. Even a skilled dream-walker would find it difficult to enter someone's mind if they had been drugged or knocked unconscious. Don't lose heart, my friend; we'll find her."

"But what if we don't get to her in time?" Tears glistened in his eyes as Ricky's voice cracked.

A new voice broke the closeness of the moment. "I wouldn't fear for Ms. Newton. Our boy kills supes, not humans. I'm sure it's just a ploy to divert our attention."

All eyes turned to the figure standing in the doorway. Adrenaline suddenly rushed Ever, causing her head to spin. A slim-yet-muscled woman leaned against the doorframe, her shoulder-length hair a mix of brown and blonde highlights. Olive skin, with the most enticing eyes—like sunlight shining through whiskey—stared back at her. This woman felt familiar. As the woman placed her hands on her hips and beamed at them, all the air seemed to disappear from Ever's lungs.

Tom stepped forward with an outstretched hand, and they greeted each other. Ever felt as if she were going to throw up. Her vision swam as she continued to watch the woman who had stepped out of her dreams and into reality.

Systir.

The word beat a tattoo in her mind, and Ever grasped hold of the edges of the table to prevent herself from keeling over. Oh God, she really was going mad.

"Ever, you okay?" Derek's voice made her drag her eyes from the mysterious woman, and she watched as his eyes narrowed and his nostrils flared, obviously seeing and scenting the fear that now ran through her veins.

"I'm fine," she managed to croak, but she felt anything but fine.

"Everyone, this is the newest member of our team, Erika Sands. She comes highly recommended from the Dublin P.I.T., and in her short time on the job, she has gained some valid accreditations in dealing with homicides—both human and supernatural."

Tom paused as he pointed out who was who in the room, but Ever couldn't breathe. She needed to get some air.

Pushing her chair back, it slammed to the floor and they all looked at her. She swayed on her feet as the woman stepped forward, the red of her lips and the concern on her face a slap against her skin. Her knees buckled, and she braced herself to hit the floor... but she didn't.

Lightning quick, even before Derek could reach for her, Erika had slid across the floor and broken the impact of Ever's fall. As soon as they came into contact, electricity sparked and Ever shuddered. What the hell was happening to her?

Sister! Sister! Sister! The words were spoken in a language she didn't know, but understood.

The word screamed inside her head as the woman brushed a strand of blonde hair away from Ever's face. Derek crouched down beside them with a glass of water in his hand and forced Ever to take a small sip. Erika leaned her into Derek and backed away, and Ever felt she could breathe again. She gulped in air and hoped the twisted sensation in her stomach would lessen soon.

"I've never had someone swoon over me before. I'm flattered." Erika grinned, more than likely trying to make light of the incident.

Donnie studied the woman. "What are you? I've never seen a being move as fast as you did. It's like you were there one second and at Ever's side the next."

Erika laughed, and it weirdly stopped the storm of

confusion that brewed inside Ever. "You could at least buy me dinner before we get naked and reveal who we are, big boy. Let's just say for now that I certainly tick the 'other' box on the employment forms."

As Ever sat up and took another sip of water, she noticed the deep dimples on Donnie's face and the scowl on Caitlyn's as he grinned at Erika. She was beautiful, but that seemed too piss-poor a word to sum up how gorgeous the newest member of P.I.T. was. Now that Ever was beginning to recover from whatever the hell was wrong with her, she studied the woman like the profiler she was.

A snug, checked shirt rolled up to the elbows was teamed with black combat pants and boots. Ever could make out the faint outline of a tattoo that peeked out from beneath the rolled-up sleeves. Strapped to her thigh was a holster containing some sort of gun. Ever had never had any time for guns, but she did have a soft spot for a nice sword; the wall of her apartment was lined with samurai swords and a stunning katana she had gotten as a birthday present from her father. Although Erika seemed to be conversing with everyone but Derek and Ever, Ever could see the woman was watching her from the corner of her eye, an amused glint setting them alight.

"I understand you've a girl missing and not a lot of time to find her. Sir, if I may?" she asked Tom, the humor gone in an instant and replaced with professionalism. When Tom nodded, she continued. "This offender kills because he has a purpose, a task he must complete. The kills he does follow through on will only be done to justify his needs and wants. Our missing human does not fit his type, and killing her would only prick at his moral compass—and yes, he does have one."

Erika moved with the grace of a dancer. She tapped the board of the crime scene photos and pointed to the crowds. "You've seen him, whether directly or indirectly. He'll come back to the scene to watch; he won't be able to help himself. The only scene he won't be back at is Melanie's abduction site, and that's for two main reasons."

She reached into her pocket and withdrew a stick of chewing gum before unwrapping and popping it into her mouth. She blew a single bubble before she spoke again. "He's wounded. The pup he tried to take bit him, and although the bite won't change him, it will take time to heal. This is his main objective. He needs to divert our attention from him to Melanie and give himself time to regain his strength. He'll keep her alive until then."

Silence filled the air while her words sank in. They had time—not much time, but a little. Tom made the first move as he lifted his handset and made a call. He ordered in food and, surprisingly, blood. Ever glanced around at her companions. She could see the tiredness etched on all their faces.

Tom hung up and turned to the vampires. "I need you guys to go get some rest. You've been running on no rest or blood for days now. We'll need you guys at full strength while Derek is out of commission tonight. The underground resting areas are being prepared for you both. No arguing, just do it."

The vampires simply inclined their heads and vanished. Derek helped Ever as she went to stand, and as her legs wobbled, she eased herself back into Derek's now-upright chair. She gave him a reassuring smile. Derek perched himself on the edge of his desk between

Ever and the new girl.

"Tom, I don't have to change tonight. We both know you need as many trackers as possible."

"Forget it, Derek. I am not pumping you so full of silver that you can barely function as man or beast. Melanie would haul your ass over hot coals if she knew you were contemplating injecting that poison into your system for her. Don't give me that look. Neither you nor I have forgotten what happened the last time you got that idiotic idea into your noggin."

Derek growled but didn't answer Tom.

"What happened the last time he shot himself up with silver?" Ever asked.

"It doesn't matter," Derek grumbled with his head hung.

"I think it does," she snapped, surprised at her own tone.

"He didn't want to miss a family event, so the dumbass injected himself with liquid silver. About two-thirds of the way into the evening, instead of turning wolf, his body began to fight the toxin, and he started to bleed silver. He fought his body's reaction to expel the silver and had a seizure. Ended up in a coma for a month."

Derek groaned. "It was a stupid thing to do, I admit, but we don't have to be as drastic. I'm sure Ever's mom has some enchanted silver that will prevent the change."

Ever shook her head furiously. "Don't ask me to do that. Too much exposure to silver can kill you, Derek. Don't ask me to do that. I won't—I can't."

The door opened, preventing Derek from replying to Ever's pleading. The smell of coffee and hot food made Ever's stomach growl in delight. When was the last time she had eaten? She couldn't remember. No wonder she was getting light-headed and felt ill. An officer came inside and laid the tray of drinks and a bag of food down on Ricky's desk. He grabbed a coffee and yanked a sandwich from the bag but just set them down in front of him.

Derek snagged two coffees and handed one to Ever. It felt strange to be sitting here, waiting around for some sort of clue to lead them to Melanie and hopefully bring her back safely. She had no idea what the poor girl must be going through, and more than ever, she wished she had some sort of magic or was strong enough to stand with Derek and his team against this monster that was just as human as she was.

She felt Derek nudge her. Ever took the box Derek was holding out to her as the smell of burger made her mouth water. She greedily took a bite, one hand reaching out for the drink cup Derek set down on the table and washed it down with the nectar of the gods. They all sat in silence as they replenished. The clock on the wall ticked loudly with every second that passed, and Ever sighed as mid-morning turned to afternoon.

Derek cracked the vertebrae in his neck and groaned as if he were sore.

"You okay?" she asked quietly.

"I should be asking you that."

She made no effort to answer him, so he sighed. "I can feel it coming, the full moon. As it gets closer, I can sense it more clearly, and my muscles ache for the change. The longer I wait to turn, the worse it will hurt."

"Then why not change now, save the pain?"

Derek shrugged. "Suppose I'm a little masochistic, I guess. The pain will remind me that I'm human. I shouldn't take the easy way out and change before it's time. I'll already be no good to Melanie when the wolf takes over."

"It's just until the sun rises. Hopefully we will have found her before then, and then all she will need from you is a hug and to know she is safe."

"God I hope so, Ever. I really fucking hope so."

They lapsed into silence again, and Ever looked over to check on Ricky. His eyes were closed again, lines wrinkling his forehead as he concentrated. His food lay untouched in front of him. Mumbled Latin spilled from his mouth, and his hands slammed down on the table. His eyes flew open, and Ever gasped as clear black orbs stared back at her. Erika moved to reach out to him but a quiet growl from Derek halted her.

"Lanie, Lanie... tell me where you are, babe. Come on."

Could he have possibly located her? If so, then they just had to be the luckiest SOBs in the world.

"It's okay, babe. Hang in there. We're coming for you. Hold on a little longer. For me... fight it."

Ricky's eyes rolled back in his head, and with a sharp inhalation, his body bucked with his head bouncing off the hard wood of his table. Derek eased off the edge of his desk and went to Ricky. He bent his knees and put a hand on his partner's arm. The warlock lifted his head, and where despair and guilt had once resided, hope filled his eyes.

"She's alive, D! Goddammit, he hurt her, but she's alive."

"How did you do that?" Derek said.

"I have no clue, but I did. She couldn't tell me where she was, but Lanie told me she hasn't left the city. He drove for like fifteen minutes before he stopped and hauled her out of the car."

Derek rose to his feet and went to the map on the wall. He circled the hospital and then he circled all the areas that would be fifteen minutes from the hospital with a red pen. "He's in one of these places. Tom, double patrols in those areas and we can see if we can lock down a place he would be holding Melanie. It's needs to be remote so that he wouldn't be heard. This is where he takes the kids. It's his comfort zone."

"He hurt her, D. She smelled of blood and fear. I don't know if she can hold out much longer."

No one answered him because nobody had the words to reassure him that Melanie could indeed hold on until they caught him. Tom called in the update and requested that patrols be doubled in the areas.

"Has anyone called her parents?" Ever suddenly asked, wondering why no one had mentioned them before.

"She's hasn't the best relationship with her family," Derek said. "Her brother is a career criminal and is disgusted his sister works for the enemy. She wouldn't want them knowing they were proved right; that she didn't belong in the supernatural world."

Ever's phone vibrated, and she scooped it out of her jeans. 'Private Number' blinked on the screen, and she pressed answer in case it was Dr. Val with an update.

"Hello?"

Nothing.

The sound of breathing made the hairs on the back of her neck stand up, and a sense of knowing hit her in the gut. She swallowed back the fear that thrummed inside her.

"Stefan, is that you?" she asked, gaining everyone's attention.

They scrambled around as she waited, listening to the tired sigh in her ear. Derek indicated for her to try and keep him talking, while Erika hissed to someone to get a trace on whoever was ringing her phone.

"Stefan," Ever said, her tone low and comforting as her heart jackhammered. "Come on, Stefan. You didn't ring just to breathe down the phone at me. At least speak to me." She pressed the speaker button and set the phone on the table for the rest to hear.

"You're a beautiful creature, Ms. Chace. Kind, compassionate. That wolf doesn't deserve to have you look at him like you do. I'd treat you like a queen. When I'm changed, I'll treat you like the queen you are."

"I'm afraid I'm terribly normal, Stefan. I'd never be fit for someone as special as you. You called for a reason. Come on, you can speak with me. As you said, I'm kind... I'll listen to what you have to say."

"It's unfair, isn't it? To be so horribly human in their eyes? To be laughed at, ridiculed. For them to have centuries, while we only have a flicker of life. I just want to live. I just want to experience it. Is that such a crime?" There was sadness in his tone, but Ever hardened her heart. He had killed innocent children; nothing could be said to make that right or just.

"I understand you, Stefan. All my life I've wanted to be special, to be magical, but I'll live as short a life as you. I will get sick, I will die."

"YOU ARE NOT LIKE ME!" he roared. "You're just like *them*—you just don't know it yet. But I like you, Ever, and I believe you when you say that you want to understand me. We will speak soon. But for now, you must hurry.

Darkness is coming, and the girl hasn't much time left." He muttered an address before disconnecting the line.

There was a moment of stillness before Derek shouted for Erika to wake up the vampires. Ricky was already heading out the door as Ever gathered herself.

The station burst into activity. People raced all over, grabbing weapons and amassing into a small army. Something niggled at her, and she placed a hand on Derek's hand to stop him moving.

"What if it's a trap? What if this is another ploy to distract us? She mightn't even be there."

The vampires sped around the corner, Caitlyn pulling her striking mass of curls into a ponytail as she moved. Derek gave her arm a squeeze as someone shouted.

"The trace came through. The phone he called from pings at the location he gave."

The sun began to dull outside as clouds darkened the sky and thunder rumbled in the distance. Derek plucked a shotgun from a rack that had been wheeled in for the officers. He checked the barrel, loaded the gun, and then pumped it twice. A feral grin darkened his face as he faced the officers who had gone silent around him.

"You heard the man. We have a location. Let's go hunting, ladies."

Skin & Bones

He disconnected the call before tossing it on the ground and stomping his foot down hard. It lay cracked on the ground, yet he knew the SIM card was still intact, possibly being tracked at this moment. They would come, and she would be dead. He couldn't really help that now.

He regretted his actions. Of course he did. This poor girl was nothing more than an instrument of distraction, and he expected that he would feel guilt over this one for his new eternity. But he had his next victim selected, and now he needed to leave before P.I.T. arrived.

A whimper snapped him from his thoughts, and he glanced over to where the girl hung from the ceiling by her arms. Silver restraint cuffs on her wrists held her aloft. Her legs dangled freely, her body twisting against the pain she was no doubt in. Her once-vibrant green eyes watched him, now lifeless and full of fear.

He shouldn't have enjoyed torturing her, but he had.

The silver restraints were simply to delay the wolf from freeing her too easily. Grief did strange things to people, and he needed P.I.T. distracted while he commenced the final phase of his plan. He would become immortal, and then they would fear him.

Packing up his bag, he tossed it over his shoulder and moved to leave. He brushed past poor Melanie and she cried out at his touch. Stripped to her underwear, a gag stuck in her mouth, she thrashed against the bindings at her wrists, and he lashed out. His palm connected with her face, forceful enough to draw blood. She stilled for a moment before the fight returned to her eyes once more.

"I could've left you alive, but I underestimated the power of your warlock. I wasn't even going to kill you, but now, alas, I must. I'll remember you fondly in my new life. If you survive, maybe I'll come back and make you mine. I'm sorry for what is about to happen."

Sirens wailed in the distance as he grabbed a fistful of Melanie's radiant red hair and yanked her eyes to his. She defiantly held his gaze, despite the fear that rolled off her in waves. With his free hand, he pulled out the knife from the small of his back and pressed the tip to her sternum. His captive shivered at the kiss of cold metal against her bare flesh.

He angled the blade and slowly inched it forward, cutting through skin until the metal met bone. It was his turn to shudder, and if he could have stayed there all day, cutting into the delicate softness of her flesh, he would have.

"It'll take time for you to die. I've made sure of it. You never know, but your warlock might get to you in time. Good-bye, my dear."

He slid the blade free slowly, and blood poured

from the open wound. Melanie struggled before her eyes closed and her breathing became ragged. He tossed the blade aside and carried on without a second glance at the dying girl.

His thoughts drifted to the lovely Ms. Chace as he slipped outside. Rain hammered down, washing the blood from his hands. He wanted to cut into her, see what hidden gems she had inside her. He longed to feel her blood on his fingertips.

As he slipped over the railings and ducked into the industrial estate, he couldn't help but ponder how good her marrow would taste when he cut it from her very-alive body.

Chapter Eleven

THE RAIN PELTED DOWN AS DEREK DROVE LIKE A maniac through the city streets, siren blaring. Cars moved out of the way quickly. Ever clung to the handle above her as a growling Derek rounded a corner and almost went head first into an oncoming vehicle. They veered and maneuvered through the rain-drenched streets, tires squealing in protest as he overtook another car.

Ever sat in the back of Derek's car with Erika seated next to her and Ricky in the passenger seat. Erika had checked and rechecked her gun a number of times, and Derek wondered why the girl was so on edge... plus why she kept watching Ever. Derek blared his horn as a car refused to move out of the way. He jammed on the brakes and cursed as the occupants of his car lurched forward. Reversing quickly and yanking the wheel around, he burst out of the line of traffic to the wrong side of the road.

"Christ, D... did you learn to drive playing *Grand Theft Auto*? You're gonna kill us all."

Derek didn't slow his actions; instead, he pressed his foot down harder on the accelerator. Night was creeping in around them, winter shortening the days and bringing darkness at a much quicker pace. His skin itched and pulled at him, and he knew he was losing the battle with his wolf. The wolf snarled and banged against the inside of his mind, wanting out, wanting to be in control. But he would hold off as long as he could, and then, if this monster lurked inside, he would shed his human skin and allow the wolf to rip into flesh and feast on death.

A growl vibrated through him, and he heard Ever clear her throat. His eyes sprang to the mirror. She tapped a finger to her brow and he looked at his eyes in the mirror. Wolf amber shone back at him. He tried to calm down, but the colour refused to leave.

They burst through the traffic lights at the top of the hill, and Derek brought the car to a screeching halt. Ricky jumped from the car before Derek. He was rushing forward to where some of the uniforms were trying to break a padlock from the gate. Ricky pushed them aside and held out his hands over the lock. Blue lightning shot from his hands as he grunted, and the lock shattered open and fell to the ground.

Derek made to go after his friend as the vampires arrived on the scene with Sarge arriving in his own car and they went after Ricky. Derek moved forward slowly as his muscles cramped, heavy like they were made of lead. He scented Ever behind him and spun around to face her.

"You have to stay here."

She snorted. "Like hell I will."

"Ever, I can't find Melanie if I'm worried about you getting hurt. Please wait here."

He beckoned Erika to follow him, and she did, her hand grasped around the butt of her gun. As Derek walked by, he barked at one of the officers to watch Ever and make sure she did not enter the crime scene. He could almost feel the anger that radiated from Ever, but he would deal with that issue later.

When Erika and he jogged up to where Sarge, Ricky, the vamps and a swat team waited, Sarge nodded and handed control over to Derek. He was used to this. It made his blood sing as adrenaline began to build up, the familiar nature of the operation ingrained in his marrow.

"This building is massive, so span out and search every nook, every square inch of the place from top to bottom. Cait, you take Donnie and go east with team one. Ricky and I will go up and start on floor two. Erika, take team two with Sarge and go west. When you meet up, make your way upstairs. Take a COM and stay in constant contact when a room is clear. Ready?"

With a nod, they all headed out, and he and Ricky crossed the floor and headed for the stairs. Derek moved in front of Ricky, his shotgun pointed out in front of him, his feet quickly double timing up the stairs. He poked his head around the curve of the stairs and angled the gun upward. The entire building was eerily hushed, with no sounds except for the beating of hearts. His eyes were still wolf, and he could see insects clambering about the floor of the abandoned building.

As they reached the second floor, Derek pressed a finger to his lips and closed his eyes. He stilled his breathing, focusing his senses on finding something concrete to tell him whether to go up or stay on the level he was on. Blood, the coppery scent of it, filled his nose, and it was coming from all over the damn place. He couldn't separate the old blood from new blood. It all just smelled like blood to him.

Making a decision, Derek chose to check out the second floor. He motioned for Ricky to follow him and the warlock did without question, a ball of blue electricity dancing in his hand. Darkness met them in a corridor with no windows, and Derek paused. Ricky muttered a quick spell, and his ball of electricity flew through the air, leading the way.

They had barely gone twenty feet when Derek caught the scent of decay. He inclined his head and pushed open the door to his right. It creaked loudly in the overbearing silence, and Derek held it open for Ricky. Another door barred their way, and Derek used his foot to kick it open, the splintering wood causing an echo to bounce around the room.

"Bravo One, everything alright up there?" Sarge's voice rumbled in his ear.

"Bravo Two, everything's fine. Just kicking down some doors."

"Ground floor clear. Moving upward."

"Me and Ricky are on the second floor. Move further into the maze out back. If we get anything up here, we'll holler."

"Copy that."

Derek pressed against the broken door, and his boots crunched over broken glass. Abandoned desks lay upturned inside the compact room. Before it had become a murder house, this building used to be a telecom office, servicing most of the country's landlines.

A fire a couple of years ago had laid the place to waste, and the owners thought it not worth the cost or hassle of getting it up and running again. You could still scent a faint smell of smoke from the burnt wood.

The scent of decay became stronger with every step Derek took into the abandoned room. He paused and looked to his left, seeing a door slightly ajar to a room off to the side. The smell was coming from inside. Derek made to go into the room when a spasm grabbed hold of him. He dropped the shotgun, and his back bowed in pain.

"D, you alright, man? Just let the change happen, man. Come on—no need to hurt yourself."

Derek braced a hand against the wall and funneled the pain. His wolf snapped and snarled at him. "I'm fine," he said through gritted teeth. He bent to pick up his shotgun and slowly pushed the door open. Blood covered the floor and a rounded conference table in the centre of the small room. It was pooled around the ends of the table, some still dripping from the edges, but that wasn't the worst of it. The table had restraints fitted at the end and the sides, with cuffs small enough for a teen. At the back of the room, a shelving unit stocked everything needed to teach Sick Bastard 101.

Bile crept up his throat as his eyes landed on various jars and utensils. As he looked closer, Derek could see that the jars were labeled with the names of the slain teens. All were half-empty of blood, and they sat next to bone samples.

"Jesus Christ, D. This is a slaughterhouse. Oh God, what if he did this to Lanie?"

Derek backed out of the room, tugging Ricky with him.

"Bravo One to Bravo Two," he called into his COM.

"Go ahead, Bravo One."

"We found Darke's slaughter room. It's as you'd expect. I'll leave it for the C.S.I's to process. Keep looking where you are. Ricky and me are gonna head upstairs and check it out. Heading to floor three."

"Copy that. Watch your six."

"Yes, Sir."

He faced Ricky, whose face had gone pale as he considered the mess and horror in the little room. Derek shifted his feet as another wave of agony iced his veins. He fought against the change. Against the creak of his bones and the pressure building up inside his head.

"Let's go up. He wanted us to see this to scare us."

"It fucking worked, D."

They headed back the way they had come, hushing the moment they left the room and cautiously making their way up the next two flights of stairs. As they reached the top, copper tickled his nose. The doors leading to the floor were toppled to the ground, building a bridge over the fire-damaged floorboards that had burnt and broken off in the fire. Derek braced a foot to test how solid it was before he planted both feet on the fallen door. He wouldn't exactly die from broken bones, but it would hurt like hell.

Ricky's ball of blue light flowed past him, and he moved slowly toward the inner door. When he reached the other side, the wood groaned and Ricky looked at him.

"Jump, I'll catch you."

"No chance in hell," his friend replied, deciding to race over the door instead of taking his time. The wood groaned louder and cracked as Ricky heavy-footed it over to where Derek waited. Derek bit down on his lip as another wave of pain hit. Pushing open the next door, Ricky ushered his ball of light forward, and Derek almost smacked into him as Ricky froze, a gargled cry of anguish ripping from his throat.

Hanging from the ceiling, a blood-soaked Melanie swung listlessly back and forth. Ricky rushed forward but with Derek's supernatural speed, he reached her first. Her vibrant red hair was caked in blood. Her face was cut, and she had a stab wound to the abdomen. Stripped down to her underwear, Melanie appeared to be dead, but Derek could hear a faint *thump, thump* in her chest.

Derek leapt up on a nearby table and reached for the restraints. His skin burnt at the contact, and he hissed. He tried again with the same result. Ricky snapped to attention and climbed up so that he could undo the restraints. Derek jumped down as Ricky touched the cuffs and muttered a word in Latin. The cuffs sprang open, and Melanie slumped into Derek's arms. He lowered her to the ground as Ricky pulled off his jacket and draped it over her, his hand pressing down on the wound that continued to seep blood.

"Come on, babe, wake up for me," Ricky pleaded, but Melanie remained lifeless. Her lips were tinged with blue, and her pulse was a dull tone under Derek's fingertips.

"Sarge! We found her. I need Caitlyn or Donnie *right now*!"

"Coming to you!"

Ricky pulled Melanie into his lap and cradled her as Derek replaced Ricky's hands with his own. Ricky kept mumbling into her ear as he rocked her. He smoothed her hair and promised to look after her, and Derek had to look away as his heart broke for the man who had dragged him out of the abyss. Sarge had saved his life, but the warlock was the one who had reminded him what it was to live and not simply be alive.

A gust of air swirled around them as the vampires rushed through the door. Donnie roared at the sight of Melanie's broken body, and Caitlyn cursed a blue streak. Derek looked at Caitlyn, and she shook her head. His shoulders sagged as despair flooded through him, and Ricky caught the movement. When he saw the answer to his unspoken question, Ricky shook his head.

"No, D, please... we can do something... we *have* to save her."

When Derek said nothing, his eyes pleaded with Caitlyn. "She can't die, Cait. Please tell me she'll survive."

There was a moment of silence as Donnie glared at Caitlyn and she, in turn, glared back at him. A force of wills was taking place in their heads, and Derek wasn't sure who would win until Caitlyn sighed.

"There might be a chance to save her."

Relief flashed over Ricky's face. "Whatever it is, just do it."

Emotion thickened her words as Caitlyn laid it out for him. "It's not something *mon ami* might have ever wished for herself. She may hate us for making this decision for her. Even when one chooses to take on this life, there are times when one regrets that the chance for their soul to be reborn has been taken from them. I can make her a vampire, but she may never be the same Melanie that you love. She may hate you for asking me to do this."

"She can hate me all she wants when she's around to do it."

"Then I need you to leave her to me. Go now; this is

not something you want to see."

Ricky pushed his chin out stubbornly. "I'm not leaving her."

"So be it. We do not have much time left. Death has already begun to seep into her bones."

Caitlyn knelt down next to Melanie and brushed the hair from her face. Gently, she pressed her lips to Melanie's forehead. "I would not do this if I thought it was something you might not want. But I welcome you into our little family, Melanie. You're now mine, and we are yours. If my daughter had lived, I would've wished for her to be like you—brave, beautiful and smart. I just wish now that you don't hate Ricky or me for making this decision for you. Sometimes, even when it has been asked, some regret being made."

"I never once regretted saying yes to being made, Cait. I live now more than I did when I was alive, and that's because of you. Melanie won't hate you for this. I certainly never have."

Caitlyn ignored Donnie, but her eyes filled with tears. She held Ricky's gaze as she said. "No matter what I do, you will not interrupt. If you do, she will die and you will not have the chance to tell her you love her. Do you understand?"

Ricky nodded, and Caitlyn began. She scored her wrist with her fangs, and blood dripped from her wound. She placed the wrist over Melanie's mouth, having gently opened it. Using her free hand, Caitlyn worked Melanie's throat so that she swallowed the blood in her mouth.

"She may still die. This close to death, it may be too late. I might not be strong enough," Caitlyn whispered.

"You're strong enough."

Caitlyn nodded. Removing her wrist from Melanie's mouth, she ran her fingers down the girl's neck until she grasped both sides and quickly twisted it as Ricky let out a strangled cry. The sound of her neck breaking, combined with Ricky's sobs, filled the room. Yet Melanie remained still.

"Now what?" Derek asked.

Caitlyn rose to her feet. "Now, I take her to my home and see if she is reborn. She will make the decision. In the end, she has some choice. I'll watch over her for the next three moons. On the third night, if she wakes before the sun rises, then she has embraced her vampire life. If not, then we can mourn her passing." She squeezed Ricky on the shoulder. "I must take her now, for this is only one part. And no, you don't want to see what must be done next, for you'll never erase it from your memories. I'll protect her and keep her safe. She's as much mine now as she is yours."

"She is ours to protect, and we will. Let me take her, Ricky." Donnie had stepped forward and was already scooping up Melanie into his arms.

Caitlyn pressed a kiss to Ricky's cheek. "I'll call with an update as soon as I have it."

And then they were gone, leaving Derek and Ricky waiting until Sarge and Erika burst in with the team. Derek laid out what had happened as Ricky sat lost below the chains that had held Melanie.

"I'll call in the C.S. I's. He might've left in a hurry and left some prints behind," Sarge said before speaking into his phone.

Now that the emergency was over and they had Melanie back, Derek felt the moon reach its highest peak in the sky. There was still a sliver of daylight outside, but the winter's moon rose sooner in the season, and it had come calling for him. His knees hit the ground, and his back bowed again with the pain. It ripped through him as if his skin were being peeled from his body. His wolf, now satisfied that Derek had done what he was supposed to do, bucked for control, and Derek was losing the battle.

Sarge turned, and his mouth hung open. Derek screamed as the bones broke and reformed in his front arms. Clothes tore and disintegrated around his reforming body, yet he had little time to worry that he would soon be as naked as the day he was born. The fiery flames of pain that burnt him from the inside out continued to sear through him. His already-amber wolf eyes blurred red, and he felt the stirrings of bloodlust. His fangs elongated, and he roared as his claws sliced through the tips of his fingers. He was halfway between wolf and human form. A thousand little pinpricks of fire punched through his skin.

It was the worst pain Derek had ever felt, almost as bad as the first change. The bones in his back broke, and then his legs, and he let out a howl of pure agony. Dear God, he was dying. Someone shouted, telling people to back off. As pain rippled through his entire spine, Derek howled, more wolf than man. The bones in his face were next, and he felt as if he had been punched in the face with a hammer.

It was then he scented her, finally able to pinpoint the scent that had lured him to her. She smelled of sand and sun, mixed with a faint hint of coconut. Somewhere in between wolf and man, Derek whimpered as Ever came forward and placed a hand on his furred head.

"Just let go, Derek. Let go of control. You did

everything you could for Melanie, and in the morning, we can hunt her killer down and get justice. Please—for me—just relax and let go. It's okay."

And with those words, he cleared his mind and let go of his control. The rest of his bones cracked and reformed, and he let out an inhuman scream before Derek was gone and the wolf was free.

The wolf took in those around him, red still tingeing his irises. He took a step toward Ever, who did not move an inch. He felt a sharp pain on his rump, and when he turned his head to the side, the wolf saw a dart sticking out from his skin. He snarled at the man who held the dart gun and tried to stalk toward him, but his paws wouldn't move on his command.

He whined as he faced Ever and his legs gave out. Resting his muzzle on his front paws, he heard a voice say, "You'll thank me in the morning, D."

As the drugs kicked in, his vision blurred, and the last thought that he had before he welcomed the darkness was how beautiful Ever looked to his wolf.

Chapter Twelve

Ever had thought the most surreal moment of her life was driving to a police station with an oversized wolf in the passenger seat. But no, travelling in the back of a police transporter with a drugged-up wolf in a cage definitely surpassed that. The wolf was making sleep yipping noises and jerking its legs around a bit. Ever had to get reassurance from Ricky that the tranquilizer dart hadn't done any long-lasting damage to poor Derek.

"Ever, I promise that D will be fine when he wakes up. Sure, he'll have a wicked headache, but considering the pain he was in a couple of hours ago, that will be a piece of cake."

Ever took him at his word, but she was loathe to leave the sleeping wolf's side. They could do nothing now but wait. Tom reluctantly phoned ahead and had a room prepared down in the basement of the station for her and Derek.

"You sure you want to stay down here with him,

Ever? He'll be out for a while," Tom asked her when they backed the transporter into the station. The back doors opened, and it took six officers to shove the cage out of the van and carry it around to the back of the station.

"I'm sure, Tom. I just want to make sure that if he's restless when he wakes, he can have a familiar face there to keep him calm."

"Ricky can do that."

Ricky snorted, hopping out of the van behind them. "Yeah, Sarge, but I'm not a gorgeous blonde with a megawatt smile. Besides, I wanna go check on Lanie."

Tom put a firm hand on his shoulder. "Leave it be, son. Caitlyn will call when she has news. She'll take good care of her. Why don't you go get some sleep."

It was an order, not a question, and Ricky trudged off with false mumblings that sure he would go get some rest... as if anyone would believe that. Until that man could see Melanie alive and well, so to speak, Ever would bet her life that there would be no rest for him.

Ever followed the officers as they struggled to hold on to the cage containing Derek as they descended a stone staircase. It was well lit for what was more or less a dungeon, with tiny spotlights leading the way down the stairs. When she reached the bottom, Ever was amazed to see a fully functional kitchen, along with four rooms that sprouted off into four different directions. Boots clattered down the stairs behind her as Tom strode down and pointed to a room on the far left. He yanked open the door for the officers, who had by now lowered the cage to the ground, and heaved it inside the room.

As the officers left, Tom stayed with Ever. She walked into the room and glanced around. Four plain, grey stone walls greeted her, windowless, with a soft light overhead the only thing that prevented her from being thrust into complete darkness. Apart from the bed, the only piece of furniture in the room was the cage, if you could even consider that furniture.

Ever eased herself down on the bed, her bones suddenly so tired that they ached. A yawn escaped her, and she tried to rub the sleep from her eyes. She heard the soft, familiar tone of Tom's chuckle, and she glanced up at him.

"Don't fight it, Ever. Get some sleep. We'll need to rest up now and regroup in the morning. There's food stocked in the kitchen as well as coffee. If he wakes early and is agitated—the wolf, I mean—there is a phone in the kitchen. Call me, and I'll send Ricky with another dart."

Ever shook her head. "I'm sure he'll be fine, Tom. Can you ring my parents and let them know I'm okay? I haven't checked in for a couple of days, and you know how they worry."

Tom came over to her and ruffled her hair, just like he used to do when she was a little girl. "I already planned to, Miss. I do not wish to incur the wrath of Samhain by not keeping her up to date with what her precious daughter is up to." He grinned before motioning his head toward Derek. "Should I leave out the bit about you and my second?"

With a grin, Ever replied, "Please. I don't know what the hell is between us, and it's best to keep them in the dark until we know what the story is."

"Roger that. But Ever, be careful with him. He's not as tough as he looks." Words of wisdom given, Tom turned and strode out the door, only stopping when Ever said his name.

"I never thanked you, you know."

Tom raised an eyebrow, and she continued.

"For finding me and making sure I was settled with good parents. I'll always be eternally grateful that you were the one who found me and gave me a perfect, loving home."

"There was no couple more deserving of you than them, Ever, and I still hold strong on my promise to help you look for whoever had to give you up if you ever want to."

Tom left with a promise to fetch her and Derek in the morning, halting only to give a code to the lock on Derek's cage. The sound of his steps echoed through the empty bunker until the door closed and she was alone with the wolf. Too tired to even take off her shoes, Ever slipped under the blankets and rested her head on the soft pillow. It smelled of Derek, wild and strong, and with one final check on the dozing, golden-brown wolf, Ever allowed her mind to clear and her eyes to flutter closed as she embraced sleep.

The sound of clashing metal was a welcome and comforting sound as she strolled along the shores of the beach, the vast beauty of her island home stretched out for miles in front of her. Sand wedged between her toes as her sandals slipped under the silky-smooth grains, but she didn't mind. The sun glistened against the crystal-clear, blue ocean that lapped against the shore and sprinkled droplets of salty water against her skin. Serenity washed over her, the complete and utter calm that came to her when she returned to the shores of her home. It was a transformation she could not explain.

"Systir!"

A cry came from amongst the trees, and she turned to see the youngest of her sworn kin race from the forest, her arms wide and her gleeful face a welcome sight. She dropped to her knees as the young girl flung her tiny arms around her neck and held her in a tight embrace. Rarely did she show outward emotions for her kin, but this little girl could draw a smile from the most hardened of warriors.

"Ever, I am so glad you have returned."

"As am I, sweet Marya, as am I. I have missed your smiling face."

The little girl untangled her arms from her neck, and Ever drank in the sight of her. Eyes of the darkest blue, skin as pale as tropical sand, Marya had a mass of dirty blonde hair that caressed her bottom. Strands of wild hair usually tended to escape from the bands that tried to bind it off her face. Today, the hair snaked down her back in a plait laced with wildflowers.

"Have you been practicing while I have been away?" she asked the little girl.

Marya shoved her shoulders back and proudly said, "I have, of course! Mother says I am almost as good with a long blade as when you were a babe."

Ever laughed, and the little girl beamed. A horn sounded before a medley of voices rang through the air. Goosebumps rose on her arms as she slipped her hand into Marya's while they walked across the sandy shore and around the corner to where the raised voices had come from.

Marya slipped free of her grasp and ran ahead, eager to join in the fray. On sight of her, the shouts and fighting halted. Everybody that spanned the beach dropped to a knee, and the warriors on the ground bowed their heads with a fisted hand placed over their chests—a show of respect, a show of loyalty, of fealty.

"Rise, warriors!" she called out before continuing on her path toward the dais where her other sisters stood. The all greeted her with a nod of the head and a fist to the heart, and she returned the gesture.

"How is the training coming along?"

"Very well, Systir. Mayhap you would like to see for yourself? You still must choose your champion."

Ever nodded, still hesitant to choose a warrior to tie herself to for eternity. Once chosen, the bond could not be broken by either. Only the final death would sever the bond and send them into oblivion, never to be reborn again. Final death wasn't the easiest to achieve for her kind.

Her sister placed her fingers between her teeth and blew, a shrill whistle calling the collection of warriors to stand to attention. Her warrior sister barked instructions, the warriors faced each other, one on one, and the slow dance began. The clash of swords and the cries of defeat set fire to her blood. She was eager to partake herself; it had been far too long since she had twirled her blade and felt the rush as metal grazed flesh.

She watched as their acquired warriors ducked, dived, wielded, and persevered, continuing on with their fists even when the coppery scent of blood marred the air. Her sisters had done a very good job of training and making the once-forgotten souls into fierce warriors in their army.

"Have we had any losses since I left?"

The hulking Danae was the one who answered her—her sister bigger than half of the warriors fighting below and twice as deadly. She folded her arms across her chest, the muscles bunching, veins almost popping free of her near-mahogany skin. "We have lost ten in total out of five hundred. But the losses that we suffered we justified; ego made them sloppy, and they challenged others. Foolish imps deserved the blade they were run through with."

Ever felt a smile tug at her lips. "And pray tell, Danae, was it your blade that sent them into the next life or another's?"

The warrior huffed. "I ran my blade through five, but the others... it was the right of the one they challenged, and he requested to be the one who ended their lives."

"I would very much like to see this warrior who thinks he has the right to make such a request from those above his station."

Turning her attention back to the demonstration, her eyes scanned the crowd in search of a warrior who might be suitable to be her champion. She had argued with Mother on numerous occasions that she did not need a champion, that the custom was outdated and she was not a typical princess to be babysat and coddled. Her mother, in return, argued that custom was important and that a champion was more than a babysitter—he was to be the second half of her soul, her confidant, and her lover... everything a queen needed to rule her subjects.

And in return for eternal servitude? Her champion would be bestowed with powers beyond his imagination. Strength, speed, vitality, and he would be the consort to the queen; he would stand beside her and command the army in her absence. They would birth the next generation of royalty, their daughters to rule, and their sons to fight. It would be the greatest achievement of his life, and supposedly, Ever would know her champion when she saw him.

The glint of metal caught her eye, and she tilted her head, narrowing her gaze so that she could focus on the pull she suddenly felt. Before her eyes stood the most gorgeous creature she had ever seen in her life. Barefooted with a naked torso, the fluid movement of his body mesmerized her as he took down his opponent with ease. Sweat gleaned from his golden skin, highlighting his toned physique, his well-defined muscles so deliciously lickable. Trimmed bronze hair completed the planes of his chiseled features, strong jaw, and high cheekbones.

As if feeling the heat of her gaze on him, the warrior lifted his head. Eyes of the deepest hazel—almost chocolate—held her own blue ones. Those eyes raked over her body, and when he brought them back up to hold her gaze once more, lust flared in his eyes and her knees felt weak.

"I see the warrior who thinks he is our equal has drawn your attention. He would make a fine champion and life mate for you."

Erika's voice pulled her from watching the warrior watch her. Her cheeks flushed as she pictured herself tracing the outline of his broad chest and shoulders as he lavished her with kisses. Her heart sped up, and her pulse jumped. How weak a woman was she that she let a man cause her to forget their objective?

"I was merely admiring his form. Perhaps he had the right to ask to be the one who divested the fallen of their second lives."

A hearty laugh erupted from her sister's mouth. "The lady doth protest too much."

Ever shouldered her sister and knocked her to the ground with a fevered grin on her face. Marya clapped her hands in glee, knowing full well what was coming next. Erika leapt to her feet, pulling her daggers from her belt. Danae tossed Ever her sword, which she caught with ease, sighing as soon as she wrapped her fingers around the hilt of it.

"You will pay for the disrespect, sister. Let us see if you have become rusty whilst preparing for politics."

Twisting her wrist around, Ever dived from the dais, landing with both feet apart in the sand, and braced herself to fight.

"Or shall we see if my absence has made you sloppy, Erika? If I entrusted our army to the right general?"

They grinned at each other as they circled one another, waiting with the patience of a hunter stalking prey. Erika struck first with her right hand, punching out with her blade, aiming for the bare skin of Ever's abdomen. Ever sidestepped easily and turned, swinging the length of her sword, narrowly missing the tender muscles of Erika's neck.

For the first time in what felt like an age, Ever felt like herself. This was what she was born for, nothing more, and nothing less. The politics of ruling their people held no sway for her, and she wished that her mother would choose one of her other sisters to rule. But Ever was the only one born from their own mother, the only one with the queen's blood coursing through her veins. It was a curse and a blessing all in one neatly wrapped gift.

She blocked one of Erika's strikes, holding her sword out and letting the weapons clash off each other, the sound of thunder rumbling as they continued to dance around each other, both evenly matched in poise and skill. All the warriors had gathered to watch them, and Ever could feel the heavenly gaze of the warrior upon her. She knew it was he without even having to look, and she delighted in the feeling that bloomed in the pit of her stomach.

After an hour of strikes and misses, Ever could see her sister waver, and she took advantage of it. With the swipe of her leg, she kicked Erika's legs out from under her. Her sister's back hit the sand, and Ever put the tip of her blade to the curve of her neck.

Her sister, far from being angry, beamed up at her and held up her hands in submission, having dropped her daggers to the ground. Ever dug her sword into the sand and held out a hand to Erika, who promptly pulled her down onto the sand next to her—an old trick they had played as children—and they both burst into childish giggles. The crowd cheered at their display of skill, and Ever felt lighthearted as Danae helped Erika up and Ever lifted her gaze to the hand that was outstretched to her.

Hazel eyes held hers as she took the warrior's hand and he pulled her to him so hard that she had to hold out her palms and brace herself against his chest. Her fingers tingled at the contact, and she slowly inhaled the scent of him. He smelled like the woods and earth. She traced the outline of his chest, and he growled.

"It is very good to have you home, My Queen."

Ever grunted. "Hush, I am not queen yet."

"You will always be the only queen I follow."

She held his gaze for a moment more before stepping back and reluctantly removing her hands from his chest. He smiled at her then, amusement dancing in his eyes.

"What is your name, warrior?" she found herself asking.

The warrior bowed his head once and then held her gaze as he fisted his hand over his chest. "My name is Deryck, My Queen, and I am your future-destined champion."

"Ever."

Derek's voice crashed her back to reality, and she bolted up in the bed, gasping for breath. Her head ached, and confusion swam an ocean in her mind. Where was she? Where were her sisters? What kind of place was she trapped in? Had she been captured by an enemy and cast aside in their dungeon? Her eyes darted from side to side as she searched for a weapon to defend herself.

"Ever, look at me. You're okay. You're safe."

Her warrior's voice reassured her, and as she looked over at his gloriously naked body, Ever remembered that she had only been dreaming, and she had awoken in the basement of the police station, and since Derek was Derek again, the sun must be up.

She swung her legs over the side of the bed and rubbed her temple. "Oh God! I'm sorry. I must've been dreaming again."

"You were calling my name."

She blushed. "Was I?"

"Yeah, you were."

She ran her gaze over him as he sat huddled in the corner of the cage, his knees to his chest, his head resting atop his knees. He looked fine, no aftereffects from the drugs. When she was certain that Derek truly seemed okay, Ever allowed herself free rein to roam her gaze over him. All sculpted muscle that came from hard work rather than hours spent in the gym, his skin was slightly tanned, his thighs thick and his shoulders wide. She drank him in with her eyes and imagined what it would be like to trace her fingertips over the hard-ridged muscle of his stomach. When he cleared his throat, she realized she had been staring at him without saying a word for a while.

"Oh God! I'm sorry. Do you want me to get some clothes for you? There has to be something lying around."

Cracking his neck, Derek replied, "There's a supply closet in the room next door with some pants and tees."

She scrambled from the bed and headed for the door.

"Ever?" Derek said, and she peered back at him. "What were you dreaming about that had you saying my name over and over? And what the hell is a Kappi?"

Chapter Thirteen

DEREK SAT AT THE COUNTER OF THE KITCHEN SCARFING down the massive sandwich that Ever had made him for breakfast. They ate in an uncomfortable silence, Ever having refused to answer his question when he'd asked what she had been dreaming about. Last night had been a complete cluster of one bad idea after another. He could still feel the wolf's lust for blood inside him, and he knew it was his own fault.

He bit into his sandwich again and savoured the delectable taste of bacon in his mouth. Ever sipped her coffee and tried her best to avoid his gaze. But out of the corner of his eye, he could still catch her watching him before a faint, kissable pink flushed her cheeks and she looked away.

Glancing at the clock on the wall, he saw it was a quarter after nine. He had shifted back to himself around sunrise, he guessed, and had awoken two hours later and watched Ever sleep. He was eager to check in with Sarge and ensure that both his partner and Melanie were doing okay, but he found he was quite enjoying the sensation of having breakfast with someone, someone who had cooked for him and refused to leave him when he was vulnerable. He was falling fast and hard for this amazing woman, and it scared him shitless.

With last night such a blur in his mind, he wanted to know exactly what had gone down when he had clashed with the wolf in him. Of course, he remembered the pain—how the hell could you forget an agony of fire like that?—and he remembered hearing Ever's voice before he got shot with the dart. But not much else.

"So how scary, on a scale of one to ten, did I get last night?" he ventured, trying to lighten the tension with a little humor.

Ever shrugged before returning his smile. "'Bout a fifteen. I honestly think a few of the uniforms pissed their pants watching you change. Although, I think they'll respect the hell out of you after watching it. *I* certainly do."

"Pfft... I messed up."

Setting her mug on the counter. "How d'you figure that?"

"I held out too long. I let myself fight the wolf, and under the moon, he'll always win. When he forced the change, I dug my heels in, refused to do it, and I enraged the wolf—set him on the path of bloodlust. Once you go there, there's no return."

Ever twisted the ends of her hair as she considered her answer carefully, her nose wrinkling as she thought. "You like to brood, don't you? It's like a hobby for you or something. Derek, there aren't many men—or wolves, for that matter—who could have held on to themselves like you did last night. The moon crept out from behind the clouds, and you remained on two feet. You helped rescue Melanie, and you sit there feeling sorry for yourself. Not buying it, buddy."

Derek burst out laughing, so much so that tears ran down his face. When he regained his composure, he said, "I have never been chastised so politely in my life. Apart from my mother, you are the only person to call me out on my shit."

"You don't give yourself enough credit, Derek."

"Neither do you."

She blinked in surprise and lifted the mug to her lips. Having taken a sip, she set it down again. "I guess I know my limitations. Growing up as I did, being normal in a not-so-normal family, I became attuned to the fact I'd never feel the rush of magic in my veins, the thrill of shifting into something other than myself. I even craved the chance to taste someone's blood, but then I thought against it. You have within you the power to save lives over an eternity when I have become nothing more than a memory of someone you used to know."

"I wish you could see yourself from my eyes, Ever. You're beautiful, smart, funny, and I've a feeling you are more than you could imagine."

The moment was interrupted by the sound of the door opening as someone stomped down the stairs. A disheveled Ricky came into view and sank down on the chair next to Derek. Ever poured and slid a warm cup of coffee his way, and he muttered his thanks. He nudged his shoulder to Derek and said, "No hard feelings for last night?"

"None at all, bro. None at all."

"Cool, 'cause I'm gonna do the same again tonight."

"I was just about to ask you to. Any news on Melanie?"

He gulped his coffee before replying, taking the half-eaten sandwich from Derek's plate and scoffing a bite. "Donnie called early this morning to say they were both doing well, whatever that means," he managed through his half-full mouth. He swallowed hard and drank more of his coffee before he went on. "He told me not to come over or Caitlyn would rip me a new one. But he's coming here for a briefing around noon."

"She'll be fine, Ricky. Melanie is tough... she'll get through it."

Ricky grunted a response as he finished off Derek's sandwich. Time ticked by, and Derek longed to soak his tense muscles in a long shower, but he suspected they didn't have time for that.

"You want me to take you home so you can shower and get some fresh clothes? Things might get a bit mental after tonight 'round here."

Derek had addressed Ever, but Ricky answered.

"No need," he said, gesturing to the duffel at the end of the stairs. "Samhain sent over a bag of stuff for Ever this morning. She said to call her whenever you have a free moment. Your dad worries when you don't call."

Ever chuckled. "Yeah, and she doesn't worry at all. Thanks, Ricky. I'll ring her there. Is there a shower down here for me to get freshened up?"

Derek pointed to the door across from where they had slept last night. "There's a shower in there. Use some of Cait's fancy stuff. She won't mind."

"Thanks," she replied with a smile, and Derek felt his stomach summersault.

Yeah, he was definitely falling for her.

He watched her as she grabbed the duffel and

headed for the shower, closing the door behind her. Cocking an ear, he listened as she spoke into her phone, and when he heard affection in her tone, he relaxed and turned back to his best friend.

Ricky had a wicked grin on his face. "Man, D, you've got it bad."

"Pot and kettle, my friend. Pot. And. Kettle."

"Touché."

Ricky's phone buzzed and he checked it before getting up from the table. "Sarge wants me upstairs. Take your time getting ready. And for God's sake, D, kiss the girl already and get it outta your system. It's been a while, I know, but you still remember the mechanics of it, right?"

His friend's teasing brought a friendly growl from his throat. "Why, Ricky? You wanna give me lessons in kissing?" he teased back.

At the end of the stairs, Ricky turned back. "Nah, man. Everyone knows witches prefer cats... You ain't my type, girlfriend." With an elaborate snap of his fingers, he pursed his lips at Derek.

Derek shook his head as Ricky left, knowing full well under all the jokes and bravado, he was hurting and hurting bad. Derek had lost many loved ones over his lifespan, but to lose someone who you were *in* love with? That would gut you from the inside out. He was only falling for Ever, and the thought of losing her was like a vice grip on his chest. When he lost him mom to old age, he had been distraught, but he had survived, same when his brother had died. He had mourned the loss of people who had known him when he was human, but his sister's death had almost dragged him down.

Derek exhaled and closed his eyes, remembering a

time when he had felt powerless.

Making his way slowly around the side of the bed, he carefully avoided the numerous wires that connected his sister to the machine that kept her alive. The faint beep, beep of the machine monitoring her heartbeat was a stark reminder that with each beep of the machine, his sister's time on earth was drawing to a close and he was utterly powerless to stop it.

"Stop brooding, Derek, and come sit with a dying woman."

He lowered himself down on the bed and looked at the woman in the bed. Hair as white as snow with a wrinkled face that showed a life fully lived; it was hard to imagine that this was his sister. The private clinic where Sylvia resided thought he was her son, and they kept it that way. Down to her final moments, Sylvia protected her brother with the fierceness of a wolf.

"You look beautiful, Sylvie."

"Hush, you charmer," she rasped. "I've already written my will."

He snickered and bent down to press a kiss to her cheek. It was clammy, and Derek could smell the scent of death on her skin. What would he do when she was gone, the last remaining person who remembered him for who he had been, not the curse that was bestowed on him?

"Shall we say our goodbyes, Sylvie? I'm sure you'd much prefer to have your children by your side instead of a reminder of what could have been."

"There is no one more qualified to be by my side than you, Derek, so shut up and listen to me one last time."

Her breath hitched, and the machine jumped. He studied her face, wishing he could erase the pain the ravaged her body. She placed the oxygen mask over her face and gulped in some air before removing it and placing it on her chest.

"I worry for you, Derek, like you were my son."

He dusted his knuckles over her cheek. "Technically, I am still your older brother. It's my job to watch over you."

Moisture glistened in her eyes. "And you have done so. But now I need you to remain alive and watch over my children and grandchildren and all those who come after that. For as long as our line continues."

She knew. She knew what he planned to do once she had become one with the earth, and she was going to make him promise not to. He ducked his head for a moment before he looked back at her. Sadness and worry—that is what he saw in her eyes.

"Don't make me promise you something I won't be able to keep." His voice cracked with emotion.

"You've never broken a promise to me yet, and you won't do it now. Derek, I can die happily if I know that you're out there watching over my family, but you need a life as well. Find a nice girl and settle down. Don't be afraid to love, and don't shut out those around you. Wolves were not meant to be solitary creatures, and neither were you.

"I love you with every fiber in my being, Derek. You survived when you could have been lost to us, and you came home. If I could stay and keep you safe, I would. But my time has come. It's time to be reunited with my Eamon."

The machine faltered again as her heartbeat became erratic. Derek didn't need the blasted machine to tell him, he could hear it with his ears—the sound of her heart giving way to the illness. He tasted the saltiness of his own tears on his lips.

"Promise me, Derek. Promise me you will live."

How could he not when she had spent her life protecting him from those around him who thought that he had welcomed a demon into his soul and was evil? She entrusted him to care for her precious children, and he would do so until death came knocking on his door.

"I promise, Sylvie. I promise you."

"Good boy," she uttered with a small smile before her eyes shut and the machine blared and the heartbreak that punched his chest wrenched sob after sob from him.

"Derek? You okay?"

Derek lifted his head and opened his eyes. Hair tousled from being towel dried, Ever stood in the doorway, dressed in ripped jeans and a black blazer snug over a white tank top. She shirked her duffle off her shoulder and came to stand by the counter, filling the kettle and switching it on. He inhaled and caught a hint of that cinnamon body wash that Caitlyn liked to wear. The wolf inside him almost bloody purred, and Derek tried to remind him that he wasn't a stinking cat.

"Derek? Seriously, are you okay? You look lost in thought."

Derek shook out the cobwebs in his mind and let himself think of other things that didn't involve dredging up the past. "Yeah, just all this stuff with Melanie made me think of my sister. She would've liked you."

"Do you miss her?"

"With every breath."

The kettle switched off, and she poured herself a fresh cup and topped his up as well. Leaning her elbows on the counter, she rested her chin in her hands. "I've never lost anyone I cared about. All my family and friends are supernatural, so it's not something I think I'll even have to worry about. But I know I'll get old. I'll get sick, and it hurts to think of my parents grieving for me like that."

He nodded. "It's true what people say when they say no parent should outlive their children. I couldn't imagine it."

"Is that why you don't have kids?" she asked, and then she slapped herself in the forehead. "I'm sorry... as far as I know you could have a whole pack of kids. It was rude of me to assume you didn't."

He laughed. "No, I can assure you that I've no kids, no girlfriend or wife hidden away somewhere. I grew up in a time when men courted women, were perfect gentlemen. When you went on dates, you went with a chaperone. The first time you even kissed a woman was on your wedding day. Ricky takes the mick and says I'm so old-fashioned."

He pushed away from the stool and rounded the corner. He could hear Ever's pulse quicken, the only encouragement he needed. She turned when he neared her, her hands glued to her sides, waiting for him to make a move. He cupped her face with his hands and tilted her head up to meet him. He gently pressed his lips to hers, and when she gasped at the touch, her lips parted slightly and he used that to trace the outline of her bottom lip with his tongue as she opened her mouth wider for him.

He kept his hands on the side of her face as he explored her mouth, Ever meeting the thrusts of his tongue with passion and lust. Her hands trembled against the hem of his tee, slowly gliding under and feathering over the taut muscles of his stomach, exactly like she wanted to do before. He growled into her mouth, and she nipped down on his lower lip, his wolf howling in approval. Neither of them needed a mate who couldn't stand up to man or beast.

Derek was dizzy from the pleasure of Ever's kiss and pulled back reluctantly as she staggered forward and blinked her eyes. He had to step away from her because if he didn't, Derek was certain he would have taken her on the counter without a second thought. He groaned as images flashed in his mind. He stepped back, his breathing ragged, delighting in the way Ever seemed as affected as he was.

"I thought you were a gentleman. You certainly don't kiss like one," she accused with devilment in her eyes.

Derek snickered. "I said I grew up in a time when men courted women and were gentlemen. I never actually said I was one. I've wanted to do that since the day you bumped into me."

She swatted at him. "Um, Mr. Agent, sir, you were the one who bumped into me, and I'm glad you did."

He reached out and twirled a strand of her hair between her fingers. "I mean it, Ever. Once this mess is all over and the dust has settled, you and I will figure this thing out between us. I'll pick you up and take you to dinner. A real date—just you and me."

"A real date... just Ever and Derek. I'd really like that." The minx came closer and bit down on his kiss-swollen bottom lip. He fisted his hands and brought them down to his sides before he lost all resemblance of control and reached for her again.

Ever's phone rang, and the smile on her face continued to radiate as she answered.

"Hello?"

Derek heightened his hearing and listened in.

"Ms. Chace, this is Dr. Val. I have some information that might help your investigation."

"Dr. Val, that's great news. We could really use that right now."

He heard the rustle of paper as the doctor rifled through some files. "I asked the oncologist if anyone fit the description of the patient you described, and he thinks he may have a suspect for you. The man begged and begged for months for the doctors to try something else to cure him. He even attacked an orderly who tried to console him. On the day Dr. Peters advised the man there was nothing left for them to try, the man did something very strange."

Ever shifted the phone to her other ear. "He took the news too well."

"Indeed, Ever. He shook Dr. Peters' hand, thanked him for all he had done, and left. That was about four months ago, and Dr. Peters hasn't heard a peep from him since."

"Because he thought he found a new way to get better."

Derek growled, and Ever waved a hand at him to hush up.

"I'm afraid I have even worse news to tell you. You see, the man was being treated for brain cancer. He was riddled with it, and he knew he was going to die a slow and painful death, Ever. He worked in the children's cancer unit."

"So that's how he knew how to take what he needed and barely leave a mark."

Dr. Val sighed. "Yes. The man you're searching for, his name is Stephen Donnelly, and he was a nurse in the hospital here."

VAL SET THE PHONE DOWN ON HER DESK AND LOOKED AT the shadows pooling her office. She heard the smack of chewing gum bursting and sighed.

"That is a terrible human habit you picked up," she said to the corner of her office and shook her head as the sound repeated itself and a cocky woman slipped from the shadows.

"Whatever you say, doc," the woman said sarcastically.

With a sigh, Val prayed for the good ol' days, a time when many had feared her and she'd held the respect of a kingdom. Now, she was forced to walk amongst the humans and be eons away from her home.

"Well... what news have you brought of your sister?"

The girl came forward and threw herself down onto the couch that ran along the office wall. She put her dirty boots up on the armrest and pulled a dagger free from her boot, proceeding to clean her nails.

"Erika," she snapped. "Do not try my patience, child,

or I will unleash all manners of hell upon you."

Erika dismissed her. "Seriously? What am I, twelve? Anyway, considering the violent reaction she had to seeing me, I would say fair Ever is well into her transition. Her champion is by her side, and he is as he always has been—a protective, overbearing, vicious SOB. So the stars are aligning and shit just got real."

Val rubbed her hands together. "Fantastic. We need her to help us reclaim what is her birthright and save the last remaining sisters. We cannot fail at this, Erika, for it would be the end of us all."

"Melodramatic much, Mother? Anyways, we are doing all we can within the limits of the rules he set forth. We can't interfere, or he will be able to kill her again. We learn from our past mistakes."

Val stood and rounded the desk before perching on the edge of it. "This is all we have left. Seventh time lucky. Keep her and the champion safe, Erika. They both need to be intact at the end, no matter how much you dislike him."

Erika swung her legs off the couch and got up, rising to her full height. "He is my future queen's chosen champion, and I will treat him with as much respect as he deserves," She flashed a mischievous grin. "But only when she's actually queen."

Sighing, Val didn't know what to say to the second of her seven. "Be gone, Erika. I grow tired of your sense of humor. Bring me another update soon."

"I love you, too, Mother."

"May the grace of the gods go with you."

"And with you."

And then Erika gave her a soldier's salute, bowing her head and fisting her hand over her chest. Giggling, the girl disappeared into the shadows, and Val was once more alone with the humans.

She considered Erika's joyful exchange. The girl had changed so much, having embraced her human life. But duty came first, and she would step up and perform her sacred vocation.

...Or the whole world would burn to ash around them.

Chapter Fourteen

The next two days passed without incident. Donnelly had gone underground, lulling them into a false sense of security with little or no leads to go on. Without their resident tech genius, the team was reduced to old-school methods of trying to track down any sniff of where Donnelly could be hiding out. All leads ran cold, frustration was beginning to set in, and darkness was festering within the group.

"How bloody hard could this actually be?" Ricky exclaimed as he slammed shut his laptop. "You'd think there'd be some clue as to where this asshat is hiding."

Derek rubbed the back of his neck. "Donnelly's covered his tracks extremely well, Ricky. No properties in his name or his alias, no properties in any family name, nothing. He sold all his estates and has no active bank accounts. Unless the rat surfaces, it kills me to say that we might never track him down."

Ricky's chair scraped against the floor as he stood

and fled the room, citing a need for air. Derek scrubbed his hand down his face. Man, he was tired. The residual sedative was lingering in his system. He had made sure that Ricky had injected him with the sedative because he wasn't sure if he could manage the wolf under the circumstances, so he had spent most of the last two nights knocked out for everyone's protection. Ever had slept in the room next door to him, not wanting to leave the station in case a break in the case came.

But after two long days, they were no further to catching Donnelly. The newest member of their team, Erika, was tracking down some former associates of Donnelly's but with half the team out of action, Derek felt they were stretched too thin. He couldn't help but glance over at Ever, who was huddled over files that she had read repeatedly. Not that she needed to—her impressive ability to recall things meant she had all of Donnelly's actions ingrained in her memory.

"Hey, you okay?" he asked as he strode over to Ever while she dredged through the paperwork.

She smiled up at him, and something constricted in his chest.

"Yeah, just pissed off that we know who he is but can't get a clue as to where he might be."

"I think everyone echoes that feeling at the moment."

"I should be asking how you're feeling," Ever said as she leaned back in her chair. "I mean, you've be injected with more sedative over the last few days than humanly possible. How's your wolf after all that?"

Leaning against the edge of the desk, Derek sighed. "More than humanly possible? Suppose it's a good thing I'm not human anymore."

An amused snort that he wrung from Ever delighted

his wolf.

"He's a little ticked off at not having been able to stretch his legs and run, but once this is done and we have Donnelly in custody, I'll let the wolf be a wolf for a few days to appease him. At least the change will be on my terms, not his."

"Sounds nice."

"And then once I've dealt with the wolf... you and me, we'll have our date."

Derek watched Ever chew on the inside of her mouth before she went to answer, but her reply was cut off as a very weary-looking Caitlyn trudged through the doors. Ever had never seen someone supernatural look so ill. Her normally porcelain skin appeared whitewashed, dark sunglasses hiding her eyes. There seemed to be a frailness to her now, and Caitlyn was anything but frail. Thinner than she had been only a few days ago, the poor vampire looked as if she were about to keel over, bite marks littering her throat.

"Caitlyn! Here—sit down." Derek dashed over to his teammate and for once, the vampire took his assistance without a word. Easing herself into the chair, Caitlyn removed her glasses, and Ever gasped. Her once slate eyes were now a hazy grey with tinges of red. A yellow bruise shaded just below her eye socket, as if she were healing from a fist to the face.

"I apologize if I frighten you, Ever. Unfortunately, I'm not at full strength at the moment."

"God, Caitlyn, you look like hell," Derek blurted.

"And you are a charmer as usual, *mon loup*."

Derek shook his head. "How's Melanie?"

Caitlyn let her lashes lower, brushing her cheekbones before she sighed and opened her eyes once again. "She's as well as can be expected. It's difficult the first few days, dealing with the Hunger and accepting your new life. She has been reborn as a vampire, but she needs a little time to adjust to the changes needed in her life."

"And the shiner?"

"A gift from Melanie after I explained what had happened to her. It's fine. It'll heal before the morning sun rises."

They lapsed into silence, nobody really knowing what to say. Derek got Caitlyn caught up on what few details they had gathered on the case, and Ever busied herself with the files on the table. Despite having read through them numerous times, they were unable to gather any useful information from the data. Tracking the phone was useless; Donnelly had discarded that as soon as the call was over. Derek wondered if Ever longed for the security of her classroom, relaying the stories of the crimes committed and solved, not being a main character in the twisted plotline.

The door swung open hard, smacking against the wall as a red-faced Ricky stormed in. "Cait, how's Lanie? Is she all right? When can I see her? Are you okay? Christ, girl, you look like you've been hit by a truck!"

Derek shook his head at his partner as Sarge walked up and clasped the warlock on the shoulder.

"Take a breath, Ricky, and let the girl have a minute. If anything bad had happened to Melanie, I'm sure that's the first thing she'd have said, right, Caitlyn?"

Derek noticed a flash of emotion in the vampire's eyes, but he was sure everyone else was too preoccupied to notice. They shared a look, and Derek nodded, understanding that some things just didn't need to be said. Derek wasn't sure that Ricky could fully comprehend how different Melanie would be now. He had been born into his powers; Caitlyn, Donnie, and himself were all made supernatural in blood and death. And sometimes, those nightmares lived with you no matter how old you became.

Caitlyn rubbed her temple, tiredness showing anew in her face.

"She came through the change well. It'll take her time to adjust. Not only has she to deal with her torture, but now she's also a vampire. As I told Derek, she will have a tough battle ahead of her. The Hunger, it is not a pleasant thing to deal with, especially for a baby vampire."

Caitlyn paused, and Ricky launched into another tirade of questions, despite an imploring look from Derek. His friend didn't seem to care about how affected Caitlyn was after what had happened. It wasn't out of malice, but rather, pure need to know that Melanie was going to be all right.

Caitlyn held up a hand. "Please, Ricky. Melanie will be fine. She just needs time. And you cannot see her for a while. She is too volatile and unpredictable to be around anyone she could break right now. Donnie's with her, and she seems to be calm in his presence. Mine only angers her now. Once she is calm and has a hold on her Hunger, then we can see, but she's not ready to be around those she cares for. She would never forgive herself if she hurt one of you."

Shoulders slumping, Ricky mumbled something incoherent and walked over to his own desk. He pulled out Melanie's laptop bag and handed it to Caitlyn. "Here, give her this. It might make her feel more herself to have a familiar item. Tell her I took good care of it and that I'll see her soon."

He left the room then, and Derek made to follow him but Sarge shook his head.

"Leave him be. He has a lot to process. We'll get more out of him once he makes sense of it all in his head."

"Who could make sense of all this?"

Sarge made no effort to answer him, turning to Caitlyn and holding the vampire's gaze. "Caitlyn, you should get some rest and feed. If Donnelly pokes his head above ground, we will need you. Can Donnie leave Melanie by herself, or will one of you need to be there?"

With a timid shake of her head, Caitlyn replied, "No, I've security at my home and can lock her inside. I can call Donnie and tell him to settle her and come here. We've work to do."

"Do that. But get some rest first, please. And the please was just to be polite, Agent—it wasn't a request."

A breathtaking smile lightened Caitlyn's face, giving everyone a glimpse of her true self. Despite the fact she was definitely a tough cookie, few people saw her for who she really was and appreciated her strength.

"Yes, sir. I'll ring Donnie on my way downstairs." She cast her gaze to Derek. "You will wake me should you find Donnelly or I'm needed at home?"

Derek bobbed his head. "Of course."

Caitlyn rose and bowed her head in their general direction, stopping at the door as if to say something before heading out.

When the door closed behind her and Caitlyn was far enough out of earshot, Derek blew out a breath. "Damn Sarge, if it takes that out of Caitlyn, then I never want to know how you actually make a vampire."

Sarge leaned back against the window. "But you understand, Derek. You hardly ever talk about how you became a werewolf."

"And bore you all with details? I was bitten, I died—sort of—and became this. No need to dredge up the past." Derek indicated to himself. In truth, Derek never talked about what happened to him because his first ten years as a werewolf had been anything but pleasant. Only a few were aware of the horror he had witnessed under the cruel reign of his once-alpha, and he'd sworn, on the day he had blooded Neville in order to win his freedom, that his family would never find out what he had been up to on his ten years gone. They'd been through enough.

Realizing he had been silent for too long, Derek deserted thoughts of blood and grief and focused on the present. Neither Sarge nor Ever mentioned his lack of conversation, having returned to the task. He went and sat at his own desk, rifling through the file he had put together on Donnelly. Derek had to hand it to Donnelly—he was smart and resourceful. How had he managed to stay within the confines of the city without drawing the attention of a single officer on the hunt for him? He let his eyes scan over the pages as he tried to get an accurate picture of who Stephen Donnelly was.

Stephen Donnelly was a thirty-two-year-old nurse who had worked at the Cork Hospital Children's Ward since he'd graduated from nursing college six years ago. Donnelly, diagnosed with an inoperable tumor in his brain, had petitioned Chester Birmingham to be made on seven different occasions.

According to the notes Donnie had written up, Donnelly had reacted violently to Chester's unwillingness to make him a vampire. But Chester only wanted to make the beautiful or unique his vampires, and Stephen Donnelly was anything but unique. Staring at the picture of the reddish-brown-haired murderer, Derek considered him just another face in the crowd, unable to stand out. There was nothing out of the ordinary about him, and Chester would have reveled in turning the dying man down.

Faced with ridicule and fear of death, Donnelly had turned to murdering innocent teens in order to fight the disease that corrupted his head. But the rot that festered inside him would never excuse the horror he had inflicted on those kids and the nightmares poor Chrissy would live with.

Derek snapped his head up as he heard Ever gasp. She looked up from the computer screen, her blue eyes wide in surprise. Ever tapped her screen.

"Dr. Val emailed over Donnelly's medical and personnel files. According to this, Donnelly was a sensitive."

Derek banged his fist down on the desk. "That's how he knew. That's how he knew they were supernatural and maturing."

"Apparently, the hospital used his ability to treat some patients who came in with unusual injuries before the big reveal. Those who were in the know helped him to hone his ability. Trained him to sniff out a supe. Goddammit.

"According to Dr. Val's file," Ever continued, "his parents noticed it when he was a child and he started to tell them that a vampire lived next door. His parents took him to a psychiatrist because they thought he was a little strange. They drugged him to try and keep the 'voices' at bay. It was only when the big reveal happened did they realize that Mr. Hayashi was actually a centuries-old vampire from Japan."

Derek growled, the sound vibrating throughout his limbs. "Most sensitives use their gift to help others. I know a few who run an anti-bullying charity to help supes feel less like outsiders in mainstream schools. But Donnelly didn't have a chance. He spent most of his life thinking we were the cause of his 'illness', and then used as a locater by the hospital. Man, if I were him, forced to point us out and then refused saving when I was told I was dying, I'd probably hate all things supernatural as well, and I might use my gift to hunt down teens in the hope of curing myself, too."

Ever folded her arms on the desk in front of her. "I think Chester's repeated refusal to make him was the final straw. There he was, a dying, desperate man who wanted all his life to be supernatural, and there was no chance of him surviving. I assume that Chester's rebuttal was less than courteous."

Sarge cleared his throat. "Chester likes to assert his power over those he views as weak. He runs most of the vampires in Cork and rules with an iron fist. He's a sadistic old git, but he has kept the murder rate within the vampire community down since he came to power. He might be a disgusting, immoral SOB, but he's a productive one."

Pacing the room, Derek was close to losing all sense of reason. He'd lied to Ever when he told her that he had the wolf under control. He was still lobbying for control despite the full moon's end. The wolf wanted the taste of blood and the feel of flesh between its teeth. The prey had hurt one under his protection, and there would be no forgiveness; he would not be taken alive.

While Derek was loathe to agree with the other half of himself, the wolf had a point. Did Donnelly deserve to be sent to prison and protected against the murderers and criminals who thought it wrong to harm a child? He would be dead soon enough anyway, the rot in his brain decaying until he died a painful death. But Derek and the wolf's death would hurt a hell of a lot more, and something dark and twisted in him felt his blood surge at the thought of it. He had the capacity to let the darkness overcome him, and on days when he welcomed it—invited it, almost—Derek was certain he could become the hunted rather than the hunter.

The door opened, jerking Derek back to the present. Ricky came back into the squad room with his shoulders hunched and a defeated look on his face. He headed straight for Sarge, and the two of them huddled in the corner, whispering. Ever didn't doubt that even though her human hearing couldn't hear a word, that Derek's could. She studied him as he continued to pace, his ears twitching slightly as he listened to Ricky and Sarge's conversation.

When he spied Ever watching him, Derek had the good graces to blush for a moment. He pulled the chair from his desk over and set it down beside Ever's with the back facing her. He hunkered himself down and rested his arms on the back of the chair. Twisting slightly in her chair so that she faced him, Ever gave him a little smile as he scrubbed his face with his hand. He looked tired, but since he hadn't had a proper, non-drug-induced sleep for a couple of days, that was to be expected.

Her fingers reached out without her being conscious of it and traced the underline of his jaw. He closed his eyes and sighed. Her petting brought him some pleasure. His eyes opened a second later, the hazel of his eyes now mixed with amber as both wolf and man looked back at her. Her own pulse quickened as she continued to dust her knuckles over the stubble.

"I really should shave," he said finally.

"Nah, I like it. You seemed too clean-cut before. This is the real you. Wild but calm. Rugged but stable. Not like the Mr. Stuck-up Agent I met a few days ago."

He chuckled. "Has it really been only a few days? I feel like I've known you all my life."

Reluctantly, Ever pulled her hand away from Derek's face. Leaning back in her seat, she bit back a smirk as she tried to calm her pulse and remember that they had a job to do. "My mother used to say that I had an old soul. That from the day she first laid eyes on me, I stared back at her, and she was pretty certain she could see the universe reflected in my eyes." She felt her lips tug up at the corners as she spoke of Samhain. "I laughed and told her that she only felt that way because she had yearned for a child for so long. Whether it had been me or another infant, Samhain would have seen the universe in their eyes because being a mother was the universe for Samhain."

"You never told me about the new dreams you've been having. I'm curious to know what dreams you've had about me." With a lopsided grin and a fluttering of those beautiful lashes, Derek tried to coax from Ever what had put shadows in her eyes for the last few days.

Ever shook her head as Erika paraded through the door, a mischievous grin on her ruby red lips.

"So, who might just have found the impossible and is the most awesome person ever?" She paused for dramatic effect, and then curtsied. "Me, that's who."

That little statement had everyone's attention. When the new girl did not attempt to carry on, Derek growled, and she scowled.

"Buzzkill," she muttered before she told the rest of them what she had found. "Okay, so I called up a friend of mine who specializes in genealogy and family trees. She has access to birth, death, and marriage records, so she put Stephen Donnelly's name into her system and went to work. She was able to confirm that both Stephen's parents died almost four years ago, and that his mother and father had no siblings."

"And how is this helpful?" Ricky snorted.

"Because up until a year ago, Donnelly thought he had no immediate family. But apparently, Donnelly's grandfather had been a very naughty boy, and Donnelly's father had a half sister who was like twenty years older than he was. She kept her mother's surname, and Donnelly didn't know about her until he was contacted by a lawyer to confirm that dear ol' Auntie June had left him a massive farm just outside the city."

"And why did we not find any records of the property?" Ricky interrupted once again.

"If you let me finish," she said and sighed. "Anyway, Donnelly had already been told he was dying, so he took the keys but never changed the name on the deeds. We couldn't find the property because there is only one record to prove that Donnelly had an illegitimate aunty—the paper he signed when receiving the keys."

"And I take it you have the address?"

Erika's grin widened. "But of course. Aunty June had a secluded farm in Watergrasshill. Shall we go?"

Chapter Fifteen

A THOUSAND FIRES BURNED THE INSIDE OF HER CHEST, and she fought with all her strength not to scream. Her skin felt like she had insects crawling all over her, and the faint glow of the afternoon that peaked through the curtains made her want to vomit. Her stomach constricted, and her brand-spanking-new fangs punched free from her gums as another wave of Hunger gathered inside her. How anyone thought becoming a vampire was glamorous, she had no idea. This sucked... no pun intended.

Her thoughts lingered on the feeling of the knife slicing through her and the sound of her heartbeat as it flickered with life before she passed out. Melanie had known she was going to die, and she had been terrified. She'd tried her best to be strong and stop herself from showing any fear, but fear was a horrible human emotion too hard to mask. But nothing could have shocked her more than awakening in a grave of dirt, Caitlyn's neck at her mouth. She knew right away what had happened, and she was afraid again, afraid of what she had become.

Melanie remained hunched on the comfy armchair, the room almost completely in darkness as she took in the exquisiteness of Caitlyn's home. Trying to ignore the raw, gut-wrenching pain that racked her entire body, Melanie focused on the delicate furniture and fixings of the quaint little bungalow. Her new twenty-twenty vision meant she no longer needed her glasses, and it was a strange sensation to be without the wide-rimmed specs perched on her nose. A lush, apricot wall was adorned with artwork that she guessed was original. Caitlyn had been alive for a very long time; it figured she would have collected some stuff along the way. Hardwood floors complimented the room with little or no personal touches apart from the one wooden box atop an ornate, black iron fireplace.

There were no pictures of Caitlyn or Donnie in this room, but this room was all Caitlyn—sophisticated and stunning. Melanie wondered what parts of the house were to Donnie's taste. She knew they lived together, but as long as she had known them, they hadn't exactly been the PDA type. Maybe it was down to Caitlyn's age... or maybe she should stop being nosy to distract her from the pain.

Another punch to the gut, and she gritted her teeth, forgetting about the fangs in her gums and scoring her bottom lip. She had been a vampire for less than a day, and she hated it already. She should have just died three days ago, and then she wouldn't be feeling as shite as she was.

Feeling restless, Melanie got up and circled the room a few times before she had to sit down again, exhausted. Where was the super strength? Where was the invincibility all vampires carried? Melanie began to wonder if she were the exception. Were the Bambi legs she was currently working with a permanent fixture, or would she grow out of this weakness fast? Surely now that she was anything but normal, she would start to see the fringe benefits soon, because right now, with the tiny pinpricks of fire in her blood and the constant weakness, Melanie wished she were back in the security of her human life.

The door to the sitting room opened slowly, and Donnie popped his head in. She smiled at him, and he came in quietly, moving with a grace and fluidity that should have been impossible for a man of his size. He perched himself on the chair across from her and tossed her a bottle, which she caught with ease now. Before—uncoordinated as she was—Melanie would have dropped the bottle on the ground, her lack of sporting ability a sore topic with her GAA-mad father who yearned for his only daughter to be as sporting as he was. But then again, he also lived a life of crime, so his opinion didn't matter... much.

Focusing her new vampy eyes on the bottle, her nose caught the smell of coppery deliciousness before she had even opened the cap, and she groaned at the scent of it. Quickly, she uncapped the bottle and chugged down the heavenly goodness, quenching the fires of Hunger for a little while at least. When Melanie had finished, she placed the empty bottle on the floor and ran the back of her hand over her mouth.

Her hand came away bloody, and she longed to lick the drops from her skin. Tears pricked her eyes with embarrassment as she looked up at Donnie, who was watching her with sympathetic eyes.

"I would've licked the blood by now if I was you. Hell, I wouldn't have been so civilized and opened the bottle. When Cait first made me, I sank my fangs into the plastic and sucked straight from the bottle. The Hunger makes us animals in the beginning, but you've shown great promise this day. Cait will be pleased."

The massive vampire leaned back in the armchair and crossed his right leg over his left, his foot resting on his knee. He then rested his massive hands in his lap and lowered his lids, as if to give her the privacy to do what she wanted to do. Only when he sensed that she was ready did he open his eyes and glance at her again.

"I'm sure you have questions, and I'll answer them as honestly as possible for you, Melanie. But some answers may not be the ones you want to hear, so be careful."

The Hunger quietly eased for the time being, Melanie felt more or less like her old self, except for the non-beating heart in her chest. She hadn't reacted well to Caitlyn when she'd first awoken to her new self, and Caitlyn hadn't been by in a long while to see her.

"Is Caitlyn mad at me? For punching her, I mean."

Donnie shook his head. "No, Caitlyn isn't mad. She just wanted to give you space to hate her without you feeling obligated to her."

"Why would she think I hate her?" Melanie gasped.

"Because it was she who made you a monster."

Melanie swept a strand of hair from her face, wincing slightly as her muscles protested. "That's not how I feel at all. She had no other option but to make me... though it hurts right now to get my head around things. She did what she had to do to save me."

"Caitlyn doesn't see it like that."

Melanie's head began to throb. "Okay... but I don't hate her."

"She'll be glad to hear that, though she may take some convincing. Between us, Caitlyn never wanted to inflict this life on another. She vowed long ago to never make another. She's only made two vampires her entire existence, and they are both sitting in this room right now."

His jaw ticked, and Melanie thought it best to move away from the subject for the time being. "When can I be around people again? I should be out there helping them catch the monster that technically killed me."

Donnie shifted in his seat, a very human act, and Melanie began to understand she would have to learn how to act human around others. "It could be a month; it could be a year. We just don't know. But from how you are today, I expect it will be sooner rather than later."

"Will I hurt other people?"

"You'll adjust to your new strength, but right now, it would be very difficult for you to be around people like Ever, or even Ricky. Their blood will call to you, and despite Ricky's power, he'd be powerless to stop a hungry vampire from snapping his neck."

She sucked in a breath—not that she needed to—and shuddered. She'd never want to hurt Ricky. Idiot that he was, she liked him.

"Caitlyn may ask Derek to help you. Train you to fight against one such as himself."

"Why can't you train me?" she enquired, not particularly keen to be on the receiving end of a punch by Derek. Somehow, she felt easier with Donnie.

The older vampire chuckled. "I've always been physically stronger, and my adjustment to vampirism wasn't as much of a change as you would imagine. True, I traded beer for blood, but being a rugby player meant I was always going to be a strong vampire. I have brute strength that comes from years of playing sports and have a more smash first think later attitude, and Caitlyn can only show you so much. You need to learn to use your power and training with Derek, a person who is used to training with new recruits from his army days and someone who will be very hard to break who'll help you."

Melanie tilted her head, soaking in all the information Donnie was giving her. Never again would she be vulnerable or weak. She would be strong and prove to Caitlyn that she had done the right thing making her. Melanie had wished for years that she would have latent magical powers that would blossom one day.

"I can see the wheels turning in your head. What're you thinking?"

Melanie snickered. "It's funny to think that I'll never be weak again."

"You weren't weak before, Melanie. Many of us would've felt blessed to have your strong mind."

"But my mind didn't protect me from being kidnapped. Ricky was right all along. I was perfectly flawed in my humanness. Now I can help others with more than my computer skills. I can be a valuable member of the team, not a liability."

Donnie rose and stretched out his long, muscular limbs, cautiously coming to stand in front of her. Then he lowered himself down so they were at eye level. Something clicked in Melanie's mind, and she knew that, no matter what, Donnie would look out for her.

Family.

She had never really had a family before, her parents too consumed with their own lives to worry about their quiet, hacker daughter. Even when she was arrested for hacking into the government database, her parents had sent the butler to pay her bail. Mom spent most of her time in Europe shopping, and her dad... Her dad had enough to do commanding his criminal empire. Then Tom had recruited her, giving her a new place to stay and a way to use her skills for good.

A thumb brushed away a tear that escaped and leaked down her cheek. "I've always wanted a family, a little sister to look after. I never had that. Sport was my escape from the horrid foster family I lived with. Cait and me, we'll be your family. You'll never feel alone again."

Melanie guffawed. "What are you... a mind reader?"

Donnie raised an eyebrow and grinned.

"No frickin' way! Where and when do I get that power? That's so cool!"

Laughing, Donnie eased himself down onto the wooden floor. "It's not as cool as you might think, sister."

Melanie returned his smile at that.

"While Caitlyn has the ability to communicate with those she has created when she wishes, my 'gift' means I've numerous thoughts running through my mind at any given time. Sometimes it's hard to filter them out, but I've learned to control it over the years.

Each gift is different. Caitlyn will tell you all about hers in time. It may take time for your own 'gift' to manifest. It normally comes from deep within us. I was always a good listener, so I guess that's why I'm now always listening."

Melanie threw her hands up in the air. "So basically,

I'm still gonna be a computer geek, but I'll be able to see inside comps and see what's wrong with them? Hardly as cool as controlling the weather or freezing things over."

"This is real life, not an *X-Men* movie."

Melanie blinked and looked at her friend, who could hardly contain his laughter.

"Mr. O' Carroll, you certainly are a dark horse."

He winked. "Wait till you seen my movie collection. It'll be nice to have someone to watch those with rather than Caitlyn's fascination with rom coms"

Melanie burst out laughing at the image of the two hardened vampires sitting down watching *The Notebook*. Tears streamed down her face as she tried to control herself. "Oh my God, that's too much."

"And I'll deny we ever had this conversation if Cait finds out I let one of her secrets out."

She held up three fingers. "Girl Guide's honor. I will never speak a word."

"How're you feeling now?" he asked.

She could feel the beginnings of the fires of hell building up inside her, but it didn't burn as much as before. She pulled her knees to her chest and rested her chin on her knees.

"I feel okay, I guess. I still want blood, but I no longer want to hurt you for not giving it to me."

"That's good. It'll get easier. As a baby vampire, you need to drink at least every two hours until it becomes too much and you just don't want or need to drink. You probably feel like you couldn't eat solid food right now?"

She grimaced, the thought of ingesting normal food repulsive.

"In time, you'll begin to be able to eat proper food

as well. You won't need it, but you can still enjoy the occasional burger every now and then."

Donnie got up off the floor. "You also don't need to be holed up in this room all your immortal life. I've my own space, as does Cait. Before she returned to the station, she told me to tell you to pick which room you feel most comfortable in and to think about furniture, colours, and anything else that you might want. If you want stuff brought over from your apartment, then that can be arranged as well."

He walked over to the door and looked over his shoulder at her. "This is your home now for as long as you need it. Never feel you have to deal with this by yourself. Both Cait and I are only a call away if you need us. Come on; let me give you the tour."

He was out the door and moving along the hall as Melanie detangled herself and followed him. She paused at the doorway, the fading sunlight still lingering in the glass hallway. Melanie gingerly raised her hand and began to inch it ever so slowly into the sunlight. Her skin crackled, and she hissed, pulling her hand back as the smell of burning flesh tainted the air.

She darted her gaze up to Donnie's retreating form and snarled. "Hey, little help here."

He stopped but didn't look back at her. "First lesson. For the first few years until you grow accustomed to it, the sun is your enemy. It'll burn you to your final death. Sunscreen mutes it, but for a while, you can only go out in the dead of night. Look to your right and flick the switch."

She did as he asked and watched as the glass tinted over. Melanie repeated her initial action, and the sun no longer burned her skin. Steeling herself against the fear inside her, she stepped forward and followed Donnie into the kitchen. Thankfully, Donnie had already shaded the windows as she watched her flesh knit back together. Donnie walked over to the fridge and removed a bottle of blood, waiting while she drained it dry, suddenly overcome with Hunger.

"Second lesson. When we are injured, we need a healthy intake of blood. The synthetic blood will do for bridging the gap between feeds, but when we are hurt, we need to feed on human blood. Right now, you're drinking donated blood because you would be likely to rip out a human's throat to feed the Hunger."

The kitchen was as minimalistic and chic as the living room with no dining table, simply a tiled, black-marble breakfast bar with hobs and a sink. The room wasn't very large, and Melanie supposed vampires didn't need a massive eating area. Two massive silver fridges were set against the only wall.

"The second fridge is stocked with blood, the first with normal food. Take what you want when you need it. Don't stand on ceremony here. There's no need."

She discarded the empty blood bottle and moved out of the kitchen to an area of the bungalow that branched into a variety of different rooms, all with their doors closed. At the end of the hall, the bedrooms seemed to carry on around the corner. Stairs to her left signaled there was another floor above that she hadn't considered would be there before.

"Up the stairs are Caitlyn's quarters. She has a self-contained living and sleeping area."

Melanie narrowed her eyes. "Do you sleep up there as well?"

A sad smile. "No, my room is the area under the

stairs. It, too, has a self-contained living area with a shower, living room, and sleep area. It's very nice and open planned, and it has an amazing view of the city at night."

Melanie didn't want to push him further. All the rooms seemed to be like luxurious apartments. She pointed to the room at the far end of the hall, the one that veered off around the corner. Somehow, she felt she would be intruding if she had her room right next to Donnie and underneath Caitlyn's.

"Can I have that one?" she asked.

"Don't you want to see it first?"

Melanie shook her head. "No need. It's still gonna be the nicest place I've slept in."

Donnie motioned for her to proceed, and she strode over, twisted the handle, and shoved the door open. Her mouth dropped at the amazing space that lay before her.

The walls were painted a dazzling shade of sky blue, the white furniture only adding to the brightness. To her right stood a gigantic bed raised up off the ground, the four posters canopied by a luscious blue silk curtain that draped over the bed. Off to the side of the bed, a writing desk and bookshelves lined up, leading off to a locked door.

Melanie's eyes grew wide when she spotted the massive, fifty-inch TV in front of the darkened windows. This was like going to the best hotel ever and not paying a cent.

Donnie strode over and opened the door, indicating the porcelain-tiled bathroom. "Bath, shower, and all that girlie crap you might need. Door to your left is a walk-in wardrobe. If you need some new clothes, Cait can order them in for you."

She just watched him, mouth open as he grinned.

"I'll leave you to get settled in. I need to check in with Cait and let her know you're doing okay."

He swept from her new bedroom as she stepped farther into the room, suddenly overwhelmed by all the changes in her life. Panic bubbled in her chest and her flight instincts kicked in. Eyes darting around for an escape, her gaze fell on a familiar friend leaning against the bed.

Staggering forward, she took her laptop bag in her hand, her fingers gliding over the badges she had sewn onto it by hand. Perching at the edge of the bed, she unzipped the bag and pulled out her laptop. She might feel a little out of her league, but she knew how to de-stress with her laptop.

Opening it up, a piece of paper slipped out, and she grasped it. Setting the laptop down on the bed, she opened the note. Tears welled up in her eyes as she traced over the words with her eyes.

Lanie,

No matter what happens, I'm here for you. You can't get rid of me that easily. See you soon, vampire girl.

It wasn't signed. It didn't need to be. Much as Donnie was the only one to call Caitlyn Cait, only Ricky ever called her Lanie. She hugged the note to her chest, and for the first time all day, despite the fire in her veins, Melanie began to think that becoming a vampire might not be as bad as she thought.

Hunger punched a vicious hole in her stomach, and Melanie doubled over in pain.

Then again, maybe not...

Chapter Sixteen

The team had already been assembled when the call came in. Night had crept in on them as silent as a predator, and the midnight blue sky twinkled with stars. If the team hadn't been gearing up to finally lay their hands on the monster they sought, then Derek might have appreciated the beautiful presence of night. There was no moonlight tonight, the overcast clouds hiding it from sight, but Derek knew it was there; it sang in his veins.

Donnelly hadn't been able to keep from his compulsion. A frantic parent had called in to say that her daughter had snuck out to meet up with a girlfriend. When she hadn't turned up, the girlfriend had called the house to speak to her, and the alarm was raised.

The girl was about to turn sixteen and ready to come fully into her powers. She slipped out of her bedroom window and into the woods behind her house that her family watched over. A nymph through birth,

Fern was the eldest daughter of her clan and the first to mature. According to reports, she had shown signs of her coming of age, and her father, a Satyr, had banned her from leaving the house because Donnelly was on the loose. Fern hadn't listened, and now they all feared she was in the clutches of the monster.

It had been decided that the team should split up with Derek, Ricky, and Caitlyn heading to the property Donnelly had acquired from his dear ol' aunt, with Donnie meeting them there while Sarge, Ever, and Erika would visit the victim's house and see what information they could gather there. Erika had sulked at not being included in the raid at the farmhouse, but she seemed appeased after being pulled aside by Derek and advised that Donnelly might come back to the scene to survey and they needed someone there other than Sarge to protect the innocents.

Before leaving, Derek had grazed his knuckles over Ever's cheek, hating the fact that he was straying from her side, but knowing she was safer and out of harm's way with Sarge. He then ducked inside the back of the black van that would drive them outside the city. The van peeled off and sirens shrieked into action as they headed down the dual carriageway. Derek checked his weapon once, then again, before slipping it into the holster on his thigh. He straightened his vest, not used to having the Kevlar on his person. Since the perp knew the team boasted a were amongst the ranks, Sarge had ordered him to wear the heavy-duty vest to protect against silver blades or bullets.

Of course, arguing that a silver bullet to the brain would surely kill him hadn't gotten him anywhere.

Caitlyn leaned forward in the van, her own black

ensemble mimicking his, sans vest. She twirled her pretty daggers around in her hands before stabbing them into the sheaths on her thighs. After her little rest, Caitlyn looked more herself and more focused than ever. Her phone chimed, and she dug it from her pocket, eliciting Ricky's attention. In the van, there was no chance of privacy.

"Yes," Caitlyn said into the handset. A smile crept onto her face as she pursed her lips. "I'm glad that you're feeling better, and have no worry, it has already healed."

There was a brief silence before Caitlyn chortled. "Yes, I promise I will as soon as possible. But first we must make the monster who took your human life from you dead, no?"

As soon as Caitlyn had laughed, the tension seemed to have eased somewhat from Ricky, the warlock leaning in closer to try and hear what was being said. Caitlyn edged away from him and shot him a glare, and he held up his hands in apology.

"Do you feel well enough to be left alone?" A pregnant pause. "We'll discuss that later. But if you're feeling well enough, can you put Donnie on the phone, please? Merci. I will tell him."

Caitlyn faced Ricky. "Melanie said to thank you for taking such good care of her computer. Donnie?" Tuning back to her call, she explained to Donnie what had happened and asked if he felt Melanie was stable enough to be left alone. She nodded her head at whatever Donnie had said and gave him directions to where they would be.

"No, I'm not at my full strength right now, but I'm fine. Do not worry. Yes, I will see you soon."

She snapped the phone shut without a farewell and

concentrated on them again. "Donnie will meet us in Watergrasshill. It seems Melanie is doing well enough to be left alone. She is taking to her new life with as much passion and zest as she did her human one. He, of course, will be setting the security on the property to prevent her from leaving."

"Gives new meaning to being grounded, Caitlyn."

She snorted—a very un-Caitlyn sound. "You've no idea, *mon loup*, no idea."

Ricky stared out of the back of the van into the darkness as the rest of the men assigned to their team tried to ignore the exchange. Derek watched them, assessing their ability to remain calm under the strain. Before the reveal, the most action these SWAT team members got were bank robberies and hostage situations. Now, backed into a corner with creatures that didn't need a gun or a knife to fillet you, he understood why a lot chose to retire.

They zipped through the tunnel and accelerated toward their destination. At this time in the evening with the city on a clampdown, they only saw one or two cars on the round. The eerie quietness unnerved him, but Derek really was unsure why. He knew the second van, carrying Ever and Sarge, would be moving at a little slower pace. According to their information, the house Donnelly had been left was a twenty-minute hike through the woods from where he had grabbed Fern. He hoped the teen could hold on for ten minutes more. That's all they needed.

Time ticked by at an annoyingly slow pace. Derek tapped his foot on the floor of the van until Caitlyn shot him a dirty look. They veered off the round and up off the dual carriageway, bypassing the school and continuing into the main village. Continuing ahead, they swept by the church and into the more rural countryside. Derek could smell the animals as well as freshly cut grass and hay.

After what seemed like an age, the van pulled over at the side of the road and dimmed its lights. Derek opened the back door and jumped down, his boots crunching against the gravel. Caitlyn was next, making no sound as she landed and glanced around. In the blackness that engulfed them, Derek thought he spotted a ghost of a smile dance on her lips as he felt a gush of wind and looked up to see Donnie standing next to them. The vampire acknowledged Derek as he ran his eyes over Caitlyn's form.

"Have we a kill order?" he grumbled to Derek, not taking his eyes from Caitlyn.

"Unfortunately not, Donnie. We take Donnelly alive if possible. Only go for the kill if your life or one of your teammate's lives is in danger. We got that?"

A chorus of 'yes sir' rang out in the still night. Derek looked around at the men and woman that surrounded him, unable to shake the unease in his gut. Something didn't feel right about this; even his wolf was angsty. But a young girl's life hung in the balance—there was no time for caution.

He motioned them all forward and flicked the switch on his COM. "Everyone copy?"

"Yes sir."

"Then let's go. Cait, you and I will head through the front of the farmhouse. Donnie, you and Ricky go 'round the back." He pointed to the SWAT team. "You three with me; the rest with the big guy over there. One of the supes will enter the house first, so no one try to be heroes. If you find the girl, you get her to safety and leave the bastard to the rest of us. The girl is our main priority. Don't lose sight of that."

Without another word, Derek took off at a jog, Caitlyn keeping pace with him, as did the three men following them. He made out the faint outline of Donnie's team as they moved through the field and circled to come through at the back of the house. Derek's team made their way up the graveled pathway, brushing past overgrown brambles and trees. As they entered the courtyard of the property, the farmhouse came into view.

Drenched in darkness, there appeared to be no sign of life inside the house at all, but Derek knew well that on occasion, looks could definitely be deceiving. The stillness of the boarded-up house and the lack of sounds nearby should have been the first sign that all wasn't right.

"About to breach the rear, over."

Derek signaled for the team to gather around. They huddled close to him, and Derek could hear the rapid beat of their hearts. As he listened closely, he confirmed it was not from fear but from the adrenaline that coursed through his veins.

"Ready at the front. On three, over?"

"On three, copy."

Derek counted to three in his head, lifting up his leg to kick in the wooden door. The wood splintered on impact, a thunderous sound echoed by the precision kick that imploded the door at the rear of the house. Derek stepped over the threshold, Caitlyn at his heels. He opened up his supernatural hearing but could only count seven heartbeats, the exact number of those team members whose hearts still beat.

"I don't like the feel of this..." he muttered low to Caitlyn.

"I agree. Something doesn't feel right about this place."

They proceeded to check out each room, the smell of must and mould indicating that no one had lived here for a long time. Where the hell had Donnelly taken the girl?

He heard Donnie shout, "Clear!" and Derek echoed him. They gathered inside the main living area as Ricky kicked out at a table and sent it flying across the room. No one said a thing because they all felt the same.

Derek cursed a blue streak, yanked his cell phone out of the pocket inside his vest, and called Sarge. He brought the bear up to speed, and his friend swore.

"It's strange, Sarge... this place would've been the perfect place to hide out. Not a neighbour for miles to hear anything, but the bastard is not here."

Caitlyn stilled suddenly, her nose crinkling. Her eyes met Derek's at the same time Donnie pulled Ricky and two of the SWAT team with him, bursting through the window. Caitlyn grabbed two more men, and Derek did the same, leaping out the window as the house shattered around them, a fiery inferno engulfing the farmhouse in a cascade of orange and red.

The sound of the blast had ruptured Derek's eardrums, but by the time he got up, they had already begun to stitch themselves back together, the ringing in his ears clearing as he checked to see if everyone made it out okay. The humans rubbed their ears, not sharing the same quick healing abilities as he and the vampires. Sirens wailed in the distance as Caitlyn knelt down by Donnie's unmoving frame. A large splinter of wood protruded from his back, and it took Derek a second to calculate where the other end would have come out. The vampire hadn't yet turned to ash, so he took that as a good sign.

He heard ringing, and his eyes landed on Ricky. A stream of blood gushed from his ears, and his friend had no idea his phone was ringing. Derek crawled over to him and slipped his hand into his pocket. Pressing the loudspeaker, Derek answered with a grunt.

"Derek, everyone alright? We could hear the explosion from here!"

"Yeah, we're good, Sarge. Couple of burst eardrums, and Donnie's down right now. Donnelly must be somewhere nearby—that bomb was set remotely. He had to know we were in there at the right time."

"I agree. Watch your six, Derek. He could still be lurking in the shadows."

"Roger that."

He hung up and slipped Ricky's phone into his own pocket.

"What the hell?" his friend yelled as he rubbed his ear. "A bomb! Seriously?"

Derek left his friend and went to crouch down beside Caitlyn. She rubbed the back of Donnie's head as he gritted, "Just pull it out, Cait. Come on."

"It'll hurt."

"Only if you enjoy it... just do it."

Caitlyn wrapped her fingers around the thick shard of wood and muttered in French. As Donnie began to argue, she ripped the shard free of his flesh, and Donnie roared. He bucked against the pain as Caitlyn flipped him over onto his back. The shard had gone straight through, miraculously a couple of inches below his heart. They'd been lucky.

Donnie closed his eyes, his chest heaving, pain written all over his face.

"Is everyone else okay?" he gritted out.

"Yeah buddy. We got everyone out. They won't be hearing much for a few days, but at least they're alive to moan about it."

"I'm going to mount Donnelly's head on a spike in return for this."

Caitlyn, in a rare show of affection, ghosted a kiss to his forehead. "Don't be cliché, Donnie. Not all vampires like to mount the heads of their enemies on pikes for all to see."

Then the tenderness was gone as Caitlyn rose to her feet, swiftly dismissing the dirt on her pants before walking away.

Derek held out his hand to Donnie, who grasped it and pulled him up. Donnie wavered on his feet but managed to stay upright.

"She loves me, really," he told Derek with a smile.

"I can see that. Come on, Romeo, let's catch up with Juliet."

"I can hear you both."

"We know," they said in unison as Caitlyn sighed.

Derek slowed his pace to match Donnie's as he timidly walked toward where Caitlyn stood with the rest of the team. The sirens grew louder as the fire engines neared, and Derek tried to catch Donnelly's scent, but the air was too tainted with the smell of the burning house. He scanned the trees, hoping to catch a glimpse of another predator watching from the cover of night and foliage, but he got nothing.

Caitlyn's phone vibrated, and she snapped it open.

Derek strode over to her as he heard her chastise the caller. He could see that Caitlyn was getting flustered, so he swiped the phone from her hand.

"Hey Melanie, how you doing?"

"I was going crazy just sitting here doing sweet FA. Please don't be mad."

Derek couldn't help but grin. "I'm not mad, Melanie. How can I help?"

The girl sighed. "So I tried to call Donnie, but his phone isn't working." She paused, as if waiting for Derek to explain, and when he didn't, she continued. "Anyway, Donnie told me where that creep might be hiding, so I kinda hacked into the city plans of the property."

"You could go to jail for that, Melanie."

"Hush, Derek, let me finish," she chastised. "Like I was saying, there are some aspects of the schematic left out of the updated maps online. Did you find anything at the house?"

"No, he kind of blew up the house while we were in it. He's not here."

"Oh my God! Is everyone okay? Is that why Donnie didn't answer his phone? Is he dead? Wait, where's Ricky?"

He held the phone away from his ear, making a mental note to teach the girl about volume tone for supes when he got the chance.

"Everyone's okay. I promise."

There was a pause on the line. "You're not lying, but you're not telling the whole truth, either."

Interesting, he thought. Hearing the lie in his words was almost unheard of if a vampire wasn't in close proximity.

"Did you check the slaughterhouse?"

"I'm sorry, what?"

"The slaughterhouse. According to the old records, the farm was also used to kill animals and sell the meat. It hasn't been used in about forty years, so that's why it fell off the surveyor's new plans."

Hope blossomed in his chest. "Where is the slaughterhouse, Melanie?"

He heard her click on the keys of her laptop. "At the back of the farm, there should be a path. I can see it here online, but it looks like the overgrowth of trees and bush might be obstructing it. About a hundred yards into the woods, the slaughterhouse should be around there. If he took the nymph anywhere, it's there."

"We got this. And Melanie?"

"Yeah?"

"Good job. See ya soon."

He closed the phone before she had the chance to speak and handed it back to Caitlyn. "You heard that, right?"

She nodded.

"Okay, let's go."

Derek turned to the men being treated on the ground. "We have a possible location for Donnelly. Caitlyn and I will continue. The rest of you get yourselves to the hospital."

Derek pivoted, ready to head out, when a firm hand grasped his shoulder.

"I'm coming, too."

Derek shook his head. "Not when I can still see into your chest cavity."

Donnie growled. Derek sympathized with him, but right now he was a liability, and Derek didn't need that. "Phone Sarge and tell him we need backup. C'mon,

Donnie... I can't watch her back if I'm watching yours." A dirty tactic, but Derek would roll with it.

"Once I feed, I'll be okay."

"There's no one 'round here able to donate, Donnie. Go get healed, and then follow us."

"Drink from me."

They all spun round to look at Ricky, who had crept up on them. When no one spoke, he blew out a breath.

"I'm serious. It's not like we'll be going steady or anything, but I still can't hear outta one ear, and three invincible Hulks are better than two."

When nobody budged, Ricky threw his arm up in frustration, pulled a penknife from his pocket, and slashed across his wrist. "Drink, you stubborn idiot, before I bleed out."

He shoved the wrist in Donnie's face, and Derek turned away, not wanting to watch the exchange. A minute later, it was over, and Derek found himself shaking his head as Donnie staggered. Ricky's wrist no longer bled, and he showed no ill effects. Donnie, however...

The big man giggled. "Man, I haven't been drunk in almost two decades, and this is the closest I've come. Damn, warlock, your blood packs a punch."

"Yeah, well, don't come looking for seconds—I'm a one-vampire type of guy. Now get your asses in gear and get that monster."

They didn't need telling twice. With no further words, Derek, Donnie, and Caitlyn rounded the still-alight house. After a short search, they located the path Melanie had told Derek about and disappeared down the trail, vengeance on their minds.

Chapter Seventeen

Tom pulled the phone away from him as the sound of the explosion boomed in his ear. The line went dead, and he tried to remain calm for those who stood beside him. Ever could see he was trying very hard not to scare the poor parents whose child had been taken. Unfortunately, Erika seemed to lack the subtlety needed to keep everyone calm and at ease.

"What the hell was that?"

Tom glared at her as he pressed buttons on his phone and scowled, continuing to press buttons until something connected. Relief washed over his suddenly tired face as Ever's heart drummed in her chest. A strange sensation tugged at her, and as she braced herself against the wall, she knew that Derek was fine... but she wasn't sure how she knew.

"Derek, everyone alright? We could hear the explosion from here!" Tom spoke into the phone, huffing out a breath when he nodded to whatever Derek had said at the other end. After listening for a few minutes, Tom grimaced and said, "I agree. Watch your six, Derek. He could still be lurking in the shadows."

Tom slid his phone back into his pocket and faced Fern's parents. "Please, do not worry. Neither Fern nor Donnelly was at the farmhouse. But my team is the best at what they do, and they will bring your girl home safely."

He called Ever's name as well as Erika's and beckoned them from the room, pausing only to get a uniform to step into the room with the parents. Tom kept moving toward the kitchen, closing the door behind them when Ever and Erika had stepped through. Ever perched on a breakfast stool, and Erika leaned against the wall, popping some luminous green chewing gum as she waited. Tom held up a finger as Ever made to speak and then flicked a switch on the wall. A radio began to play a classic eighties song at a low decibel.

"Okay," he began, "there was an explosion at the farmhouse. Nobody was seriously injured. A couple of burst eardrums as far as Derek could tell. They will survey the area, try and find a lead, but Donnelly knew they were coming."

"And he rigged the place to blow? How did he know what to do?" Erika asked. "Donnelly was a nurse, not a frickin' bomb maker."

Ever shrugged. "Anyone with access to the Internet nowadays can see how to make a homemade bomb. Donnelly trained as a nurse, but he would have some concept of mixing chemicals, and that, I assume... would have made it easier for him to rig the place. Nobody was hurt too badly, that's all that matters."

Tom sighed, and silence hung heavy in the kitchen.

Ever chewed on the end of her thumb, anxious and a little jealous. Some part of her wanted to be out there, kicking ass and taking Donnelly down, but a mere mortal couldn't compete with the supernaturally strong. And she chided herself for even thinking that Melanie, her only human ally, had now gone to the dark side and left her. God, that was such a horrible thought to have, considering what the girl had been through.

Ever was dragged from her thoughts by the chirping of Tom's phone.

"Ricky? You okay?" Tom barked into the phone.

The bear chuckled at whatever sarcastic quip Ricky had slung back at him. Then, as he continued to listen to the warlock speak, his gaze narrowed and a flash of green blazed as the man's eyes merged with the bear's.

"Christ, I'll never get used to that," Erika whispered from over her shoulder.

Ever glanced over her shoulder and raised an eyebrow, which made the mysterious girl grin. She waved her hand and said, "Strange coming from a supernatural creature, right? Where I come from, we don't see a lot of shifters and the likes."

"And where's that?" Ever ventured.

The girl's grin widened, a glint sparkling in her eyes. "Gotta keep some secrets, Ever. Maybe one day I'll tell you all about it."

Ever shook her head and turned back to Tom, who had just hung up with Ricky. Her godfather closed his eyes and scrubbed a hand over his face. Tom had never seemed to age whilst Ever was growing up, but right now, the bear looked every bit of his age.

"Melanie seems bored already with her new life and has decided to do some investigating on her own.

Apparently, when the county council rezoned a lot of areas in Cork to accommodate pack living areas, the person who redid the plans for Watergrasshill omitted an outer building that Donnelly's sister had used as a slaughterhouse. Ricky said Derek and the vampires have gone to see if that's where Donnelly has taken Fern.

"That monster took her to a slaughterhouse?"

The yelp startled them. With the music playing, no one had heard the young girl slip in the door. Tears brimmed, and she spun round, rushing from the kitchen and taking the stairs two at a time. Tom cursed, and Erika winced, but Ever stood to go after her.

"Ever, you don't have to go after her. I'm sure the family will make sure she's okay."

Ever gave him a brief, almost bitter smile. "They don't understand. She's human and in love with a supernatural. They'll never understand how helpless she feels, knowing she will grow old and die while the woman she loves won't age. I do, to some extent. Maybe I can comfort her in some way."

"Ever..." Tom began.

Ever pressed a kiss to his cheek. "It's okay, Tom. I know who I am and where my place is in this world. I may not be content with that, but that's my issue and I can deal. Now, let me go talk to the girl. I'll be fine."

Slipping from the room, Ever tried to ignore not only the pitying looks she got from Tom and Erika, but also the tremendous pain that had spread throughout her chest. Here she was, planning on exploring this thing between herself and Derek, while he would have to feel the loss of her when she aged and eventually died. Could she do that to him? Be selfish and condemn him to such a life? Because even now, after only knowing him for a short amount of time, Ever wasn't sure she could leave him.

Just outside the kitchen door, she paused, gathering herself together before she went in search of Fern's girlfriend. Closing her eyes, she took in a breath and could hear Erika and Tom talking from her spot outside.

"I can't wait to go back to my hotel and shower. I think I could sleep for a month after this."

"Why are you sleeping at a hotel?" Tom questioned, and Ever wondered the same thing.

A pop of gum sounded, and Erika replied, "When the transfer came through, I was told it was immediate. I just shoved a case into my car and left. Not much time to hunt for somewhere to live or anything. If you know of anyone looking for a roomie, let me know."

There was a lull of noise, and the hairs on Ever's arms stood up. She had the strange urge to storm the kitchen and protect Tom. Her fingers twitched, and absentmindedly she reached behind her to grasp nothing but air. What the hell?

"You should ask Ever. She has an apartment above her garage. I'm sure she wouldn't mind if you stayed with her for a while." His voice sounded robotic—almost forced—but Ever considered she might just be a little paranoid.

"Cool, boss! I'll ask her for sure." Another pop of gum, and the unease dissipated. Shaking out her tired limbs, Ever walked away from the kitchen and headed for the stairs. She could hear stifled sobs as she came to the top of the stairs. A door to Ever's left was slightly ajar, and through the little gap, she could see the young girl cuddled up on a bed, holding a massive grey bear to her chest.

Pushing the door open slowly, the girl's head jerked up. When her eyes met Ever's, she could see pain, fear, and despair all swirling around in the girl's pale blue eyes. Ever gently set the door ajar again and went to sit on the edge of the bed. She gave the girl a little time to dry her eyes.

Glancing around the room, it made Ever smile to think of Fern as nothing more than a typical teen. Band posters and pictures littered the walls. Clothing was tossed on the floor, and textbooks were stacked high at a desk that was covered in more clothing than space available.

"She really is a slob. I'm always telling her to clean up and her dad might let her out more. But then she smiles and says one neat freak is enough in a relationship and opposites attract."

"I get that," Ever smiled. "She seems like such a free spirit, but then again, most nymphs are, right? I'm Ever."

"Siobhan."

Ever turned on the bed and bent her knee, letting it rest on the blanket. She braced her elbow on her knee and tried to give Siobhan a smile.

"Is she dead? I wish someone would just tell me so I can know how I'm supposed to feel. Her parents don't like me because I'm not one of them, but they can't throw me out until we know."

Ever tilted her head. "Nobody will throw you out, Siobhan. And your Fern is not dead. My team is tracking her down right now, and my..." What had she called Derek?

Champion, Kappi.

The voice was back, whispering words of madness in her mind, but she squashed it down. "My friends will do their very best to bring your Fern back to you."

Hugging the bear tighter, Siobhan leaned back against the solid-wood headboard. "They all think it's a phase for both of us. That Fern wanted to try out a human, and I wanted to try out a supernatural. But we love each other. I knew from the moment she walked into school that I loved her. Do you believe in love at first sight?"

Of course you do... did you not lay eyes on your champion and know you had to have him? Think, Ever...

Ever's breath hitched. Calmly, she waited until she could articulate a sound, and then she answered, "I'm not sure. I've never been in love before, so I can't really understand what it is that you feel for Fern. But the way you talk about her, the way your face lights up at the mere mention of her, if that's what love looks like, then I can't wait to experience it."

The girl rubbed the back of her neck. "Thank you."

"For what?"

The girl shifted positions on the bed. "For treating me as an equal even though I'm young and human."

Ever reached out and nudged her knee. "We 'mere humans' need to stick together."

Siobhan's eyes widened. "You're human?"

"Yup, and I hang out with supes every day. You can hold your own, I bet."

The girl considered her words, and a thought ran through her mind before she giggled and replied, "Fern says that I must have been supernatural in my past life because I'm as ruthless as a vampire, as loyal as a wolf, and sometimes as much a pain in her ass as her brother. God, if she's not okay, I don't think I'll survive it."

Ever shifted closer to Siobhan and took the girl's

hand in her own. "If Fern was able to make a strong, resilient, young woman like you fall in love with her, then she's as determined to get back to you as you are to hold her in your arms again. She'll come back to you."

The girl's shields cracked, and she launched herself at Ever, throwing her arms around her neck and sobbing into her shoulder. Ever hushed and whispered reassurances to the girl, suddenly aware they were no longer alone in the room. The door creaked slightly as a boy a little older than Fern stood in the doorway. Eyes red from crying, the boy had pale, freckled skin with brown hair that was tinged with a berry shade of red.

"Fern will be fine, Siobhan... she's too stubborn not to be." His voice was musical and bewitching, and Ever sensed that he was using his magic to calm down his sister's girlfriend. He nodded at Ever in greeting.

The girl detangled herself from Ever and sniffled. "Do your parents want me to go, Finn? I know your dad hates me, so I can go wait outside if he wants."

Finn strode over with an elegant glide and ruffled the girl's hair. "My da doesn't hate you, Shivs; he's actually quite fond of you. He's just afraid for you both. There's a reason why most supes date within their own kind. You're welcome in our house anytime."

Turning to Ever, he held out his hand, and she shook it, surprised by the firmness of his shake. For someone who moved with the fluidity of a dancer, Finn was stronger than he looked. Then again, for all her beauty, Ever was certain there was a ruthlessness behind Caitlyn that very few lived to talk about.

"Do you really think Fern will be brought home safe?" he asked her, his tone wavering slightly for all its sternness.

"Yes, all of those searching for your sister will fight tooth and nail to bring her home safe and sound. Just make sure that you are there for her when she comes back. She'll need all your love and support."

Her phone vibrated in her jeans pocket, and she reached in to pull it out, hoping it was Derek saying the girl had been found. Ice covered her veins as she read the text and stood up abruptly. Both Finn and Siobhan watched her, and she forced a smile onto her face.

"It's just my mom checking in... even when you're a grown-up, your mom likes to fuss over you. You guys okay if I head out to give her a call?"

Finn inclined his head. "Sure. I'll make sure Siobhan is okay. My sister will kick my ass if I don't."

That brought a genuine smile to her face as Ever headed out the door.

"Ever."

She peered over her shoulder.

"Thanks. For a mere mortal, you're kinda special."

"Right back at ya', hun."

She left the two teens behind and fumbled her way down the stairs, pulse racing and fear blossoming deep inside her. Ever just needed to slip out unnoticed, and everything would be okay. Peering into the family room and spying Tom with the family, she passed the room quickly and quietly. Thankfully, Ever managed to make it to the kitchen without attracting anyone's attention.

"Where you off to?" A pop of gum sounded, and Ever realized she wasn't alone. Erika was perched on the countertop with a tablet in hand. She flicked through it without looking up, and Ever began to think about how she was going to get around the woman.

"Was just going to get some air." She stepped forward,

stopping short when Erika's suspicious eyes met hers.

"Before you do... Tom said you had a spare apartment that you might be willing to let me crash at for a bit. I'll pay rent and stuff, just don't wanna be stuck in a hotel for ages."

Eager to get by her, Ever nodded her head. "Sure, no hassle. Once we get done here, I'll show you around the place."

Beaming, Erika said, "Awesome! Cheers, Ever. 'Preciate it." Her gum popped again, and Ever inched her way toward the back door.

"You want some company? You shouldn't be by yourself out there at the moment."

She held up her phone. "I need to call my mom. She's been hitting my phone up all night to check in. I'll be fine. I'll stay close to the house. Promise."

"Okay." The girl dropped her gaze and continued whatever she was doing on her tablet.

Ever let out a sigh of relief and tried to walk calmly to the back door. She hurried and sent a text as she closed the door behind her, stepping down onto the lush, wet grass. Stars twinkled in the sky, faint hints of lights against a navy skyline, the three-quarter moon mostly hidden behind grayish clouds. Under different circumstances, Ever could have sat for ages admiring the stark beauty of the night.

The wind gathered, and Ever caught the faint scent of smoke on the wind. Trees rustled, and an owl hooted in the distance. She began to have second thoughts, wondering if she shouldn't have told Erika exactly what was going on, but it was too late now. Her phone buzzed again, and she checked the screen.

Her gut told her it was a bad idea—a tremendously

stupid idea—but with a quick glance around to make sure no one was watching her, Ever put one foot in front of the other and delved into the forest. The smell of trees and rain surrounded her as she made her way deeper into the forest until the lights of the house had vanished and the only light that paved the way was the barest hint of moonlight through the trees.

Panic began to set in, and she suddenly wished Derek was here and safe and they could leave all this mess behind them. A fox scurried across her path, and she jumped in surprise, barely managing to stifle the scream that bubbled in her throat. Rain began to fall, a light drizzle muddying the ground around her.

Ever kept an eye on her phone, hoping it would ring and she could make a run back for the house.

You are a warrior... act like one.

The voice scolded her, and she staggered. Maybe she was really going insane. It wasn't like she knew anything about where she came from. Maybe her mother had been a schizophrenic. She knew the illness manifested in your early to mid-twenties. Could she really be going mad?

A tear leaked from her eye, and she brushed it away, unwilling to admit that she might be losing the only thing that made her in any way special—her mind.

A thump dragged her back to awareness, and Ever clenched her fists by her side. The air suddenly turned from the smell of trees and rain to wrongness, like something wasn't right. Her senses pricked and tension built up in her neck.

"I knew you'd come. Like an angel sent to save me, I knew that you'd come."

She shivered at the tone of his voice as the monster

stepped out from behind the cover of a tree trunk.

"Hello, Stephen."

He stood only meters from her, nothing remotely human about the man who now faced her. He took a step in her direction, and she backpedaled. He seemed amused by her actions.

"You came to save the girl and the wolf. That doesn't surprise me, Ever. I knew from the first moment we met that I had been searching in all the wrong places. That you would be my salvation, my way to becoming immortal."

"And how are you going to do that, Stephen? I am utterly human."

He pulled a silver blade from his hip, and fear drenched her.

"I'm going to eat your skin and bones before you mature into your powers because you, my sweet, delicious Ever, are anything but human."

Something clicked inside her, but Ever didn't have a chance to process anything as Stephen lunged for her with death in his eyes.

"HELLO, STEPHEN."

She had come. A goddess surrounded by golden fire, she had come to save his life and make him immortal. Her sacrifice would not be forgotten, and while he might take enjoyment from slicing her flesh from her bones and tasting her marrow, he might regret having to kill her. But there was no one else like her. The power inside her was mounting, waiting to surge forward, and he had to have it.

"You came to save the girl and the wolf. That doesn't surprise me, Ever. I knew from the first moment we met that I had been searching in all the wrong places. That you would be my salvation, my way to becoming immortal." He couldn't mask the eagerness in his voice. He needed to taste her, wondering for too long if she tasted like honey, the same way her hair smelt.

"And how are you going to do that, Stephan? I am utterly human."

She didn't know... and now she would never know. Death had come too soon for her.

He pulled a silver blade from his hip, and he could almost taste her fear on his tongue.

"I'm going to eat your skin and bones before you mature into your powers because you, my sweet, delicious Ever, are anything but human."

He waited a second before he lunged for her, knife in hand, hoping to strike out before the wolf came after him.

All the others had whimpered and begged for their lives, and he'd expected Ever to do so, too. But he was not prepared for her to fight back... hadn't predicted it, and hadn't anticipated her attack. When her foot connected with his stomach, he flew across the forest into a tree.

They assessed each other, his prey looking startled by her own actions, but she braced herself for a second-wave attack. And he couldn't disappoint her, now, could he?

CHAPTER EIGHTEEN

THE NIGHT WAS SILENT AROUND THEM WITH NOT EVEN a peep from the animals that roamed the night. The predators that hunted before them were far deadlier than any of them could ever be. The wind began to gather, a marginally soft howl amongst the trees, their footsteps not making a single sound. Derek normally found the night soothing, but at this very moment, the sound of his rapid breathing and the thumping of his heart seemed to unease him. Something pulled at his gut, but he had to focus on finding the nymph before Donnelly had any more time alone with her.

The thick foliage hampered their line of sight, and even though he could see through the eyes of the wolf, vampire vision saw a lot more. He let the vampires lead the way, pushing all his alpha instincts back. A growl vibrated low in his chest, and it was met by a hiss from Caitlyn. Guess he wasn't the only one feeling on edge.

Whatever potency had come from Ricky's blood

seemed to have completely healed Donnie. The normally stoic vampire was racing through the woods with a stupid grin on his face. His pupils were dilated, fangs extended as if he were high, and maybe he was. Perhaps his partner hadn't been as forthcoming as to the extent of his magic. Caitlyn scowled at her progeny, uttering several curses in her native tongue that had Donnie grinning even wider.

After running at a supernatural pace for almost ten minutes, Derek slid to a halt when Donnie held up a hand. He motioned them forward and then crouched behind a thick, leafy bush looking out into an open field. Light sprawled across the dirt ground, illuminating the way and possibly giving their position away if Donnelly was watching. Darkness seemed to eat up the rear of the field, and from the beacon of light in front, Derek could make out the faint outline of steel.

Switching from human to wolf eyes, Derek allowed his other half to see what the man couldn't. A steel unit stretched out across the field, the main entrance situated under the light. It ran down until the back of it trailed off, and Derek knew that without his wolf eyes he could not have made out the full length of it. Steel against steel, the outhouse was built to withstand the adverse Irish weather, the only chink in its armor being the glass roof... unless the glass was specially designed to take all kinds of weather, which Derek was certain it had been. Otherwise, under the strain of a blustery winter's night, the glass would have shattered long ago. The scent of blood and fear tainted the air, but from Derek's nose, he was unsure if the blood was old or new.

"I don't think Donnelly simply forgot to turn off the light," Donnie said.

His tone was still slightly slurred, but it seemed the high was evening out. Good—they needed his muscle.

"Indeed." Caitlyn swept a curl from her face. "I think it's a distraction. Donnelly knows we will hunt him. After the bomb, I'm weary of his methods. Nothing will be as it seems."

Derek considered their words and knew they were right. "I think the light is a diversion so that we go in the back, and I bet he has it rigged. That means the only way in is through the front, but I could be totally wrong and he has both doors rigged to blow."

"Well, that is encouraging." Caitlyn snorted.

"We do have another option, though—one Donnelly couldn't have known about." Donnie stared at Caitlyn, who shifted uncomfortably under his scrutiny.

"Pour l'amour de Dieu!"

Caitlyn shifted out of her customary ankle-length duster, and Derek caught the hunger in Donnie's eyes as he watched her. Ignoring them both, she pulled a hair tie from her wrist and gathered her thick curls into a ponytail. She glared at Donnie and then at Derek.

"You speak a word of what you see, and I swear that what I do to you will take an eternity to heal. I'll make it so you never have little puppies of your own, much less romance your human. Understand?" Caitlyn hissed out, murder in her eyes.

Derek nodded, trying to hide the grin that threatened to derail the whole scene. Donnie was already grinning like an idiot, there was no need for him to follow suit. Caitlyn gave Donnie a hard push on his shoulder, but the mountain of a man didn't as much as budge. Like a panther in the night, Caitlyn slipped through the overgrowth, and in the time it took Derek to lower his lashes and raise them again, Caitlyn was at the side of the slaughterhouse.

She turned to glare once more at them as Donnie shuffled closer to Derek. Crouching low, Caitlyn bent her knees, and then she was in the air. Derek's mouth hung open as she levitated over the glass roof of the building. With ease, she ghosted her feet onto the roof, testing its strength until she was assured it would hold her weight. Legends were legends for a reason, and although rumours quickly spread through the supernatural community, Derek understood fully why Caitlyn would want to keep this a secret.

"Amazing, isn't she?" Donnie whispered.

"Did you know she could do that?"

The burly vampire nodded. "Since the night she changed me."

"And only members of a certain line are rumored to hold such power?"

"Indeed."

Derek blew out a breath. He still had so much to learn about Caitlyn. When he first met her, the French vampire had constantly looked over her shoulder. Now, he knew why.

"Can you do that?" Derek asked.

"Nope... not yet, anyway... Cait said it manifested in her around her fifth decade as a vampire, but I think my talents lie elsewhere."

He wanted to probe further, the wolf curious as to what, exactly, those he considered part of his pack might be hiding. But everyone was hiding something; Derek himself couldn't feel any grievance toward the vampire's being guarded. He respected it. The wolf was designed to sniff out anything that might be useful should he need some leverage, but the man was simply curious, especially if Caitlyn had been made by whom he suspected.

Derek shook his head as a sharp whistle jerked his head up. Caitlyn stood like an avenging angel upon the roof, her hair mussed in the wind, hands firm on her hips and feet spread slightly apart. Caitlyn took a step off the roof and landed on the ground very catlike. Derek and Donnie jogged over to where Caitlyn waited, tapping her foot, a guarded expression marring her face.

"Was I right? Did he have the doors set to blow?" He had promised not to mention her ability, and he would hold that promise until she spoke to him about it.

Relief flooded her face. "The back door is indeed rigged with explosives. Not as much to kill but to definitely maim. The main door isn't rigged at all. I smelled the scent of a nymph and heard a heartbeat, but only one. I don't think Donnelly is here."

"Damn it!" Derek snarled, clenching his fists and wishing he had something to punch. Instead, he brushed past Caitlyn and tried to lift the latch on the slaughterhouse door. It creaked, obviously needing a little oil to loosen it, but didn't budge. Gritting his teeth, he fisted the latch in his hand and yanked with all the strength he had. It snapped in his hand, and the steel doors inched open a smidge. Derek inclined his head at the vampires and slipped inside, pushing the door open fully and waiting for a click or indication that the place would blow.

When nothing happened, Caitlyn and Donnie followed him, and as Derek breathed in the repugnant air, the scent of old blood and raw meat stirred the wolf in him, causing it to snap, snarl, and bang itself against the corners of Derek's mind, baying for control. He pushed at the wolf, snapping a metaphysical leash on him and reminding the wolf that he, the man, was in charge. The wolf swiped a paw in his mind and Derek flinched, but then the wolf simply paced inside him, unhappy but controlled. For now.

The smells were affecting the vampires as well, more so Donnie than Caitlyn, but he guessed age had something to do with that. Their eyes were ringed with red. Caitlyn shook her head, the red dulled, and her normal grey eye colour returned. Derek moved forward, eager to find the girl and go after Donnelly. He couldn't smell his scent, but he could smell the nymph, her earthy scent laced with terror.

The slaughterhouse floor was slick with blood, and Derek found himself thankful for the boots he wore. Rows of metal containers ran down the length of the slaughterhouse. Derek knew that if he looked inside them, that they would resemble what he'd seen in the room when they had gone in search of Melanie. He didn't get the smell of flesh, so he knew that the blood that covered the floor belonged to those already dead—something he would look into later.

He heard the creaking of a chair as his ears pricked at the sound of a struggle. No doubt, the girl had sensed them break the lock and was terrified her captor had come back. A muffled sound of pain caused Derek to speed past all the rooms to a chamber a mere foot or two from the device at the back door. He put his hand on the door where he scented the girl and went to open it, yet it didn't budge. Hitting it with his shoulder, he barely made a dent in it.

Growling, he stepped aside and looked at Donnie,

who simply shrugged and put both palms against the door. He pushed, but it looked like he was doing barely anything. He heard the steel door groan and crack under the vampire's strength, and the wolf studied him as he would any other predator. The wolf huffed, content in the knowledge that this was friend not foe.

The door gave one final groan in resistance before it crumbled under Donnie's strength and fell to the floor. Derek tilted his head, very wolf-like, saying, "Your talents lie elsewhere, eh?"

"Damn right."

Derek went into the room first, and his wolf almost bashed against his skull as they spotted the girl. Tied to a chair, she had a gag in her mouth, eyes wide and darting all over the room. Her strawberry-coloured hair was matted, and Derek sniffed dried blood. She struggled against her restraints, and the scent of fresh blood tickled his nose. Her eyes settled on Derek, and tears welled in her eyes. A noise made her look behind him, and she immediately stank of fear.

Vampires were known to be bloodthirsty and violent, nightmares that parents told supernatural children at night so they wouldn't venture too far into vampire territory. It was obvious Fern had heard such stories, and after what she had just experienced, Derek wasn't about to frighten her any further. He glanced over his shoulder as Caitlyn leaned in and whispered into Donnie's ear, both vampires retreating a little.

Derek cautiously edged toward Fern. He needed to reassure her that she was safe and he could take her home. "Fern." His voice was low but held an edge of assertiveness that made her look at him. "My name is Derek, and I'm with the police. I've come to take you home. Your parents are worried about you. Do you trust me?"

Her nose wrinkled as she got a whiff of him. "Yes, I'm a wolf, but I won't hurt you. I'm going to remove the gag first if that's okay. I just need you not to scream."

She nodded and blinked away the tears in her eyes, which the wolf approved of.

Derek gently untied the gag, and Fern gulped in a couple of breaths. As she did, Derek bent down and untied the restraints at her ankles as well as her hands tied behind her. Fern brought her arms forward and rubbed her wrists.

"Am I really safe?" the girl whispered.

Derek gently ran his knuckles over her cheek. "Yes, we can take you home now. I'm sure there are a lot of people who want to see you. But can I ask you about the man who took you? If you don't want to talk, I won't force you."

He had bent his knees so that he was eye level with her. Fern jutted her chin out, determination replacing the fear in her eyes. "No, I'm okay. Ask me."

This girl would survive and be stronger for it.

"Where did he go? And why leave you here alive?"

The girl cleared her throat. "He said I wasn't enough, that he needed more. He talked to himself a lot... like, argued."

Donnelly was devolving, sinking deeper into the madness.

"He told me that he had to hold back and stop himself from killing me. He had to resist my flesh." The girl shuddered, and her lips trembled. "He said I was to distract the police from his objective. He mumbled a name over and over, and when he closed his eyes, I could tell from the look on his face he was imagining what he was going to do to her."

Another brush of knuckles over her cheek, and she stopped trembling. "You're doing very well, Fern. Do you remember what name he said?"

"Ever... he said he was going after Ever."

The wolf howled and banged against his skull. The pain sent shockwaves throughout his body, and he stiffened. Rising, he pressed a kiss to the girl's forehead. Hands shaking with anger, he pulled the phone from his pocket and dialed Sarge's number. The bear answered.

"We have the girl. She's safe. Put Ever on the phone." He growled the order, not caring that he was the subordinate and Sarge was his boss.

Something in his voice made Sarge obey, and he called Ever's name. His heart pounded in his ears as he heard Erika say that Ever had gone outside for air about twenty minutes ago and hadn't come back in. There was a lull in conversation, and then Erika spoke.

"She's gone. There are mud prints, though, and they seem to head into the forest."

Derek snarled. "Donnelly has her, and I'm going to break his neck." He snapped the phone shut, and his eyes meet Caitlyn's.

"Go... we will protect the girl with our lives."

"You're leaving?" the girl whimpered behind him.

"I have to, sweetheart. The girl he took belongs to me... she's mine. I need to go to her. I trust these vampires with my life and yours, but I have to go."

"She's yours like Siobhan is mine... Go get your mate; I'm okay."

Mate.

Both man and wolf liked the sound of that. And she

was, he realized, his mate. It was why he was so drawn to her, why he wanted her with such passion and need. Why he felt calmed by her presence. Donnelly had taken what belonged to him, and he would feel the sharp edge of his teeth. Seems the wolf would sink its fangs into blood sooner rather than later.

He rushed from the room, satisfied that the girl was in safe hands with Donnie and Caitlyn. The wolf clawed and snarled at Derek, and he began to rip the clothes from his body, the need to be wolf overwhelming. He wasn't worried about bloodlust because he would sate it by gorging on Donnelly. He made it out into the open, shucking off his boots when his knees gave out.

Bone crunched, cracking and shattering as human bones made way for lupine. His eyes morphed to amber, and his jaw broke, reforming with his muzzle and rows of sharp canines. His back bowed, and he groaned as the fire that was the change ignited his body and made man into beast. Long limbs stretched out in front of him, massive, powerful paws that could claw out a man's throat in an instant. Fur coated his naked skin, and in one final, excruciating surge that rippled throughout his body, Derek the man was gone, replaced by a chocolate wolf that shook off the remnants of pain and raised its muzzle to the half-hidden moon.

A howl ripped through the dead silence, a vengeful sound that held the promise of blood and death. Derek, still able to form sentences in his mind, urged the wolf forward, telling him that their mate was in trouble.

The wolf understood what the man was saying, understood 'mate' as well, and needed to seek justice for the blood the monster had spilled. He would be the seeker of justice and would present his dead body to their mate as a present. The wolf grinned, its tongue lolling to the side of his mouth. The man pushed harder, and the wolf snarled but listened.

Gloat later... kill now...

The man snarled like a wolf, and the wolf loped off at a fast pace, eager for the taste of blood and the scent of his mate. They raced through the trees, braches smacking against his fur as his paws galloped through the forest. He wasn't sure where he was going, pure instinct carried him as he went. The draw to the girl who would be his mate pulling him as if they were attached by a string.

He followed that string as rain fell down, splashing on his fur and nose, drawing a sneeze from him. When the wolf breathed in, he caught the scent of his mate. Sun. Sea. Sand... That was what his mate smelled like. The wolf was not a fan of the water, but when her scent embedded in his nose, she smelled right. His.

Ours.

The man who was part of him reminded him that he had to share, and the wolf decided he was okay with that. They gathered speed as the scent of their mate became heavier, closer. They heard the sounds of a struggle, of a fight, and they snarled, muzzle ticking with anger. The wolf slowed his pace and went down on his belly. Creeping forward through the bushes, he stuck his nose out and watched as their mate fought with such beauty, such grace that they were mesmerized by it.

Their mate wasn't a fighter... but she certainly looked like it.

Man and wolf watched unnoticed for a few minutes, hidden in the shadows and waiting for their chance to strike. It took all the wolf's control to keep the man at bay as he lunged forward in his mind to go help their mate. But they waited and stalked farther into the bush, their teeth wanting to feel bone in their grasp.

...And they would not let go until the last breath was wrung from he who would hurt their mate.

Chapter Nineteen

EVER DODGED AWAY FROM HIS LUNGE WITH A SPEED SHE did not possess. She rolled on the ground and quickly regained her footing. Bracing her feet, she felt an onslaught of adrenaline flush her veins.

This is who you are... a warrior... a defender of the weak...

Believe it. Remember it.

The crazy was back in her head, but she couldn't let that distract her from Donnelly. The moment she hesitated, the second she dropped her guard, he would have the upper hand, and she would die. Death surrounded them like a blanket of fear and power. Ever didn't want to die, so she would have to kill Donnelly to survive. But would she been able to wash his blood from her hands?

You have slain many in battle... do not become weak of heart now...

She swallowed hard and shook away the thoughts

in her mind. Donnelly studied her, the glint of his own madness visible in his eyes. For some reason, Donnelly believed she was his salvation, but he was deluded, blinded by bloodlust and possibly his tumor. Ever's only hope was to hold him off for as long as it took the team to realize she was gone and come for her.

She had to believe they would come for her.

Ever also had to bury the questions the bubbled in her mind. How had she been able to fight back? It wasn't as if her love of martial arts movies could have taught her anything like what it had taken to beat Donnelly back. She certainly had never used a roundhouse kick to divest anyone of his or her weapon as she had Donnelly...

Feet apart, she took a defensive stance, unsure how she knew where to place her feet and hands. Her fists clenched, and she felt no fear... only an eagerness to fight.

"Muscle memory is an amazing thing, is it not, Ever?"

Ever blinked her eyes but didn't respond, and Donnelly took that as permission to continue.

"You see, when a patient hasn't used certain muscles in a long time, it takes a few goes before the muscle will remember to act how it should. But it will always remember."

His eyes roamed over her, and she stifled a shudder. She let him ramble on because it bought her a little more time. Her phone vibrated in her pocket, but she couldn't risk taking it out. That would anger the monster before her, and she was already trying his patience.

Donnelly started to circle her, and she moved her body to echo his. He smiled, a feral thing that made her skin itch. Time ticked by at a slow pace as the forest remained quiet around her. Part of her felt she should have stayed in her cozy little classroom where she was safe from monsters, and part of her reveled in the rush of excitement that seemed to boil her blood.

Or maybe it was just the fact she was heading on the train to Crazy Town.

"You told me if I came to you, then Fern and the team would be safe. Did you keep your word, Stephen, as I have?"

Donnelly tapped his index finger to his lips. "I have. The wolf should have the girl by now, unless the property went kaboom like my aunt's house. I left a little message for him with the nymph... I'm sure he is on his way now. I wouldn't want him to miss watching you die."

Derek was coming for her—she could feel it in her heart.

"He won't let you kill me, Stephen. Is that how you want to die—mauled to death by a werewolf? If you stop this now, we can get you to a hospital, make you comfortable, and ease your pain."

Donnelly sniggered. "I won't feel the pain for much longer, sweet Ever. Once I kill you, I will be reborn. If there was another like you, then maybe I could have kept you, but alas. You, my dear, are special."

Ever snorted out a laugh. "I keep telling you, Stephen, I am not special at all. If you kill me, it will not save you, only bring you a step closer to death. Can you not feel it? Death—it lingers around us, snapping at our ankles for a taste. If it's coming for us both, Stephen, then I can accept it... but can you?"

"Shut up!"

His scream of fury startled her, yet she didn't even flinch. She let him mumble to himself and bang the side of his head with his hand. She waited for him to lash out, and then either she would die or he would. She readied herself for his attack, but it never came.

In an instant, the air of madness was replaced by a façade of calm. "Stop trying to anger me. What's amazing is you really do believe that you are as human as me."

"You're not human. You're a monster."

"True," Donnelly agreed. "But it still doesn't negate the fact that I can feel the power under your skin, waiting to show through. I read all about you, Doctor. Ever Chace... abandoned at birth, raised by a witch and a Druid. Maybe your real parents were more than human. Don't you think you should have found out sooner? I've never sensed anything like you before... you are anything but a mere human, Ever."

Ever couldn't stop the blaze of hope that flooded her. Could he be right? Was she what she had longed for all her life... to be more than human... to have a purpose? Her eyes must have given her away, as Donnelly curled up his lips at her.

"You feel it, too, now—don't you? The realization that you could have been more? That you could have been feared and revered for who you are? You could have been worshipped, and now *I* will be."

She blinked, and that was all he needed. He sprang forward, and his fist connected with her cheek. Pain blistered, sending a shockwave of agony throughout her body. Ever stumbled back but didn't lose her footing. He came at her again, wildly tossing his fists about in the hopes that another would connect. As he went left, Ever kicked out again with her right foot. He grunted but kept up his assault.

Punching upward, her fist connected with his jaw, and blood splattered from his mouth as Donnelly went down. Her hand burned as Donnelly shirked backward and slowly got to his feet. He ran the back of his hand over his mouth, wiping the blood from his lips, but not the blood that stained his teeth. Ever caught a glint of sliver and cursed as Donnelly had somehow managed to get his hands on the blade once again.

"Oh, to have a night with you, Ever. To explore, to taste, to cut... but I grow tired of you now, and it's time you prayed to whatever God you worship."

He roared and came at her, and Ever braced for impact... one that never came. A blur of chocolate fur flew past her and knocked Donnelly flat on his ass again. The wolf wrapped its teeth around Donnelly's wrist, and Ever winced as she heard the crack of bone under the wolf's grip. Donnelly let out a wail of pure agony as he tried to pull his wrist from the jaws of the wolf. He was unsuccessful.

A growl so sinister it made the hairs on her arms stand to attention erupted from the wolf's throat. Donnelly attempted to get up, but the wolf sank its jaws tighter around the man's flesh, and Ever saw fear in Donnelly's eyes.

"I should've killed you, wolf, when I had the chance," Donnelly grunted, earning a skeptical huff from the wolf.

Seemingly, the wolf didn't believe Donnelly could hurt him, much less kill him.

"Derek?"

The wolf turned to look at her, and she saw Derek in his eyes. She held his gaze and smiled. The wolf let go of Donnelly's wrist and padded toward her. She sank down to her knees, and as the wolf stopped in front of her, she ran her fingers through his fur, the bristles a comforting sensation.

"Thank you for coming for me."

The wolf simply narrowed his gaze as if to say, *Don't be ridiculous, of course, I would come.*

Mate.

The word sounded in her head, and it was Derek's voice that had spoken. The wolf tilted his head as he sat down on his haunches. He pawed at her knee, and she continued to run her fingers over his fur.

Mate.

Ever smiled and nodded. "We'll see. You owe me a proper date first."

The wolf sneezed, and she laughed.

Lost in sensation, neither of them seemed to notice Donnelly drag himself across the ground, wrap his fingers around the blade, and lunge for Derek. Ever fell back as the wolf twisted away from her with such speed—but not enough to avoid the stab of silver to his stomach. The wolf howled and snapped its teeth.

The wolf felt the silver enter his bloodstream and begin to take hold. His body trembled, but he had to ensure his mate was safe before he could lie down. He felt the blade leave his body before it entered again at a different point. He swiped out with his paw, leaving his claws free, and as his vision blurred, he caught the scent of copper and knew he had hit his target. He needed time to catch his attacker off guard. The wolf let his eyes close, almost whimpering at the horrible sound of his mate's cry.

Donnelly kicked the wolf before he cut into his leg with the silver blade. The animal didn't move. He turned his focus back to Ever, whose eyes spilled over with tears as she clasped a hand over her mouth to keep herself from crying out.

"There's no one to stop me now, Ever. Your wolf is dead... but you'll see him soon." Donnelly raised his arm, the blade raised high, and Ever closed her eyes, ready to accept her fate.

A gurgling sound snapped her eyes open, and she watched as her wolf ripped Donnelly's arm from the rest of his body. Ever knew wolves were strong, but to rip an appendage from a body took serious strength, and even laced with silver, Derek had done it.

A paw pressed down on Donnelly's throat, and Ever heard a crack before the wolf whimpered, Donnelly managing a cheap shot to his injuries. The wolf fell to his side and whined, his paws twitching, trying to get up, to protect her.

Ever clambered to her feet, ready to take on Donnelly, when a blur of motion came into the clearing. Fangs bared, eyes a glorious blood red, Caitlyn gave Ever her best feral grin as she strode over to Donnelly. She placed a boot where Derek's paw had been and eased her weight down. Donnelly struggled under her boot but was unable to move.

"You have caused terror and slain innocents in your quest to become immortal. It's not a blessing. It is hell on earth, but you will soon be in your very own hell. I wish Melanie were here and that she could exact her vengeance upon you. Yes, she survived, but you won't. I hope you burn a thousand deaths in hell, you son of a bitch."

Donnelly's larynx crushed under a swift pressure from Caitlyn, and he stopped moving. He was dead; it was over. Ever rushed over to where Derek remained unmoving on the ground. He tried to lift his head when she came near, and she felt the tears stream down her face.

"Change back, you stubborn man. We cannot help you as a wolf."

Caitlyn's voice seemed to spur him on. Ever heard bones crack, and the wolf convulsed, his entire body going into a seizure. Fur disintegrated to be replaced with flesh and hair, paws became hands and feet, and the wolf became a man in a wave of snapping bones and pain. Derek rolled onto his back, and Ever looked on, horrified at the deep lacerations on his torso and leg. She pulled off her hoodie and draped it over him as he shivered.

She placed her palm on his chest, and he shuddered.

"Is Donnelly dead?" he rasped out, his body convulsing, reacting to the silver.

"Yes. He won't be hurting anyone else."

"Good." His eyes drooped shut, and she tapped him lightly on his cheek.

"Hey, no sleeping. If you think dying will get you out of your promise to take me on a date, you have another thing coming, Mr. Broody Agent."

His eyes slowly opened, and when he looked at her, she felt as if he were looking right into her soul. "*Mate,*" he growled and lifted an unsteady hand to cup her cheek.

"You said that already when you were wolf. We can discuss it after you're better."

His hand dropped as Ever heard Caitlyn bark orders into her phone. She then crouched down beside Ever and watched helplessly as his breathing became shallower and his pulse harder to detect.

Ever cast her eyes to Caitlyn. The vampire's own eyes were wet with tears.

"Say good-bye, Ever. He hasn't long left."

"No," Ever said sternly. "You can't just die on me, Derek. You can't bring me into your world and let me... let me fall for you... and then leave me alone. Please, hang on a little longer. For me."

But Derek didn't respond, and all hope evaporated from inside her, leaving a gaping hole, a void she didn't think she could fill again. And to think she had been afraid she would die and leave him alone. He looked so frail, so humanly fragile, and Ever wished with all she was that she could save him.

You can, you know... save him. Remember what it's like to be who you really are. He's not dead yet. Command his soul to remain in his body. He will obey, for he is yours and you are his.

Ever blinked away her tears.

Come now... it's like riding a bike. Close your eyes and concentrate on your wolf. Look inside and focus on what you want. Demand it. It is your birthright. It is who you are.

Valkyrie...

Ever let out a strangled cry. God, she was mad... a certifiable wacko. But her hands moved of their own accord as Derek sucked in a harsh breath. Her hands tingled as she placed them on his chest. Caitlyn called out to her, but Ever pushed her away. It was then she felt it, felt the absolute beauty of Derek's soul—the kindness, the strength, the sheer courage of what made him Derek. It flickered inside him and began seeping out, readying to move on to the next life.

But Ever wasn't going to let that happen. He was hers. She felt it bone-deep inside herself, and while she thought she should be afraid, she wasn't. Not one bit.

Close your eyes, Ever. Believe in your heart and soul

that you can do what you are trying to do. Let who you are set you free. Save your champion, for he, in turn, will be the one who saves you.

Crying out, Ever closed her eyes and reached inside Derek. It was instinct, pure and simple, and she let her body and mind take over. She felt her fingers grasp hold of his soul and grab on tight. The soul squirmed and tried to escape, but one roar from Ever stilled it. Derek's body jerked, and she felt overcome with a rush of power that made her head spin.

"I forbid you from passing over. I own your soul, warrior, and you will be mine for eternity. You will live, for I command it. Now, live!" she yelled before clamping her mouth down onto Derek's lips and breathing life back into his body. His body jerked as his heart stuttered and began to beat again.

His hand slipped to the back of her neck, and his tongue met hers—hard, rough, and possessive. The wind gathered and whipped around them, and Derek's eyes snapped open to see a translucent shimmer of gold surrounding Ever's eyes. He broke the kiss and his hold on Ever loosened as she stumbled back. The silver burned inside him, and he was drowsy, like he could sleep for a month.

Ever knelt before him and began muttering in a language he didn't understand. He reached out to touch her, but she was drunk on power and slapped his hand away. Caitlyn stepped forward, and Ever lashed out, knocking the vampire off her feet. Struggling to sit up, Derek moaned, but Ever was lost to him.

"I am power, I am might. I was born to rule, and rule I shall. Vengeance will be mine, and I will respond in kind to those who hurt what belongs to me. Blood will have blood."

Lightning flashed and thunder rumbled as Ever dropped to her knees and screamed. His body weak, Derek dragged himself toward her as blood began to trickle from her ears. He was aware of people coming into the clearing but being held off by Caitlyn.

The light vanished from around her, and Ever's eyes returned to normal. She slumped forward, but he caught her, cradling her head against his knee. He brushed his lips against her forehead, and her eyes fluttered.

"It seems I must leave you once more, my love," said a voice that was not his mate's. "Deryck, he is coming for us... for my kin. I have no strength left to defeat him."

Her voice held a strange lilt as he hushed her. She stirred in his arms, her fingers reaching out to graze his skin.

"Until our next life, my love."

Then her eyes rolled back in her head and she lay limp in his arms. Both man and wolf roared in grief.

Mate. Mate. Mate.

The word rebounded in his head, and he made a split second decision. Man and wolf became one in their single-minded quest. He accepted the urge to make Ever his, and baring his fangs, he latched onto Ever's neck and bit down hard, tasting blood. He ignored the shouts and yells around him and concentrated on Ever. He forced the mating bond into her mind, felt it snap into place.

Derek...

Her voice was a symphony in his mind.

Mate.

Mate, he agreed.

Pushy wolf.

He felt the laughter in her words, but she refused

to wake. He knew she was being dragged under by the darkness, and so was he. Derek barely heard Sarge call his name, and he reluctantly opened his eyes.

"Jesus, Derek, what did you do?"

The wolf came forward at his tone. "Mate... mine," he growled, and he heard his friend suck in a breath before he followed Ever into the abyss.

Chapter Twenty

"He cannot have what is not his!" Her voice echoed in the still of the island, for neither a tree nor an animal dared to disturb the stillness and risk her wrath. She had never felt so angry in her life. He who was her father had relinquished claim over their home to her, his only daughter, and he could not have it back. Ever slammed her fist down on the ornate wooden table, and little Marya jumped at the sound.

They gathered at the back of their home, the decking overlooking the sandy beaches that surrounded them, the golden brown such a tropical sight that it was strange to feel angry in a place so beautiful, so untainted by the outside world. Perched at the top of the table, Ever addressed her sisters who had come to her—some standing, some sitting, but all attuned and ready for attack. An attack was imminent.

Somewhere in the distance, she heard the crashing of the waves against the cliffs, and it eased her somewhat.

The sea always had a calming effect on her, and today, when everything was at stake, she needed to feel centered. Ever glanced around at her sisters, the ones who had been able to gather here today, all dressed in the finest of battle attire—from the powerful Danae, to her second, Erika, and even little Marya wore clothing fit for a warrior. The littlest of all her sisters also wore a stunning short blade that Ever had used herself when she had been nothing but a babe.

"He will not take it from us without a fight, Systir. We are who we have been for centuries, and your father cannot change that. You have a choosing ceremony to prepare for."

Ever narrowed her gaze at Joslyn's words, the tall, dark-skinned warrior reminding her that she had to choose her champion today and that was why she was dressed in the ridiculous clothing her mother had forced her into. A long, flowing, golden gown sat atop her skin, the straps thin with a neckline that plunged down to reveal her cleavage. The dress ghosted the sand as she walked, her bare feet the only comfortable thing about the ensemble. Today, she would be wed, taking her champion as her own, and be blessed as queen—a burden she felt tightening like a noose around her neck. It panicked her. She no more wanted to be queen than she wanted to wed, but something about her chosen champion made her insides quiver.

"Do you not think we have far more important complications than my having to pick a champion?" she scowled.

"Since it is evidently clear who you have chosen as champion, we see no need to prolong this any further, My Queen."

Her cheeks flamed at Joslyn, and her sisters laughed—a welcome sound as doom came riding through the night like a horseman of the apocalypse. Ever fidgeted with her dress as she leaned back in her chair. Her sisters straightened, suddenly becoming serious as a familiar aura came upon them.

"You sisters are right, Ever. It will do morale good to finally usher you in as queen." Her mother ran her knuckles over her cheek in affection, but the affection was gone in an instant, only to be replaced with the face of a hardened warrior, one who had no issues dealing out death. Her mother may be considered by most as the person to invoke for love, but Freya was far from a romantic, and she was considered—amongst those in the know—a death goddess.

Ever huffed, causing Erika to lean in and whisper, "Must we remind Mother that you have already had a taste of your champion? Or does she not know that he sweeps from your room before dawn most mornings?"

Lashing out at her sister, Erika simply chuckled and dodged out of her way with the biggest grin on her face. Freya sent them both a rather disapproving stare, which sent them both into fits of laughter. When they managed to compose themselves, Freya strode around the decking as if these warriors were her own. She tightened the breastplate on Marya before ruffling the little girl's hair. Marya growled, but her eyes lit up at Freya's attention. Not only mere mortals worshipped Freya.

"Who is watching over Folkvang, Mother?"

Freya sighed. "I have left Almira in charge for a time. The girl seems more at home there than I ever have."

Ever understood. Despite Almira being a full-blooded Valkyrie, the young warrior did not hold the stomach for battle and would likely get herself killed. She lacked the lust for blood that the rest of them seemed to hold. She would be much happier in Folkvang. Ever had only ventured there once, and the place had been so peaceful it had creeped her out. But the light that emanated from Almira as she wandered through Folkvang proved the girl was meant for different things.

"I blame her mother," Freya snarled.

Yet, like most of the warriors who were destined Valkyries, they had been given to Freya at birth to train for their destiny. None except for Ever herself knew for certain who had given birth to them, yet now, Ever suspected that Freya knew more than she let on... if the whispers on the wind were true.

"Enough of this," Ever insisted. "Mother, we need to plan on how to contain Father. He does not wish for me to become queen and accept the claim I have on Valhalla. It is my birthright to rule and bring warriors over from the brink of death to join my army. We cannot let delusions of a centuries-old myth allow us to go back to the mead-bearing wenches that history appraises us to be. We, the Valkyrie, are powerful warrior women who are not in need of a man to dictate to us how we should rule our kingdom. I will not allow it. If you want me to be queen, then Father has to be banished from Valhalla; his rule no longer is valid here."

"Such a pretty speech from my beautiful daughter."

The scrape of metal ripped through the air as her sisters pulled their blades from the sheaths at their hips. Ever raised her head, smiling at the massive sword that rested in Danae's palm. It was almost as tall as her sister, and nearly as bloodthirsty. There was a reason why Danae called her sword the god slayer.

Holding up her hand, Ever held her nerve and refused to turn to acknowledge the man responsible for her birth. "You are not welcome here, Father, and if you had wished an audience, then it should have been done through proper channels."

"Can a father not simply show up to see his beautiful daughter on her special day?" he questioned, stepping forward so Ever could make out his profile out of the corner of her eye.

"Not when you have murder in mind, Father."

He leaned down and brushed his lips over the top of her head. Ever dug her nails into her thigh so she would not flinch away from his touch. His power spread out over her, crawling across her skin and forcing bile to race up her throat. But she had learned as a young babe in Odin's care that a sign of weakness or fear would not be permitted in his presence. A daughter born of his blood would not be weak.

"It is customary, in the human world, for a father to walk his daughter down the aisle on her wedding day."

"It is also customary for old men to die and leave their children in peace. Could you do that, instead?"

Odin boomed with laughter, and then struck out, his palm making a cracking sound as it met with Ever's cheek. The face once caressed so lovingly by Freya now bore the marks of Odin's rage. Much like Freya, the world at large had Odin confused. He may wear the guise of an old man, complete with white beard and wrinkles, but Ever knew her father. He was a cruel, power-hungry god who craved ultimate dominion over the world. All of his children had turned their backs on him, and it displeased him.

"Odin!" Freya screamed. "Do not dare test me. You are

lucky that her sisters have not run you through with a blade and ended the curse that you are."

Odin rounded on Freya. "Do you think me so easily disposed, lover? Many men have tried to take me out and failed. Our privileged whelp will not succeed where better men have failed."

He was a cocky SOB, her father.

Odin turned back to face Ever, who had remained seated without having moved an inch, as if the wallop to the face had caused her no harm. Oh, it had hurt; Odin had the strength reminiscent of the great leader of men he once had been; yet Ever would not react to him.

"Say your piece, Father, and leave us. We will not entertain the ramblings of an old fool."

Odin dragged his fingers through his beard, assessing the situation before edging toward Ever once more. Erika slipped from her seat with the speed only Ever's second possessed. She twirled her twin blades in her hands and stepped in front of Odin and Ever. Ever rose and rested a hand on her arm. Not breaking eye contact with Odin, Erika eased her stance and retreated, but only a margin, still ensuring she would be able to lay down her life for Ever if needed, as was her sworn duty.

"I have come to take back what is mine, Ever. Valhalla should belong to the gods. I need to take hold and prepare for the impending battle. The first rumblings of the prophecy have come to pass. Heimdallr has already been lost to us... Ragnarók is upon us."

With a snort, Ever shook her head. "Ragnarók is a myth, Father. You have succumbed to the madness of old age. Many have tried to restart the world before, and it has never been a success. Thousands would die, but Ragnarók is a bedtime story told to keep the gods in check. I will not let you ruin those men and women who have joined us in battle. I will not let your berserkers into our home to pillage and plunder."

Odin clenched his fists, and lightning flashed in the clear blue sky. Odin, it seemed, was not as composed as he was made out to be in stories, his anger sending dazzling and dangerous flashes of lightning into the sea. Ever swallowed hard and waited for another strike, which didn't come. Odin's eyes slowly closed as he breathed in and out for a number of minutes. When his eyes snapped open, the lightning flared in his eyes.

"I would think you would be more cautious with your words, Ever, since you have already lost two of your kin. It must hurt to know you could not protect your sisters. It would be a shame if you lost any more, would it not? Some of your sisters are quite young... bones will break quite easily." His lips curled into a vicious snarl as he shot a look at Marya. A testament to her fire and spirit, the girl stood up, straightened, and returned his stare.

Dismissing her with the wave of his hand, Odin's focus turned back to Ever and Freya, who had come to stand by her daughter's side. "Ragnarók is coming sooner than you think. It is necessary to rid the world of the perversion and evil that clings to the humans like a shadow. You cannot prepare the warriors for what is to come. You do not have a choice in the matter, Ever. Do as you are told!"

The command rang true in his voice, yet Ever simply folded her arms across her chest. "I do not bow to you, Odin. I have held the traditions of Valhalla for many centuries without your aid or input. The Valkyrie has evolved since your rule, and we will not go back to being lesser beings to men who wish us to serve and bed them.

Change is coming, and you, Father, do not have a place here."

"Well said, sister dear."

A voice from behind them was enough to wring a groan from almost every being standing on the decking. A deep chuckle eased her tension as she drank in the sight of the male entering her line of vision. He was femininely beautiful, her half brother, with high cheekbones, angular facial features, and long, dark lashes that had caused more fair maidens to weep then Ever could count. Dark eyes accompanied those lashes, and when he smiled, she knew the trickster had mischief on his mind.

Whipping his long, black hair from his shoulder, Loki bent down to kiss her cheek in obvious affection, and Ever gently tapped her fingers across his cheek. He beamed at her, but Loki's charms were lost on her. She knew behind the beauty and smiles lay a conniving and manipulative creature who delighted in causing havoc.

"Hello, Kyria." Using a name given to her at birth by Odin, the old meaning of Valkyrie as a term of endearment... the name she used more often, Ever, a name given to her by Freya.

Dressed in simple black combats and an emerald woolen sweater, he looked like any normal twenty-odd-year-old human, if power did not leak from every pore, that is. When he slung a protective arm around her shoulder, Ever delighted in the look of pure rage on Odin's face. Just because his children had deserted him did not mean they had deserted each other. Sometimes, having overprotective brothers was a blessing by the gods.

"Sorry I'm late to the party. I was reluctant to leave the bed of the human beauty who I spent the night with... legs for days, that girl had, and a very wicked—"

"Loki, please," Ever scolded, her tone light and affectionate. "I'm sure Marya does not want to be tainted by your exploits in the human world."

Marya giggled, and Ever peered up at Loki, who had stuck out his tongue at her.

With a sigh, Ever asked, "What brings you to Valhalla, Loki?"

"I came to interrogate your champion. See if he is worthy of bedding my sister."

"Too late for that..." Erika mumbled, and Loki laughed again, the sound so melodic and calming that she knew he was doing his best to influence those around him.

"Enough." Odin gnashed his teeth. "Ever, you will hand over the keys of Valhalla to me, or I will lay waste to all of your kin and end the line of Valkyries right now... Their blood will mingle with the sand and become no more."

"Jeez, Dad... melodramatic much?" Loki said in his best human voice. "I may have a solution that could put a halt to all of this bloodshed and fighting. A powerful seer has advised me this is the best course of action. Let Ever prove she is capable of ruling Valhalla without you. If she wins, you leave, and if you win, then Ever will hand over the keys to Valhalla."

Narrowing her gaze, Freya spoke for the first time since threatening Odin. "What are you up to, trickster? Why interfere in matters that do not concern you?"

Loki installed himself in Ever's chair and slung his boots atop the table. He leaned the chair back and grinned widely up at Freya, who stood just over his shoulder. "Of course matters concern me, evil Step Momma! I love Ever as much as I could love anyone, and her health and life matter to me. But Odin is right. The first warnings of Ragnarók have begun, and I, for one, do not wish to be lost in the chaos. I quite like earth when I visit. They adore me."

"I am curious, son. What do you propose?"

He conjured an apple and began to chew earnestly on it before he answered the all-father. "I propose a test. Terms will be laid out, and both parties will agree before it can commence. Ever will be cast into the world with no knowledge of her powers or who she is."

A startled cry left the lips of her kin, but as Ever held Loki's gaze, something whispered seductively in her mind.

Trust me, Kyria. I wouldn't hurt you.

And she did trust him... more fool her.

"She will be reborn and left to discover her true nature by herself. If she is destined to be queen of the Valkyrie, then fate will intervene and bring her back to us. If not, then Odin will have Valhalla to lessen the blow of Ragnarók. Though we all know if Ragnarók happens we are all dead, regardless."

"You cannot expect Ever to venture through the human world by herself. No, this is ridiculous," Erika yelled, fear a pungent scent around her.

Ever had yet to open her mouth, she simply motioned for Loki to continue.

"Right, so, of course we cannot leave Ever alone in the big bad world of humans. We will set her champion on the same course as well. The Valkyrie queen's champion is supposed to be written in the stars, right? So let them stumble upon each other on earth. And before you complain, Odin, they will have no knowledge of each other—merely a cosmic pull that may or may not lead them to one another."

Odin tapped his finger to his chin. "And what is to prevent me from slaying her before she discovers who she is or finds her champion?"

Loki's smile grew wider, and his eyes danced under the sun. "The rules, of course. There is nothing I can do to stop you from killing her, but I think since you are all mighty and powerful that Ever needs a little advantage as well."

They all waited for Loki to continue, but the trickster simply let his chair fall back down and leapt from it. He slid across the floor like a dancer and twirled Erika around, ignoring the growl emanating from her chest.

"So the rules will be that you cannot tell Ever who she is or imply to her what she is, but we can assist her in her endeavors. You can become friends, allies, and steer her in the right direction. If anyone tells her, then Ever's life is forfeit. Ever and Ever alone must uncover her destiny."

Ever let his words sink in but she felt no fear. Deep down, bone deep, Ever, despite all her hesitations, knew that this was who she was meant to be. Queen of the Valkyrie, saver of souls and defender of the weak. If she had to prove herself to do so, then so be it.

"I also think, since I know what Odin is contemplating, that we will not be able to track her or know where she is reborn. And since Odin plans on killing you as soon as he locates you, Kyria, I propose a gift from me to you."

"I'm not sure I like your gifts, brother. The last time, it was that horrific pink dress. The one you thought would look—what did you say? Fetching? —on me."

"This gift you will like, I swear it." He circled around and raised his hands up. "As there are seven Valkyrie sisters left alive, Ever will be gifted with seven lives. Each time she is slain before reclaiming her throne, she will be

reborn as a babe, the slate clean. If, after attempt seven, Ever is no longer alive, then Valhalla will become Odin's once more."

"I agree," Ever told him, her voice firm and her will strong.

"As so I," Odin chimed in.

Freya grabbed Ever's face in her hands. "You cannot agree to this, Ever. Odin will kill you if you are human."

"Then help me remember that I am not, Mother. I do this for our kin. For the sake of all Valkyrie."

Loki clapped his hands together. "Fantastic. Now, if anyone breaks the rules, Ever will die, but Odin, if you break the rules and set your berserkers to hunt Ever, then for each rule you break, you will lapse into slumber for a year, essentially giving Ever a head start. Do you agree?"

Loki had tricked Odin into thinking he was a step ahead, and Ever silently thanked him for it. Odin simply grunted.

"Excellent. Now Ever, come here," Loki demanded, extending his hand that she took. He pulled her close and planted a kiss right on her lips for a moment before he let her go. Her lips tingled, and she felt magic seeping into her. He leaned in and whispered in a low voice.

"I have faith in you, Ever. Hold strong. I'm betting on you."

Louder to everyone else he sang, "It has been agreed, and the rules set. We shall wait with baited breath as Ever finds her way back to us. Now, bring her champion so we can begin the spell."

There was a flurry of movement, and suddenly Odin had his arm around her chest with a dagger to her throat, the tip pressed against her skin.

"Round one to me," smirked her father, but she

had already reached for the blade under her dress and stabbed backward, sticking it right into Odin's eye as he sliced her open with his blade.

Odin bellowed, and she heard a roar in the distance and knew Deryck was coming for her. But life faded from her as the crimson mess that was her blood began to seep into the wood at her feet. The life she had lived for centuries faded away in front of her eyes, and as she felt death tug at her, Ever was certain she saw the trickster wink before she was no more.

CHAPTER TWENTY-ONE

EVER CAME AWAKE IN A HAZE OF PAIN AND CONFUSION. Her whole body ached, and when she tried to open her eyes, the lights above shone so brightly that she let out a groan of pain. Instantly, the lights dimmed, and she cracked her lids open again a fraction. A cold cloth dampened her eyes, wiping away the crust and dirt that seemed to prevent her from opening them completely. She shifted from her prone position, but agony tore through her and she whimpered in pain.

"Hush now, Ever. We need to let the wolf sleep, or he may awaken grumpier than usual."

The familiar voice eased the tension and fear that crept up as she tried a third time to open her eyes. Caitlyn balanced on the edge of the bed, a worried expression darkening her features. Ever opened her mouth to speak, yet a croak was all she could manage. Her throat was dry, and she reached for something to drink. Her hands trembled, but Caitlyn snared the cup for her and held it to her lips. Ever took a sip or two, then nodded, and Caitlyn removed the cup.

"Better, *chère*?"

"Yes, thank you... where am I?"

Sweeping her hair off her face, Caitlyn studied her for a moment before she spoke. "You're in hospital, Ever. You've been unconscious for three days. You both had us all very worried." She inclined her head to her right.

Out of the corner of her eye, she could see a dark-haired figure asleep in the bed next to her. His chest rose and fell, causing relief to spread throughout her. Ever rubbed her forehead, her memories hazy. She was alive, Derek was alive, and she had no clue how.

Ever made to sit up, but nausea and dizziness halted her. Silently, Caitlyn slipped her arms behind Ever and hoisted her up, slipping another pillow behind her for support. Returning to her spot on the edge of the bed, she watched Ever with great trepidation.

"What happened, Caitlyn? Is Donnelly dead?"

Caitlyn's grey eyes flashed red for a second. "Do you truly not remember what happened in the woods?"

Ever cast her thoughts back, but the last thing she remembered was Derek lunging for Donnelly in wolf form. She tried to think harder, to clear the haze in her mind, but pain laced through her head.

"I don't remember much. I remember Donnelly blackmailing me to come to meet him and then Derek coming to help me. After that, it's all a blur."

"That is what *mon loup* says as well."

Ever breathed in through her nose and out her mouth. She breathed in the scent of wood and Derek, a familiar scent now ingrained on her very self. "Has he been here all along?"

Caitlyn answered with a weary smile. "He has refused to leave your side since he woke. He hissed like an alley cat any time someone tried to remove him from the room. I told them, it is not wise to get in between a wolf when he has chosen his mate."

Mate...

A flash of memory reminded Ever of what Derek had done to keep her alive. She touched her fingers to her neck, where he had bitten her. "He pushed me into mating with him so he could force his strength into me. To keep me alive."

"Yes, he returned the favour you bestowed on him. I was witness to it all, and I have not told a soul. But there are things we need to discuss when you are well."

Confused, Ever found it hard to comprehend what the stunning vampire was saying. She rubbed her temple, eager to get Caitlyn to elaborate, but something in the vampire's expression told her to leave it alone for now.

"He may be a wolf, Ever, but Derek is an old soul. He protects what is his, and now he has claimed you as his mate. Now he will be twice as possessive, twice as stubborn, and twice as likely to argue with you. Do you love him?"

Caitlyn's question caught her off guard. Casting her eyes to Derek's sleeping form, she asked herself the same question... and was a little taken aback by the answer.

"Yes. I do."

Caitlyn grasped her hand. "Good. That is good. I like you, Ever, and would hate to have to hurt you if you hurt him. Derek is my family, and I would bleed anyone who hurts him."

Ever gave Caitlyn's cold hand a squeeze. "I have no plans to hurt him. I wasn't expecting to find him or to fall so quickly, but the wolf has my heart in his teeth. He has the power to undo me."

Seemingly satisfied with her answer, Caitlyn smiled. "You may do after all, Ever Chace." She leaned in and continued in a hushed tone. "I don't know what you are, but you are far from human. What I saw? What you did? *Mon Dieu*, it was as if you were possessed and a divinity had overcome you. You breathed life back into a dying man's body."

At Ever's wide eyes, Caitlyn said, "I haven't shared what I've seen with any other soul. And I will not. The others happened on you both as Derek made you his mate but do not know the rest. Once you have had time to heal, we will revisit what happened in the woods."

Suddenly tired, Ever closed her eyes, and when she opened them again, she was alone in the room with a sleeping wolf. She could hear the faint sound of his snoring in the darkened corner. His back was to her, but she could make out the outline of his shoulders, muscular back, and that gorgeous, chestnut hair that made her want to reach out and tease her fingers through it. He was beautiful, her wolf, and her heart fluttered knowing he was hers.

Quit looking at me like that, Mate. I can't sleep with you staring at me like that.

Ever let out a squeal and instantly put her palm to her forehead as pain lashed out again. Swearing, she heard him move in the bed and watched as he pulled the wires free from his bare chest. The machines shrieked, and a nurse ran in, quickly retreating as Derek growled and pulled the plug on the machine.

"That wasn't very nice."

"I never claimed to be nice. Push over."

His voice was thick with emotion as Ever budged over and Derek climbed into the bed with her. He yanked her against his chest, and a rumble of pleasure rippled through him. She leaned into him, trying to ignore the pain in her body. For some reason, the tenderness of being held caused tears to well up, and when Derek pressed his lips to her forehead, the dam broke and sobs wracked her body.

Derek simply held her and murmured comforting words to her. After what felt like an age, the tears dried up and embarrassment surged through her.

"I'm sorry. I snotted all over you."

"I'm a big wolf; I think I can handle a little snot." He chuckled.

She sighed against him. "Are you okay?"

"Watching you lie there like that almost killed me, Ever. I could feel the bond here, ya' know," he tapped a finger to the side of his head, "but I couldn't get you to wake up. What happened in the woods? Caitlyn says you don't remember."

Ever shook her head. From the look on Caitlyn's and now Derek's face, Ever wasn't sure if she really wanted to know what had happened. Maybe some things she was better off not knowing. "I'm sorry. It's still all a bit fuzzy."

Pressing his lips to her forehead again, he ran his hands down her arms, and she shivered under his touch. Her heart raced, and she swallowed hard as Derek bent at the neck to press a kick to the side of her neck, where he had bitten her. She bit back a moan as heat lit up her veins, but she tilted her head so Derek would have better access.

A very satisfied grin pressed against her skin. "I'm sorry I didn't wait until we did this right, but you were dying, and neither man nor wolf could let that happen."

Ever pressed her hand to the side of his face, and he all but purred. Maybe Caitlyn was right and Derek was part cat. He nipped at her ear as if to chastise her, and Ever knew then she had projected her thought into his head.

"It's gonna take a little time to get used to having you in my head."

"Ditto," he replied before becoming serious once again. "Are you sure you're not mad? You understand why I did what I did, right?"

Turning her head, she looked up at him and saw the fear in his eyes. He was afraid she would leave him. That forcing her to mate him might have ruined whatever it was they had. For as long as she could remember, Ever had only wanted to feel like she belonged because too many times she had felt so alone. Falling in love with a werewolf was not in her plans, but destiny was a funny thing. She felt safe in his arms, as if she finally belonged.

"I'm sure. It happened before either of us had planned, Derek, but what's done is done. Now we need to figure out how we deal with everything else."

"Like?" he enquired.

She shrugged. "To be honest, I'm not sure, but we can't rush us. I won't move in with you or anything like that."

When he growled, Ever sighed. "Not yet, anyway. We need to get to know each other. Likes and dislikes. And you still owe me a proper date. That's a major stipulation of this mating."

"Okay. Okay... a date. I think I can do that. But now I really need to kiss you. It's instrumental to my recovery."

Ever laughed with an eyebrow raised. "Oh really?"

A devilish smile lit up his handsome face. “Yup. Doctor’s orders.”

“Well then, how could I refuse?”

His chest vibrated before his mouth found hers. It was tender at first—Derek simply tasting her—before he nipped at her bottom lip, causing her to gasp, and his tongue invaded her mouth. The kiss turned hungry rapidly, and Ever traced his stomach with her fingers.

“My eyes! My eyes! Need to scrub them clean... will have nightmares!”

Ricky’s cry dragged Derek’s lips from hers, but she could only smile.

“Perfect timing as always, Ricky.”

Wagging his finger at Derek, a smirk a mile long on his kisser, Ricky said, “Sarge is on his way up. Thought it best to interrupt so her *godfather* doesn’t rip you a new one.”

Derek simply scoffed at Ricky’s cheerful quips and wrapped his arms around Ever. Sarge stalked into the room, shot Derek a look, and came to give Ever a hug. She returned the bear’s affection, and as soon as Sarge let Ever loose, Derek wrapped his arms around her again.

“Your mother’s not happy with you mating a wolf.”

“My mother’s not happy I’m seeing anyone at all. Is she here?”

Tom shook his head. “No. Samhain left to take care of a coven meeting, and your dad is still in Europe. He should be home by Friday. She and Dr. Val have been having quite the conversations about you, Ever, and Samhain left strict instructions for you to call when you woke up.”

Ever groaned. “I’m still asleep. For a little while, anyway.”

That brought a smile to Tom's face. "Okay, but do call her. She was worried about you. As were we all."

"Yeah, Ever, you circled the drain a couple of times, girl. Did he tell you about the wall he decimated when you coded in the ER?"

"You decimated a wall?"

"You died... twice."

Fair enough, she supposed, but she still slapped him softly on the chest. Laughter filled the room, and Ever finally breathed a sigh of relief. Everything was good. Donnelly was dead. But could she really go back to being a teacher now that she had seen the darkness that lurked around the corner and survived?

"No."

Derek's voice snapped her from her thoughts.

"Damn it, Derek! Stay out of my head until we learn how to stop some thoughts from going through." The hurt on his face made her soften her voice and say, "I just mean that I need to be able to keep some part of myself, and even though we're mated, you can't order me around. If I want to ask Tom to join the team, I'll do it and you can't stop me."

Derek growled and glared at Tom, who held up his hands. "Don't look at me, she's *your* mate. I could've told you how stubborn she was if you'd have listened."

"Hey!"

"Look at it this way, D," Ricky moved to stand by the table, plucked a grape from the punnet of grapes, and swallowed it, "if Ever is consulting with us, then you can keep a better eye on her. Closer she is, the less grumpy you'll be, too."

The door to the room swung open, and Dr. Val entered. "Ever, it's so good to see you awake. Now, I need to give Ever the once-over, so gentlemen, that means you have to leave. That includes you, too, Derek."

Derek growled, earning a slap from Ever. "Go. I'll be fine."

With a quick peck to her cheek, Derek slipped from the bed and caught the T-shirt Ricky tossed him, the warlock muttering about Derek causing a riot if he went out shirtless before he slipped from the room, Derek in his wake. As soon as Derek had left, Ever called Tom back, asking Dr. Val for a moment to speak with the bear.

He sat down on the bed and held her hand. "You okay, love?"

"I'm okay. Just a little confused."

Have you already forgotten who you are?

Her tormentor was back to drive her to madness. While she could cope if she were going mad herself, she was now linked to Derek, and she could not let the madness seep into him. She would not let it destroy him, even if it took her over.

You're not going mad, sweetheart; simply waking up.

"Of course you are. A lot has happened. You just woke up after being out for a few days. Time will make it easier. Now, what can I do for you?"

She had a second to back out, but her mouth worked of its own accord. "Remember when you said if I ever wanted to find my biological parents you would help? Does that offer still stand?"

For five heartbeats, Tom studied her before he finally answered. "Of course. But Ever, be sure you want to go down this avenue, and realize you may not get the desired result. Why now, when you were adamant that you had no interest in locating them?"

Did she dare tell him that she thought she was

losing her mind? He would usher in a psychologist, and it would turn into a circus before too long. If she was to go mad, then she wanted as much time with Derek as possible.

Shrugging, Ever explained, "Maybe this whole almost dying has made me realize I'd like to know where I'm from. And I think I'd like to understand why my mother abandoned me. It's a new feeling."

"Alright then, leave it with me. I will do my best to look into it."

Tom rose to leave, but Ever grasped his hand tighter. "Please don't tell Samhain. She will be upset, and there is no need to tell my parents anything until we know something, right? And Derek doesn't need to know, either... just us, okay?"

Tom eyed her suspiciously, but nodded. "Not a great way to start out a relationship, Ever, but okay. For now, it stays with us. Caitlyn might be able to help as well if you don't mind her knowing. She will be discreet."

"That would be good. And Tom? Thank you."

Tom gave a shake of his head, his greying hair sparkling with the lighting. "No thanks needed, Ever. You are family. And if Derek hurts you, I'll break both his legs."

"How could he dare when I have two dads to hunt him down?"

Tom left swiftly after her comment, and she reckoned he didn't know how to respond to it. She did look at him as another father figure. Anxiety spread across her chest at the thought that she may hurt her parents by looking for her biological parents. She would tell them, but only when she finally sorted out what was going on in her head.

Closing her eyes, Ever leaned into the pillows and exhaled a breath.

Do you seriously think that we would leave you in peace to forget about us? You will remember, Ever, and it will all come back to you in one swift rush. Your champion is by your side. Your powers are unleashed. Remember what you are now... believe it.

Valkyrie.

A sob bubbled in her chest and her eyes sprang open as Dr. Val strode into the room. With one look at Ever, she came to stand beside her and smoothed her hair away from her face. "Now dear, don't cry. It's been a long few days, and you need to rest. Dry your eyes, and let me give you a quick check. Then you can sleep for a while before your wolf comes hunting for you again."

Ever nodded and closed her eyes again as Dr. Val checked her over. But Ever was afraid she would never sleep again. The nightmares that stalked her when asleep were beginning to plague her during the day. Death scented the air, and Ever breathed it in as Dr. Val injected her with something and told her to rest for now. So she did.

EPILOGUE

THREE WEEKS AFTER LEAVING THE HOSPITAL, EVER stood in front of her mirror and assessed herself. Dressed in a sky blue, knee-length dress—which she had learned was Derek's favourite colour—she slipped her feet into black heels that should add an inch or two to her height. Tonight was her first official 'date' with Derek. They had been so busy the last few weeks that it had been almost impossible to make arrangements before now.

Not that they hadn't seen each other over those three weeks, but they had both secured a night off, and she was excited. Draping a shawl over her shoulders, she left her room and made her way downstairs. The thumping of Erika's heavy-metal music vibrated from the guesthouse and brought a smile to her face. Despite her reservations, Erika had turned out to be a good tenant, and late-night movies and chats had made them firm friends.

As had Caitlyn. The vampire called her at least once

a day to check on her but still had yet to divulge what had happened that night to her... and neither had Derek. Her wolf had managed to evade her questions with kisses to distract her anytime she broached the subject.

Pushy wolf.

Glancing at the clock on the wall, she noticed that it read seven-forty pm. Derek was late. Her wolf tended to be over-punctual, arriving at the very time he had promised to be there. She tried not to worry, to elevate the knot that had managed to twist in her stomach. Reapplying her lipstick, she kept glancing at the clock.

Derek?

She sought out the bond that connected them, but all she got was silence. Maybe the shields that Caitlyn had helped her build were working too well.

Her phone rang, and she groaned when she saw the station's number show up on her caller ID. If he was calling, it meant he wasn't on his way. She pressed Answer and tried for her best pissed-off voice.

"Oh no, Mr. Agent, you're *so* not cancelling our date. We've had this planned for *ages*," she drawled. "Unless someone is dead or dying, don't even try to cancel. Come on, Derek. I wore a dress and everything. If you think you can smooth this over with promises of making out with me or the likes, I will just taunt you by telling you about the brand-new underwear I bought..."

"Ever! TMI, TMI!"

Her skin flushed red.

"God, Ricky, why didn't you say something sooner?"

"You wouldn't let me get a word in edgeways. Ever, I need you down here. Derek's been arrested."

"What happened?" she asked as she raced upstairs to change.

There was a hesitant pause before the warlock answered. "Police burst into an apartment this morning after a disturbance was called in by a neighbour. They found Derek asleep next to a girl. He was covered in blood, and she was dead."

She knew it couldn't be true, but she gasped. Derek had been with another girl when he'd wanted to go slow with her. Betrayal stung, but what Ricky said next changed everything.

"She was in bits, Ever. They're claiming Derek lost it and ate her. It's not possible... it's D... but the body was ripped apart.

They're saying he ate her fucking heart while it still beat in her chest."

To be continued...

Acknowledgements

WRITING A BOOK IS A SOLITARY EXPERIENCE, BUT publishing a book is not.

I need to give a big shout out to all the CTP ladies, Courtney, Rebecca, and Marya, for their constant support, reassurance, and faith in my books. I get to live my dream because of all of you, and words cannot express how thankful I am for that.

Oh, and for loaning me your names for the series!

The real life Melanie Newton, who inspired a character that I love so much. You are worth more than gold, and I feel so honoured to call you my friend.

Cynthia Shepp for doing such an amazing job at editing my story. I have no doubt Skin and Bones wouldn't be the same without the work you put in.

My family, whose love, support, and constant cup of teas mean so much to me.

Lj and Taylor, I love you both so very much. To infinity and beyond.

Michelle, my best friend and often my therapist. Thanks for always being there for me.

Helen, me ole partner-in-crime. Distance may separate us, but can never tear us apart.

My work Biatches, y'all know who you are! Thanks for keeping me sane, making me laugh, and being kick-ass women.

And finally to the readers. Thank you for reading Skin and Bones. I wouldn't be able to call myself an author without any of you.

About the Author

Susan Harris is a writer from Cork in Ireland. An avid reader, she quickly grew to love books in the supernatural/fantasy genre. When she is not writing or reading, she loves music, oriental cultures, tattoos, anything Disney and psychology. If she wasn't a writer she would love to be a FBI profiler or a PA for Dave Grohl or Jared Leto.

Susan Harris is the author of Shattered Memories.

Playlist

Music and writing come hand in hand to me. With over a hundred songs on the list, here's a shortlist of most listened to.

Running with the Wolves—Aurora
Cry—The Used
Last Damn Night—Elle King
Livin' on the City—John Butler Trio
Dead inside—Muse
Catch me if you can—Walking on Cars
Pray to God —Calvin Harris ft Haim
Bloodstream—Ed Sheeran ft Rudimental
Shut up and Dance—Walk the Moon
It takes a lot to know a man—Damien Rice
Wish—Paper Route
Desire—Meg Myers
Fireproof—Against the Current
Smoke—Pvris
Crazy Train—Ozzy Osbourne
Blood Hand—Royal Blood

ANGEL OF SMALL DEATH AND THE CODEINE SCENE—Hozier
TEAR IN MY HEART—Twenty One Pilots
SICK LIKE ME—In This Moment
SHOTS—Imagine Dragons (broiler remix)
WELCOME—Fort Minor
STRONG —London Grammar
RAISED BY WOLVES—Falling in Reverse
FLOODS—Fightstar
TRUE FRIENDS—Bring Me the Horizon
BAD BLOOD—Jess Glynne
THE RECKLESS AND THE BRAVE—All Time Low (Acoustic)
DANCING ON MY OWN—Kato
PREDICTABLE—Good Charlotte
MONSTER—Meg Myers
HOW THIS GOES—The Coronas
AUDIBLE JOES —State of Frustration and Sin
WOULD YOU STILL BE THERE? —Of Mice and Men
ITCH—Nothing but Thieves
STAY WITH ME—You Me at Six (Acoustic)
BLANK SPACE—Our Last Night (Cover: Original by Taylor Swift)
CREEP—Daniela Andrade (Cover: Original by Radio head)
HOLDING OUT FOR A HERO—Nothing but Thieves (Cover: Original by Bonnie Tyler)
CRAZY—Denmark & Winter (Cover: Original by Willie Nelson)

Full list can be found on Spotify!
spotify:user:11135970205:playlist:3LtD8bN2DaZNaS-Ra7CvJEF

CPSIA information can be obtained at www.ICGtesting.com
Printed in the USA
LVOW10s1834020916

502629LV00002B/19/P